I0773496

Big Secrets, Little Lies

BUTLER FAMILY LEGACY

PAT NICHOLS

Big Secrets, Little Lies by Pat Nichols
Published by Armchair Press
ISBN: 979-8-9860519-2-5
Copyright © 2023 by Pat Nichols
Cover Design by Elaina Lee
Edited by Sherri Stewart

Available in print from your local bookstore or online.
For more information on this book or the author visit:
https://patnicholsauthor.blog
Printed in the United States of America
Big Secrets, Little Lies is a work of fiction. Names, characters, and incidents are all products of the author's imagination or are used for fictional purposes. Any mentioned brand names, places, and trademarks remain the property of their respective owners, bear no association with the author or publisher, and are used for fictional purposes only.
Library of Congress Cataloging-in Publication Data
Nichols, Pat.
Big Secrets, Little Lies/ Pat Nichols

All rights reserved. No portion of this book may be reproduced in any form, stored in a retrieval system, or transmitted in any form by any means—electronic, photocopy, recording, or otherwise—without written permission from the publisher or author, except as permitted by U.S. copyright law.

Books by

Pat Nichols

Women's Fiction

Willow Falls series

The Secret of Willow Inn
Trouble in Willow Falls
Star Struck in Willow Falls
Bridges, Books, and Bones

Butler Family Legacy series

Big Secrets, Little Lies
Truth and Forgiveness
New Beginnings

Contemporary Romance

Jenny's Grace

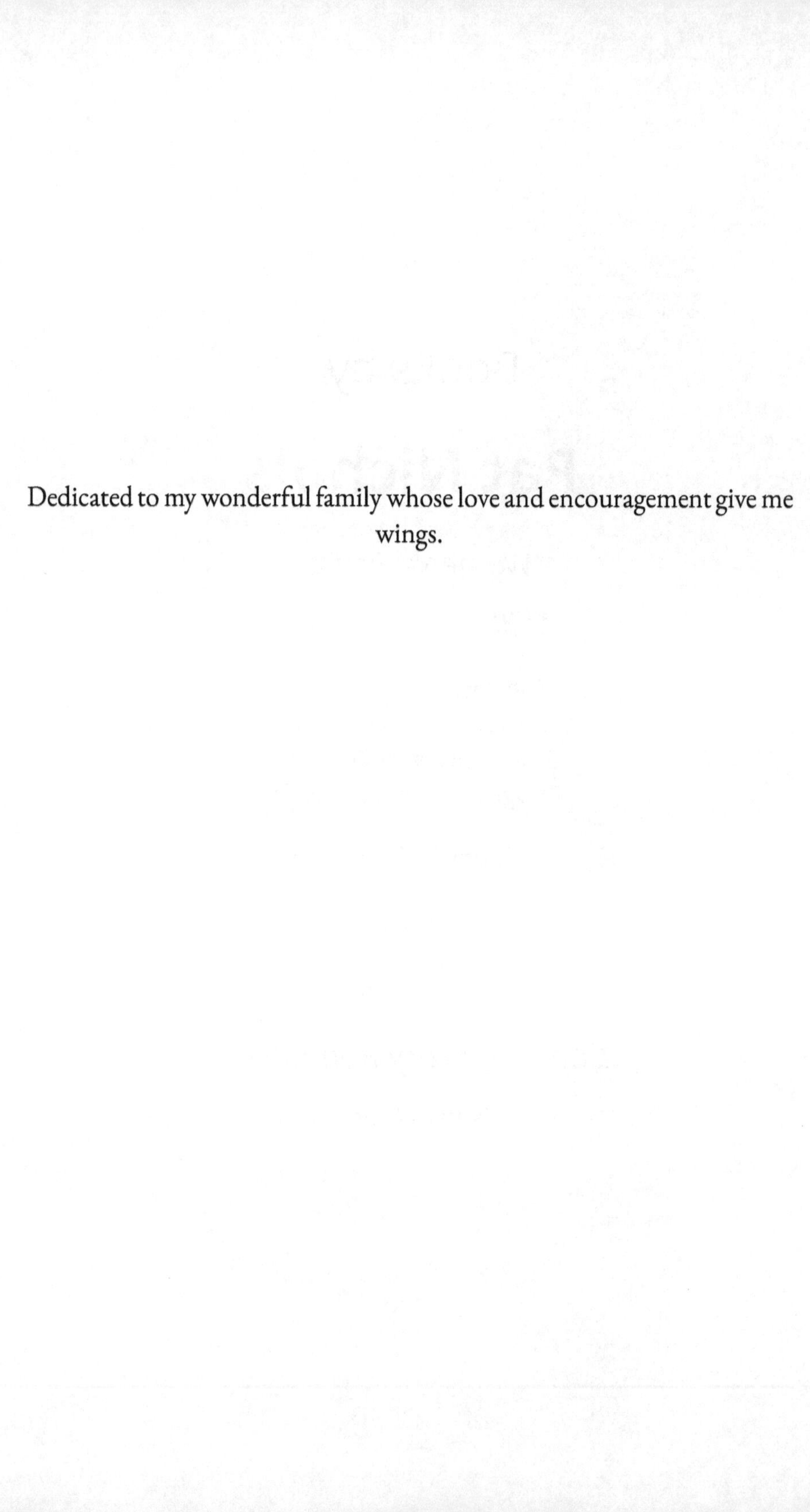

Dedicated to my wonderful family whose love and encouragement give me wings.

Chapter 1

Daisy Butler's heart pounded as her eyes darted back and forth between six elevators. Every junior associate understood that a summons to the top floor in the Manhattan high-rise office building meant something significant had taken place. Sometimes positive, other times not so much. Hopefully four years of undergraduate work and three of law school, plus two more years accumulating an insane number of billable hours for barely enough salary to cover her rent had paid off. Unless—

A ping. The second elevator door on the left yawned open. Daisy stepped inside and pressed the button for the fiftieth floor. Sweat beaded on her upper lip and dampened her palms. What if an associate had stumbled on the truth about the assumption she had failed to correct and forced the senior partners to send her packing? Back to Georgia. A fraud. A failure.

Another ping. The door slid open.

Daisy breathed deeply and tucked her shoulder-length, dark blonde hair behind her right ear, revealing a faux-emerald earring a shade darker than her eyes. She squared her shoulders, held her head high, and strode into the lobby for the second time since the day she'd first arrived in the city.

A smartly dressed, attractive woman smiled from behind a tall, granite-top reception desk. "Ms. Butler?"

"Yes, ma'am."

The young woman's left brow raised.

Why did some women balk at being addressed as *ma'am*? Grateful she hadn't called her *honey* or added *y'all* to her response, Daisy pasted on her best smile. "Yes, I'm Ms. Butler."

The woman's brow relaxed. She stepped from behind the desk and motioned Daisy to follow her down a short hall and into a room warmed by wood paneling and a crystal chandelier. "Mr. Warner will join you shortly." She strolled out, leaving the door ajar.

Daisy eased toward the massive conference table holding center stage, encircled by fourteen plush-leather chairs. She ran her fingers along the smooth-as-glass dark wood surface. Nothing like the hand-hewn table in her parents' humble kitchen, marred by nicks and spills from years of family meals and school projects.

Grateful for a moment alone, she strolled to the wall of windows and gazed down at the iconic Plaza Hotel and beyond to the oasis awash in autumn colors floating amid a sea of buildings. Central Park's massive outdoor space appeared far more magnificent from the Warner Law Firm's inner sanctum than from the cramped office she shared with two junior associates. At least if today marked the end of her career, she'd spend the last few moments in a room lower-ranking attorneys seldom entered.

"One of the best views in the city."

Daisy turned toward the deep male voice. Her breath hitched at the sight of Mr. Warner, the senior partner and founding member of the prestigious law firm. Michael, his handsome son and heir to the family fortune, accompanied him.

"Daisy is an interesting name for a corporate attorney." Dressed in a dark suit, white shirt, and solid blue tie, the silver-haired senior Warner approached.

"All the women in my family are named after flowers." She pressed her damp palms to her skirt. Why had she uttered that bit of irrelevant information? "On my mother's side, sir. I suppose it's a southern thing."

Mr. Warner stood ramrod straight at the head of the conference table. "We're fortunate a bright, young corporate attorney from a prominent southern family accepted a position with us."

"I'm the one who's fortunate, Mr. Warner." Had the senior Butler's reputation cinched the employment offer? Daisy stole a glance at Michael, touted as one of the city's most sought-after bachelors. What about the morning three months earlier when he'd bumped into her in the ground-floor coffee shop and spilled cappuccino on her blouse? A mishap or an excuse to invite her to dinner to apologize? One evening at a trendy, high-dollar restaurant followed by five more—the last two ending with a kiss.

"Our corporate division represents an impressive number of successful companies." Mr. Warner's tone exuded confidence. "Curtis Butler's business empire is highly respected."

Sweat trickled between Daisy's shoulder blades at the mention of her grandfather and the truth she had failed to reveal during her first interview. The fact she had never met the eighty-year-old man, or that no one in her family dared mention his name in her dad's presence. The wealthy, powerful grandfather who most likely had no idea she existed.

"Another reason we're pleased to promote his granddaughter to the position of senior associate."

Daisy blinked. Had she heard Mr. Warner correctly?

Michael edged closer. "The partners are impressed with your work, Daisy. Which is why we've made the decision to fast-track you toward a partnership."

She gazed into his hazel eyes and breathed in the musky scent of his cologne. Had her efforts and work ethic led to this moment? If word about dinners with Michael or her family-connections leaked, would associates tag her as an opportunist profiting from her grandfather's reputation?

Michael smiled. "We're expecting a lot from you, Daisy."

"I won't let you down." She swallowed a sigh, grateful she remained employed.

Mr. Warner glanced at his watch. "Michael will share the details of your promotion." He pivoted on his heel and headed toward the door. "One more thing." The senior partner paused and peered over his shoulder. "Michael will escort you to an event at our Southampton home this coming Saturday." He walked out and pulled the door closed behind him.

Daisy's chest tightened. How many attorneys promoted to senior associate had he commanded to appear at his private residence? Her eyes landed on one of three paintings adorning the paneled walls. Rumor among the associates claimed the partners had insured the firm's artwork for untold millions. Was the same true of the Warner's private residence? "Does your father know we've had dinner a few times?"

Michael leaned his hip against the conference table's round corner. "You mean that I've dined with a southern beauty who's ambitious and as smart as any Ivy League-educated attorney?"

Daisy's eyes narrowed at the not-so-subtle remark about her southern education. "You didn't answer my question."

"Here it comes, ladies and gentlemen of the jury. A cross examination from our newest senior associate who's high-heeled clad feet are firmly planted on the path to the big prize. Partnership in a world-class law firm."

Daisy turned away and meandered to the window. A stretch limousine pulled in front of the Plaza Hotel's entrance fifty stories below—a symbol of wealth and position. Everything her mom wanted her to achieve. Everything her dad detested. "At what cost, Michael?"

He strode to her side. "Why the suspicion?"

"Call it curiosity."

"Yes, my father knows we're seeing each other socially." He touched Daisy's shoulder. "Trust me, your promotion is based on merit and what you bring to our firm."

She faced him. "You mean my family connections?"

His brows raised. "Is that a problem?"

More like a landmine. Daisy squared her shoulders. "Of course, it isn't."

"Good. Now, about your promotion..."

As she listened to Michael outline details about her new salary and responsibilities, one all-consuming mission took root. Before the truth about her grandfather surfaced, she had to find a way to make her connection to her dad's elusive family count for something without breaking his heart and dashing her mom's dreams for her future.

Chapter 2

Poppy Fowler Butler rolled down her sleeves, donned a wide-brimmed straw hat, and grasped a pot of flowers for her daily trek to the clapboard structure twenty paces from her family's commercial greenhouse. Her private retreat—a space without mirrors, where she could forget the dark wine-colored birthmark that stained her left cheek and scarred her soul.

She stepped inside the tiny structure her sister called 'the little house', and closed the door. The warped floorboards creaked as she walked six feet to the window, pushed it open, and placed the flowers on the sill. A waft of late-October, coastal-Georgia breeze cooled the air and fluttered the sheer white curtains that added a touch of elegance to the rustic space.

Poppy hung her hat on a hook before settling on a hand-hewn wooden bench. She stroked the empty space beside her. How she missed Daisy, her oldest, and although she would never admit it, the favorite of her three children. Her confidante. The child she'd encouraged to achieve success worthy of the Butler name. The daughter who lived the life denied her by a disgraceful past and her tainted appearance.

The tabby cat charged with keeping the greenhouse rodent-free sprang onto the windowsill, stretched, and yawned.

"I know *you* won't divulge my secret." Poppy reached across the narrow space and lifted the lid on an ancient trunk. She removed the thick scrapbook she'd kept hidden from everyone except Daisy. The collection of newspaper clippings from Savannah's society and business pages featuring her husband's family.

Images surfaced of the only time Poppy had come face-to-face with Danny's father, Curtis, thirty-three years earlier at his hundred-acre ranch a mere ten miles away. His name was never spoken in their home after that gut-wrenching encounter.

Poppy flipped the scrapbook cover open and ran her fingers over the handwritten title. *The Butler Family Legacy.* She turned to the last entry. A newspaper photo of Danny's mother taken during a fundraising affair at the Butler's grand estate. She closed her eyes and mentally replayed the one time she had seen the woman in person. The day she and Daisy drove to Savannah to shop. The courage she'd found to glance out the passenger window as her in-law's driveway came into view. Her surprise when she spotted Mrs. Butler clipping stems from a rose bush. Watching the woman she had only seen in pictures turn in their direction as Daisy slowed to a stop. The brief moment their eyes met followed by the shame burning her cheeks as she pressed her hand to her birthmark and looked away.

"Yoo-hoo, Sis," Pansy Fowler's cheery voice rang out. "Are you hiding out in there?"

Poppy snapped the scrapbook closed, set it in the trunk, and lowered the lid seconds before her sister's face appeared in the window. "Come on in, sweetie."

"Okay." Pansy breezed in, followed by Boots, her black, sixty-pound rescue dog with white front paws. Her sister plopped her plump body down on the bench and removed her ball cap, one of dozens she had collected over the years. Her dark bangs clung to her forehead above twinkling brown eyes and pink cheeks. "I finished another story about what happened to Mama."

"How many different theories have you written about her disappearance?"

"Lots." Pansy placed a thin stack of stapled papers on Poppy's lap. A colored-pencil drawing of a rainbow arched over a castle graced the top page. "This one's the best."

Poppy slid her arm around her sister's shoulders—the child-like, middle-aged woman who made it her lifelong mission to solve Rose Fowler's mysterious disappearance thirty-five years earlier. "Is this one a happy or a sad story?"

Pansy's face beamed. "Happy." She twisted toward the wall behind the bench and touched her name scrawled in red paint. "Remember how we used to hide in here every time a client visited Mama and gave her money?" Her smile evaporated. "Will we ever find out which of those men are our daddies?"

Poppy stared wide-eyed at her sister. "You've never asked that question before."

"Doesn't mean I haven't thought it." Pansy popped up and lifted the cat off the windowsill. "So, do you?"

Poppy couldn't count the number of times that question had crossed her mind. "Not without a DNA test."

"I don't like tests."

"Neither do I." Poppy flicked a gnat away from her face. "Which means the answer is no."

"Okay." Pansy dropped back onto the bench. She stroked the cat's back until it leapt from her arms and darted past Boots out the door. "When are you gonna read my story?"

"How about tomorrow night after we celebrate Danny's birthday?"

"I have his present all ready."

"Good for you." Poppy stood and retrieved her hat. "Right now, what do you say we go bake him a cake?"

"We've gotta make it chocolate." Pansy followed her sister outside.

"Of course. With lots of fudge icing." They strolled under a canopy of autumn leaves formed by mature hardwood trees.

"Remember how Mama loved chocolate kisses?" Pansy swiped her bangs away from her eyes. "And how she kept that big ole jar filled with 'em on the kitchen counter?"

Rewards for hiding out in the little house and not asking questions. "We for sure had our fill of kisses."

"Sometimes I put 'em in my pocket and they turned all melty." Pansy popped her cap back on her head. "I'm glad you and Danny moved into Mama's house after you got married."

"So, you didn't have to move out of your room?"

"Uh-huh. I'm wanna buy some paint and make the walls a pretty shade of yellow, like the sun."

"If you keep adding layers of paint to the walls, your room is gonna shrink."

"That's silly." Pansy giggled. "Rooms can't shrink. As soon as Danny opens a flower shop in town, I'm gonna work there."

Poppy rolled her eyes. How many times had she explained that the unincorporated wide spot in the road she called a town was too small to support a full-size grocery store, much less a flower shop? "You know we'd be lost without you helping out in the greenhouse every day."

"I like watering all those pretty flowers. Petunias are my favorite, 'cept for roses." Pansy leaned down and plucked a leaf off the ground. "Do you think Mama's still alive?"

At least that question wasn't unexpected. Although logic dictated a no, and half of Pansy's stories about Rose Fowler ended with her dead, Poppy couldn't bring herself to utter the word. So, she deferred to her standard reaction. Redirect. "Besides chocolate cake, what should we fix for Danny's birthday dinner?"

"Meatloaf, mashed potatoes, and green beans right out of our garden. Those are his favorites."

"Maybe we should fix something fancier."

"Danny doesn't like fancy, 'cept for flowers."

"You're right." Poppy understood her husband detested anything that smacked of money or status. "We'll add corn on the cob to make supper extra-special."

"And homemade biscuits with lots of honey."

"Your favorite." Poppy followed Pansy up the steps to the screened back porch stretching half the length of the single-story frame house. A fourth bedroom occupied one end, the second of two rooms Danny had added over the years to accommodate their growing family. After hanging her straw hat on a hook, she lifted a bucket of potatoes off a bench, carried it into the kitchen, and set it on the new floor. Last year's birthday gift from Danny—fashioned with wide-wooden planks harvested from an abandoned barn.

Poppy lifted her apron off the back of a vintage ladder-back chair—one of six around the table. Her mama's prize possessions. Gifts from a satisfied client. She turned the radio to a country station and settled into the roles she'd been cast. Wife. Mother. Sister. Living in a world insulated from strangers' stares and ridicule. The world she'd encouraged Daisy to leave behind.

Chapter 3

The open suitcase on Daisy's fold-out couch conjured images of an animal trap poised to snap shut at the slightest touch. Why hadn't she refused Michael's request to spend Saturday night at his parents' home? Especially today, her dad's fifty-fifth birthday. He would scoff at his daughter dating a wealthy man from a prominent family. Especially one from the north. At least no one other than her mother knew about her dinners with Michael.

Daisy faced her laptop and eyed the Google Earth view of Meadow Lane in Southampton—the two-lane road that stretched across a narrow strip of land dotted with mansions the size of hotels. Which shoreline estate belonged to the Warner family? One with a pool and a tennis court?

Maybe she should call Michael and claim the sudden onset of flu or a severe case of food poisoning. Daisy snapped her laptop shut and zipped her suitcase closed. She couldn't let anxiety jeopardize her career or her budding relationship. Somehow she'd find a way to fit in with his crowd, like the cream of Savannah society pictured in her mom's scrapbook.

Daisy slipped into a royal blue knit dress—the one designer outfit she owned, thanks to last year's end-of-season triple markdown. Maybe no one would notice her off-brand shoes or costume jewelry.

Her phone pinged a text from Michael. *Waiting out front.*

She peeked out her third-story window at the double-parked silver convertible with the top down. Chances were the sports car cost more to garage in the city than she paid for a month's rent. She propped her sunglasses on top of her head, shouldered her purse, and lugged her suitcase off the couch. After a quick glance around her tiny studio apartment, she made her way down to the ground floor and out to the sidewalk.

Michael popped his trunk as Daisy stepped off the curb. She eyed his white denim jeans, tan boat shoes, and untucked long-sleeve polo shirt. "I hope I'm not overdressed."

"Are you kidding?" He leaned close, smelling of his signature cologne. "You look gorgeous."

"I'm glad you approve."

He hoisted her bag into his trunk then scooted to the passenger side and opened the door.

She slid onto the seat, set her purse on the floor, and traced her fingers over the luxurious leather while Michael moseyed to the driver's side. "Gorgeous car."

"Hope you don't mind the top down."

Why would anyone ride in an open convertible in October? "Not at all."

"If the ride's too cool, I'll turn on the heat."

Daisy stifled a giggle. Top down with the heat on. What else would she learn about a lifestyle made possible by extreme wealth?

Michael checked his sideview mirror before easing into traffic. "Your first trip to Long Island?"

Daisy pulled her sunglasses down. "First time outside the city. Except for my trip home in July." Why had she made that comment and opened herself up for questions about her family? Questions she didn't want to answer. "What sort of event are we attending?"

"Mother's annual fundraiser for a local art center."

A newspaper clipping in her mom's scrapbook touting her paternal grandmother's successful fundraising event slithered up from Daisy's memory. Tens of thousands raised for a worthy cause. She peered at Michael's profile. "I assume your mother will expect guests to ante up."

"Her friends always try to out-donate each other." He braked for a red light and placed his hand on the console shifter knob. "No need for you to worry. She won't hit you up for a check."

She stared at Michael's Yale School of Law ring—a symbol of wealth, influence, and brains. "Because I'm a newcomer?"

"As well as my guest."

A horn honking from behind prompted Michael to glance in the review mirror. He lifted his hand from the shifter and waved over his shoulder. "Give it a break, pal."

Daisy ran her fingers along the edge of her seatbelt as Michael drove through the intersection. "I've been thinking."

"Crucial talent for a rising-star corporate attorney."

"I have my moments. Anyway, maybe you shouldn't mention my grandfather to anyone."

"You want to shine on your own merit, right?"

"Something like that."

"Believe me, I understand." He drove onto the RFK Bridge entrance ramp. "I'm curious—"

"Crucial quality for a defense attorney."

"Touché." Michael checked his sideview mirror before maneuvering into traffic. "Why didn't your father opt for a position in his father's business empire?"

Daisy's muscles tightened. How much did he know about the Butlers? Did he have a clue about her dad dropping out of high school in his senior year and enlisting in the Marines the day he turned eighteen? Or that he would choose starvation over working for his father? "I suppose because he prefers to work with his hands. Dad grows flowers and plants for landscapers."

"One of the benefits of family money to fall back on—pursuing one's own path. Where did he earn his degree?" Michael blasted his horn and uttered an expletive at a delivery-truck driver who swerved and missed slamming into his car by inches. "Are we invisible?"

Shaken, but grateful for the distraction and the chance to redirect the conversation, Daisy employed a skill she'd learned from her mom. Diversion. "Tell me about your parents' home." According to the firm's associates, Michael's family owned two houses plus a condo in Florida. "The one we're headed to."

"It's big and impressive. You'll see."

She had to keep him talking. "Is that where you grew up?"

"Until ninth grade."

"What happened?" Daisy giggled. "Did you become a juvenile delinquent and run away?"

"I hopped a boxcar and traveled the country. Hung out with vagrants around trash-barrel fires and ate canned beans." He eyed her and winked. "Actually, I spent four years at Philips Academy. A Warner family tradition."

Daisy made a mental note to research the school.

"What about your high-school experience? Private school?"

"Public."

He shot her a questioning look, as if no one worth their salt attended state-run schools.

How could she explain without offending him? "Some public schools are as good as private." She had to change the subject again before he asked more questions. "Other than work-related trips, how often do you leave the city?"

As Michael droned on about pleasure trips he'd enjoyed, she prayed he wouldn't ask about her family's vacations, which other than a few trips to the beach were nonexistent. The moment he transitioned to the perks of city life, Daisy's shoulders relaxed and allowed her to admire the Long Island scenery. Wide stretches of trees and a profusion of autumn colors interrupted buildings and bustling towns, reminding her of home.

When Michael turned onto Meadow Lane, Daisy pictured the Google Earth images she'd viewed. Which driveway would lead to the Warner mansion?

"We're here." He turned onto a winding driveway guarded by elaborate metal gates standing open. High-dollar cars lined both sides. "Looks like Mother's event is another huge success." Michael drove past a tennis court and stopped in front of an elaborate two-story home covering a wide swath of land.

Daisy's gaze shifted to a pool and a separate structure on the right side of the house.

A uniformed man dashed to the driver's side. "Good afternoon, Mr. Warner."

"How's it going, Jenkins?"

"Couldn't be better."

"Good to hear. Ms. Butler and I are here until tomorrow afternoon. Our bags are in the trunk."

"Yes, sir." Jenkins opened Michael's door. "I'll park your car beside the garage and take care of your luggage. Your guest is staying in the Champagne suite."

"Appropriate." Michael tossed Jenkins his keys, rounded the rear of the car, and opened the passenger door. He extended his hand. "Welcome to the Warner Estate."

Daisy struggled to keep from appearing awestruck. After all, Michael knew her dad's family was one of the south's wealthiest, even though she would never see a dime of their money. "Beautiful house." She accepted his hand and stepped out. "How many bedrooms?"

"Eight. Twelve and a half bathrooms."

Daisy pressed her lips tight to keep her jaw from dropping. Why would any family need that many bathrooms? She clung to Michael's arm as they made their way up a short flight of stairs and into a grand foyer. Daisy blinked to avoid gawking at the curved staircase, marble floor, and massive crystal chandelier. Piano music perked her ears as she breathed in the sweet scent wafting from dozens of yellow roses spilling from an elaborate vase centered on a round glass table.

A tall, slender, silver-haired woman wearing stilettos and a blue and white seashell-patterned dress approached and kissed Michael's cheek. "I'm delighted you're joining us for the weekend, dear."

"Hello, Mother. I'd like you to meet Daisy Butler."

"Ah yes, the firm's newest senior associate." She smiled while extending a manicured hand. "Welcome to our home."

"Thank you, Mrs. Warner." Daisy eyed her elaborate blue diamond ring while accepting her firm grip. "Your home is lovely."

"Michael will give you the grand tour a bit later." She released Daisy's hand. "First, I want you both to meet our museum's new curator. He was educated in Europe and comes highly recommended by the most influential art experts." She linked arms with Michael and Daisy while escorting them into an elegant room awash in shades of blue, white, and gold. Dozens of guests mingled and spilled out onto a deck overlooking the Atlantic. A tuxedo-clad gentleman played a Broadway tune on a white grand piano.

After Mrs. Warner introduced Michael to the curator and hyped his credentials, a uniformed server took their drink orders. Two more servers carried trays of appetizers while circulating among the guests. So, this was how the elite raised money. Spend a fortune to raise a bundle.

Mr. Warner strode over and clasped his hand on Michael's shoulder. "Your mother's outdone herself this year." He smiled at Daisy. "Did you enjoy the ride over?"

"Yes, sir. My first trip to Long Island."

"I hope not your last. Make sure Michael gives you the grand tour, and be sure to try the lobster-and-brie tartlet. It's worth the price of the ticket." Mr. Warner spun around and approached an arriving guest.

Michael chuckled. "Dad's a lobster fanatic. Before we indulge, I'll introduce you to Southampton's most prominent residents. Starting with our next-door neighbors." He leaned close. "New money. The guy's a software genius."

"Who's the man taking all the pictures?"

"Reporter for the local paper."

A newsworthy event, just like her elusive grandmother's big affairs.

Three hours after Michael's first introduction, Daisy's cheeks ached from smiling and her brain reeled with names and tidbits of information. Thank goodness no one had asked about her family. Maybe the Butlers weren't all that well-known north of the Mason-Dixon line.

"Don't know about you, but I'm ready for a break." Michael steered Daisy out to the veranda that stretched from one end of house to the other. "I'm curious."

"Are you in a perpetual state of curiosity?" She gazed past the narrow stretch of beach to lazy waves depositing salty foam on the white sand. "Or only today?"

"As you said, an important lawyer quality. Anyway, now that you've met Southampton's elite, how does this compare to your family's big events?"

She pictured her family sitting around the kitchen table, celebrating her father's birthday with homegrown food. How could she respond without veering too far from the truth? Her mind drifted to a photo in her mom's scrapbook of her aging grandmother hosting a Savannah fundraiser. The woman she had never met, elegant in her eighties—her shoulders straight and chin held high to project an air of superiority and privilege. "Other than the guests' southern accents, I'd say they're about the same. Except for this view." Clever comment that couldn't possibly qualify as an outright fib.

"Speaking of the view, how about a walk on the beach?"

"After I talk to my dad. Today's his birthday."

"A big celebration?"

She shook her head. "Family dinner." In a house not much bigger than the Warner's great room—a house with a scandalous past. "Do you mind if I slip away to make that call?"

He placed his hand on her back. "I'll show you to your room."

"The Champagne suite?"

"He leaned close. Largest guest quarters in the house."

"Is that its name or its description?"

"Both." He led her to the foyer, up the grand staircase, and down a wide hall to an open door. "My room is the next one over. After your phone call, we'll take that tour."

"Give me half an hour." She stepped into the extravagant suite decorated in shades of gold and white, illuminated by tabletop lamps. The Atlantic Ocean, barely visible in the waning light served as the backdrop. She settled on a white love seat adorned with gold throw pillows and fished her phone from her purse. Awe mingled with a sense of guilt as she pressed her dad's number. No Face Time tonight. She didn't dare reveal where she was calling from.

Chapter 4

Poppy's fork froze halfway to her mouth as Daisy's ringtone resonated. She set it on her dessert plate, grabbed Danny's phone off the kitchen counter, and pressed the speaker icon. "Hi, honey. Your sister and brother-in-law are here." She peered across the table at Lilly, the daughter who inherited her father's hazel eyes and wavy, dark hair. "Basil called a half hour ago. He's coming home after his tour is up in two weeks."

"I can't wait to heckle my little brother."

Pansy waved at the phone. "Hey, Daisy." Her dog stretching out on the floor beside her chair emitted a muffled bark. She reached down and stroked his muzzle. "Boots says hi too."

"We know you called to talk to your dad." Poppy pushed the phone to her husband.

Danny leaned his six-foot, muscular frame forward. "Good to hear your voice."

"Happy birthday, Dad. Sorry I couldn't make it home to help you celebrate. Did you open my gift?"

"I'm wearing it." He touched the logo on his chest. "Good-looking shirt. Hope it didn't cost too much."

"You know I only shop for bargains. Fifty-percent off." Daisy paused. "I have some exciting news to share."

Lilly leaned forward. Her long hair cascaded over her shoulders. "Did you meet a handsome man and fall in love?"

"Even better. A couple of days ago, the law firm promoted me to senior associate, which is one step away from partner."

Poppy kept her eyes focused on Danny while struggling to curb her excitement. "Congratulations, honey. We're all proud of you."

"Thanks, Mom. The promotion comes with more responsibility *and* a bigger paycheck."

Danny brushed his fingers through his thick hair, showing hints of gray at his temples. "I suppose that means New York will continue to hold you captive."

"I know the city is a long way from home, Dad, but once I became accustomed to the noise and the crowds I discovered it has a lot to offer."

Lilly's eyes lit. "I'm dying to hear about all the famous people you've met."

Poppy reached across the table and touched her daughter's arm. "I imagine your sister's much too busy to go looking for celebrities."

"All she has to do is keep her eyes open when she's walking to and from work."

Pansy dipped her fork into the dessert's thick icing. "Me and Poppy made a chocolate cake for Danny. I'll save you a piece, Daisy. For when you come home."

"You're a sweetheart, Aunt Pansy, and Mom's right about my work schedule, Lilly."

"Still." Her sister tapped her finger on the table. "I can't imagine you haven't seen at least *one* celebrity."

Andy elbowed his wife. "Give it a break, sugar pie."

"Come to think of it, Lilly, I've probably passed by a dozen or more famous people and didn't notice. Folks up here always seem to be in a rush. Like they're late for an appointment or running from the law. Anyway, I miss y'all like crazy."

Poppy leaned closer to the phone. "We're counting on you coming home for Thanksgiving. It'll be the first time since Basil enlisted that our family can celebrate together."

"I wouldn't miss it."

"Before you hang up, Daisy, Andy and I want to give Daddy our present." Lilly lifted a small yellow gift bag off the floor and handed it to her father.

"I hope you didn't spend too much."

"We know you don't like expensive gifts, Dad."

"Wasting money on presents doesn't make sense." Danny removed the tissue paper and pulled out a white coffee mug. His eyes widened as he read the inscription. "The World's Best Grandpa?"

Poppy pressed her hand to her chest. "Oh, my gosh. You're pregnant?"

Lilly's face radiated joy. "We're due a week before Daisy's birthday."

"What a wonderful way to celebrate turning a year older." Daisy's tone made it clear she was smiling. "I'm thrilled for you both."

A grin spread across Andy's face as he stroked his wife's arm. "The best news is we're having a boy."

"A grandson." Danny's chest puffed. "Maybe he'll become a carpenter like you."

"Not if I have any say. I want my son to go to college and make something of himself."

Danny planted his forearms on the table. "There's nothing more important than an honest day's labor, Andy. Where would the world be without first-rate builders?"

"Sorry, Danny. I didn't mean to imply anything."

He pointed his finger toward his son-in-law. "Don't you or Lilly ever forget that hardworking men and women made this country great."

"They won't dear." Poppy pulled his arm down. "Anyway, I'm glad your sister saved the news until you could join in, Daisy."

"So am I."

Pansy scooped a dollop of icing off the plate with her finger. "I remember when you were a baby, Lilly. All soft and cuddly. Know what? I'll make a picture book for your baby boy. A story 'bout his great-grandmother, Rose."

"We'd love a story written especially for our baby by the best aunt in the whole world."

"Maybe Mama will come home one day soon." Pansy snapped her fingers. "I almost forgot to give Danny my present." She popped up, scooped an envelope off the counter, and scooted to her brother-in-law's side. "Special for you." She leaned down and kissed his cheek.

Poppy exchanged glances with her husband as he opened the envelope and removed Pansy's standard gift for every occasion. A handcrafted card with a single lottery ticket inside. Always the same numbers.

"Prettiest birthday card yet. Thank you, Pansy."

"That one's for the *big* drawing. After you win, you can give some of the money to Lilly and Andy for their new baby, and you and me can open a flower shop."

"Will you put it in the tin with the others?" Danny handed the ticket to Pansy. "For safekeeping."

"Uh-huh." She carried the ticket to the hutch and pried the lid off a floral tin her mama Rose had used to collect spare change for trips to the local thrift store.

Poppy smiled at her sister who believed that discarding losing tickets would jinx the next one. Somehow, she failed to grasp the fact that possessing more money than one needed to live a modest life represented everything Danny despised. Fortunately, the chances of winning the lottery were as improbable as lightning striking on a sunny day or Danny ever reconnecting with his family.

"Well now, everyone has given you a gift except me." Poppy opened a bottom cabinet and removed a bottle of top-shelf Kentucky Bourbon.

"Let me guess," said Daisy. "Mom is giving you the one luxury you allow yourself."

"Restricted to one drink a week." Danny leaned close to the phone. "In case you haven't noticed, there are plenty of law firms here in Georgia."

"You don't need to worry about me, Dad. Anyway, y'all enjoy the rest of the special day, and give each other hugs for me."

The moment the call ended, Poppy touched her husband's hand. "Time for my birthday gift part two." She stood and pulled two glasses from the cabinet. "Our weekly date."

"What about the dishes?"

"You two go on, Dad." Lilly reached for his empty plate. "The three of us can handle kitchen cleanup."

"Okay, then." He clutched the bourbon and escorted Poppy outside. They strolled through the backyard to a wooden swing anchored to an arbor entwined with a climbing jasmine vine—his gift for their second anniversary, when she was pregnant with Lilly. She breathed in the sweet floral scent and settled on her spot facing west to view sunsets.

Danny sat beside her. After pouring two drinks, he set the bottle on a homemade table beside the swing.

"Happy birthday, sweetheart." She held up her glass and waited for his next move.

He clinked his glass to hers. "To us."

Poppy smiled. His verbal response meant the chances were fifty-fifty the man of few words would talk during their time alone. Maybe he'd even reveal a bit of information about his troubled past and add to the story Poppy had knit together over the years. Private assumptions she kept hidden in her heart in hopes that one day he would find the courage to share the truth with her.

Halfway through his drink, he spoke. "Daisy needs to move back to Georgia."

"Are you worried about her living in New York?"

"Too many temptations."

"We taught her well. She'll keep her priorities straight."

"I hope." He took another sip and fell silent.

Poppy sighed when reality set in. Tonight she wouldn't learn any of the secrets he kept buried deep.

Chapter 5

Daisy set her phone on the coffee table. She fingered a satin throw pillow while mentally picturing her family sitting around the kitchen table, enjoying each other's company while delighting in Lilly and Andy's announcement. Her parents valued living a simple life, unencumbered by possessions, yet shackled by a past no one dared discuss or question.

She stretched her arm across the back of the love seat and eyed moonbeams spilling across the water. How would her dad and sister react if they could see her in this room surrounded by unabashed luxury? No need to dwell on that now. She checked her watch. Five minutes before Michael showed up. Time enough to unpack.

Daisy tossed the pillow aside and peered around. Where was her suitcase? Had Jenkins neglected to bring it up? She strolled across the room and opened the closet. The suitcase lay on the top shelf. Her clothes hung on padded silk hangers beside a fluffy white bathrobe sporting the Warner crest. A pair of matching slippers peeked from underneath. She found the remainder of her clothing in the top drawer of a dresser beside a handwritten note.

Welcome, Ms. Butler. Please let Mrs. Warner know if I can be of further assistance. I hope you enjoy your visit.
Nancy

Should she ask Michael about Nancy or pretend that someone unpacking her clothes wasn't more than a little creepy?

A knock startled her. She pushed the drawer closed and opened the door.

Michael leaned against the doorframe. "Is your dad enjoying his birthday?"

"He's especially excited to learn his first grandchild is due early next year." Michael's wide-eyed expression triggered a laugh. "My sister's pregnant."

"Another Butler to share the wealth. I hope Nancy took good care of your luggage."

Best to pretend she wasn't freaked out. "She did."

"Good." He held out his arm. "Are you ready for the five-dollar tour?"

She grasped his bicep. "Are you giving me the bargain rate?"

"Definitely."

Twenty minutes into the tour, Daisy's head spun with details about expensive paintings and priceless possessions. After forty minutes her muscles twitched. She'd had enough. "This has been great, Michael. But right now I'd welcome something cold to drink."

"Make that wine and you have a deal."

"You're on."

He led her from the formal dining room to party central and requested two glasses of white wine from a roving server. When the man stepped away, Michael leaned close. "I was wondering how long it would take you to stop me."

"From what?"

"Trying to impress you."

She stared at him. Maybe she should tell him that her maternal grandmother was a prostitute who had disappeared without a trace more than three decades ago. Would that bit of juicy gossip impress him? From the corner of her eye, she caught sight of his mother heading their way.

"Has my son completed the tour?"

"He has, and your home is beautiful, Mrs. Warner. Your decorating taste is exceptional. Especially your paintings. They're exquisite."

"I assume you're an enthusiast. Who is your favorite artist?"

Uh-oh. Painted into a corner. Daisy stifled a giggle at the irony while racking her brain for a name. If only she had taken at least one art class in college. "I'm particularly intrigued by French artists."

"Excellent choice. You must let Michael take you for a stroll on the beach." She eyed Daisy's dress. "October evenings are quite chilly. Did you bring a wrap?"

"A sweater."

"I'll ask my personal assistant to bring you something more appropriate."

What did she consider appropriate? A mink coat? Was her personal assistant the mysterious Nancy who unpacked her clothes? "Thank you, you're a gracious hostess."

"My pleasure."

The server returned carrying two glasses of white wine.

"I'll leave you two to enjoy the rest of the evening."

Daisy's eyes followed Mrs. Warner strolling toward guests gathered around the piano. How would a woman whose demeanor screamed of privilege respond to her mom's thrift-store wardrobe or her humble, down-home manner?

Michael swirled his wine glass, then sniffed and sipped. "Montrachet Grand Cru. From Dad's cellar."

How could he tell from one swallow? She tasted while mentally replaying their tour of the dark wood-paneled, temperature-controlled room filled with hundreds of wine bottles. "Delicious." Was that how rich people described expensive wine from private cellars?

He leaned close. "I suspect this bottle was reserved for family and a few of Dad's closest buddies."

"Lucky me. Hanging out with the number-one son." Daisy speculated how much each swallow cost while trying to remember the names of guests she'd met. Maybe it didn't matter. None were people she'd hang out with or even see again. Unless she and Michael became one of those New York power couples featured on society pages, attending gala black-tie events and dining at the most exclusive restaurants.

Michael plucked a baguette topped with cream cheese and a slice of smoked salmon off a tray balanced by a server. "Perfect accompaniment for the wine."

"Indeed." Daisy followed his lead.

A middle-aged woman wearing a gray suit approached. "Mrs. Warner asked me to bring this to you, Ms. Butler." She handed the white leather, fur-lined jacket draped over her arm to Daisy. "I hope you found your clothing hung properly."

Mystery solved. "Yes. Thank you, Nancy."

"My pleasure." The woman nodded, then spun around and strolled from the room.

"That's our cue." Michael set their wine glasses on a table and escorted Daisy out back, across the veranda, and down a weathered ramp. He stopped at stairs descending to the beach. "If you don't want sand in your shoes I suggest you go barefoot." He kicked off his deck shoes and rolled up his pant legs.

Daisy breathed in the salty air while slipping out of her shoes. Gentle waves lapped onto the sand as the cool evening breeze tousled her hair and sent goosebumps popping out on her skin. A giggle escaped as she donned Mrs. Warner's jacket. "I should have asked for fur-lined beach booties."

"If such an item exists you can bet Mother owns a pair."

She pulled the jacket tight across her chest. "I imagine sunrises are beautiful from here."

"They are. However, there's nothing more spectacular than viewing the sun setting over the city from my penthouse terrace."

An idle comment or extended an invitation? Daisy eyed the handful of guests lingering on the veranda, their shapes illuminated by gas flames flickering in post lanterns. "I'm curious. Of all the people I met, you didn't introduce any as an attorney from the firm."

"For good reason. Other than you, none were invited."

"Should I be flattered or wary?"

"Is suspicion a character flaw or a by-product of our profession?"

Daisy stole a sideways glance at Michael. "Answering a question with a question is definitely a professional ploy."

"Did I mention that you're the first attorney from our firm I've dated?" His arm brushed hers as they stepped onto the sand and headed toward the surf.

"Character flaw or personal preference?"

"More like my good fortune. You're also the only woman I ever doused with cappuccino."

Her good fortune. Daisy stooped to pick up a beach pebble. "For your mother's collection." She brushed sand off the smooth surface.

"So you noticed her rock-filled Baccarat and Steuben vases."

Did all rich people tout brand names? "How could I miss them? I mean, there's a collection in half the rooms." She reached for another pebble. "Does your mother come from a wealthy family?"

"Her father owns one of the largest private yachts in existence, complete with a helicopter pad." Michael slid his arm around her shoulders. "Does that answer your question?"

"Perfectly." Daisy turned up the collar on Mrs. Warner's jacket. If her relationship with Michael continued evolving, she'd need a lot more pebbles to come close to fitting in with his family.

Chapter 6

Poppy smoothed the collar on her long-sleeved dress, one of two reserved for church-going with her sister. She unplugged her cell phone, dropped it in her purse, and headed to the kitchen.

"Time for Daisy's weekly call before you and Pansy head out?" Danny's eyes remained fixed on the weekend newspaper lying open on the table. A clear indication he remained steadfast in his determination never to step foot inside a church.

"Almost." After tucking her purse under her arm, Poppy strolled to the backyard and breathed in the fresh-morning air while closing the distance to her private retreat. Inside, she set her purse and phone on the bench, removed her scrapbook from the trunk, and leafed through the pages. Daisy's ringtone brought a smile. She pressed Face Time. "Hi, honey."

"Hey, Mom."

"I can't wait to hear more about your promotion." Poppy's heart swelled with pride as she listened and watched the sparkle in her daughter's eyes. Her firstborn was accomplishing everything she had wished for her. "I'm proud of you. Are you celebrating big this weekend?"

"If you consider attending a fundraising event at the Warner's Southampton estate celebrating, yes. Michael and I drove up yesterday. We're a few hours from the city, so we stayed the night. Their house has twelve-and-a-half bathrooms, Mom."

"That's a lot of toilets and sinks to clean."

"I doubt Mrs. Warner ever cleaned anything. They call this room the Champagne Suite." Daisy turned her phone and slowly scanned the space.

"Oh my, everything's white and gold." While Daisy described other rooms she'd viewed, Poppy imagined her daughter living in a grand house, with staff to keep every surface spotless. Hosting big, fancy parties for important people after choosing an outfit from a closet filled with expensive clothes. "Michael inviting you to his family's home sounds like your relationship is becoming more serious."

"He's way out of my league, Mom."

"Nonsense." She'd spent years inspiring her daughter to aim high and reach her full potential. "You're a beautiful, intelligent, educated young woman with Butler blood flowing through your veins."

"It takes more than blood to fit in with this crowd. Good news is, I survived my first introduction to the Warner lifestyle, so maybe I'm up to the task."

"No maybes about it, honey."

"Since talking to Dad yesterday, I've been thinking a lot about our family dynamics. Do you suppose enough time has gone by for him to move beyond his past and introduce me to my grandfather?"

Poppy's chest tightened. What possessed Daisy to even think about asking that question? "Why after all these years do you want to meet him now?"

"Curiosity?"

She wouldn't have asked if she understood the depth of her husband's hatred for his father. Maybe the time had come to reveal what truth she understood. "I never told you about the day I came face-to-face with Curtis."

"You've met him?"

"Not exactly. A couple months after your dad first showed up at my door, Curtis was hosting a Memorial Day party at his ranch. I didn't want to go, but Danny insisted. A big white tent stretched over dozens of tables, all covered with white cloths and fancy centerpieces. There was a stage with a band. Hundreds of people milled about. No one seemed to recognize Danny. They stared at me, then looked away without saying a word. We found Curtis in his stable showing his newest thoroughbred to a group of men."

Poppy paused, swallowing the lump rising in her throat. "A look of disgust clouded his face the second he saw us. He spun away and led the men to another stall. At that moment, I understood that in addition to not being invited, we were not welcome."

"I'm so sorry, Mom. I had no idea."

"It took a while for me to come to grips with the fact that your dad used me to embarrass and humiliate his father."

"Yet, you stayed with him."

"Yes." Poppy eyed a scrapbook photo of Curtis posing with the governor and a U.S. senator. Had she spent far too much time and energy over the years touting Daisy's connection to the Butler family? "I don't know why Danny hates his father. All I know is that his hatred runs deep."

Daisy sighed. "Obviously an introduction from Dad isn't possible."

"It would take a miracle." Poppy closed the scrapbook and set it back in the trunk, confident Daisy had abandoned the idea. "The news about Lilly and Andy's baby is exciting. Your sister's more of a homebody, like me."

"You mean unlike your oldest daughter."

"You're living the life some of us can't, honey."

"Yoo-hoo, sis." Pansy's voice drifted from outside. "Time to go to church."

Daisy chuckled. "Does she know we talk every Sunday morning?"

The door swung open and banged against the wall. Pansy bounced in with Boots trailing behind her. "Hi, Daisy."

"There's your answer." Poppy aimed the phone toward her sister.

"Hi, Aunt Pansy. You look extra pretty this morning."

"Do you like my new dress? I found it at the thrift store. Cost me five dollars. When Danny's lottery ticket comes up a winner, I'll buy a closet full of fancy dresses."

Poppy turned her phone around. "Time to say goodbye until next Sunday. Enjoy the rest of your weekend, honey."

"I will. Love you, Mom and Aunt Pansy."

"We love you too." Poppy ended the call and slipped the phone in her purse.

"How soon can we go visit Daisy in New York?"

"New York's a long way from here."

"We could drive up in Danny's truck or ride on a train or a big airplane. Maybe Mama's there. We could look for her and bring her back home." Pansy touched her mother's gold cross necklace hanging an inch below her neck. "She wore this every Sunday while we did pretend-church in our front room. I'm glad we can go to real church now."

Especially since Agnes Watkins became too ill to attend the public service. "It's time to go, sweetie."

They walked out and headed toward the driveway. Pansy shooed Boots onto the back porch before climbing into Danny's truck. Poppy slid onto the driver's seat and drove down the long driveway, past the wooded area to the two-lane road.

Ten minutes later, she joined the half-dozen vehicles parked in the gravel lot beside the small white frame church. She held Pansy's hand while they walked in and slid into the last row. As the service began, Poppy counted the people sitting in the other nine rows. Thirty-seven. Typical Sunday morning. Her eyes drifted to an empty front row. Agnes's private pew. She cringed at memories of the spiteful old widow. The hateful way she had waggled her finger at them the day Rose dared take her daughters to a service. Her claim that the devil's cursed offspring weren't welcome in God's house. The part-time pastor who refused to comment. According to what their mama had told them, without Agnes' financial support, he'd be forced to preach for free. She blinked to erase the image and tuned into Pansy singing along with the familiar hymn.

When the pastor sauntered to the podium to begin his sermon, Poppy's attempt to focus on his words was dashed by a fly buzzing in and out of flowers adorning the lady's hat two rows up. It landed on one of the flowers seventeen times before the message ended.

Pansy's elbow jab drew Poppy back to reality. "The piano lady's 'bout to play the last song."

One fact never changed. The pastor's sermons were always short. Poppy led her sister to the exit before the song ended.

"Can I walk over to Willy's and buy us ice cream bars?" Pansy's tone radiated excitement.

Same routine every Sunday. "Of course." Poppy fished a five from her purse and placed it in Pansy's hand. "I'll drive over and pick you up."

"What flavor do you want?"

"Surprise me."

"Okay."

Poppy returned to the family truck and waited for Pansy to dash the half block to the corner and cross the street to Willy's gas station and convenience store—the one place on Agnes's land that sold food. The moment her sister entered the building, she pulled out of the church parking lot and drove past the two-story, brick thrift store. At the corner she braked for the three-way stop and peered at boarded-up storefronts lining the side street—a testimony to Agnes's insufferable demeanor.

She drove across the intersection, pulled into Willy's parking lot, and turned the radio to a country station. Her foot tapped to the beat until a car she didn't recognize pulled in beside her. Poppy pressed her hand against her left cheek and dropped her chin to her chest. Would she ever find the courage to allow strangers to see past her birthmark and into her heart?

The passenger door swung open. "I bought us our favorite." Pansy scooted in and handed over a chocolate covered-vanilla ice cream bar.

"Perfect choice." Poppy's heart warmed at the sight of her sister peeling off the wrapper and biting into her Sunday treat.

Pansy pulled another ice cream bar from her pocket. "I also bought one for Danny."

"Oh, dear. We'd better hurry home before it melts." As Poppy backed out of the parking space and turned onto the main road, her mind wandered to her earlier conversation with Daisy. Something beyond simple curiosity had prompted her to ask about meeting Curtis. A litany of possibilities raced across her mind. All of them saddled with dire consequences.

Chapter 7

S tunned by the revelation about her dad's hatred for his father, Daisy stood at the Warner's guestroom window. Why had she considered surprising her mom with a question about meeting her grandfather without laying a smidgen of groundwork a good idea? Maybe she should call back and tell her the truth. A seagull soared above the surf then dove to the water and snagged an unsuspecting fish. Forget about calling her mom back. She had created enough anxiety for one day. A yacht sailed on the distant horizon. Who was onboard? A rich family out for a Sunday cruise or a wealthy businessman impressing clients?

Daisy spun away from the window, dropped her phone in her purse, and debated whether to pack her clothes or find out if Nancy would show up and tackle the task. What had other guests who had slept in this room done? What would a law-firm partner do? Take charge. That's what. She pulled her suitcase from the closet and set it on the bed. While packing she wondered what it would be like living in a grand house with servants.

A knock.

Daisy closed her suitcase and opened the door. "Good morning."

"I slept right through the sunrise." Michael smiled. "I assume you found your room comfortable."

"It was perfect." As if surrounded by luxury and snuggling between satin-smooth sheets under a down comforter could be anything other than comfortable.

"Mimosas are waiting for us in the morning room."

Had they missed that space during yesterday's tour? Did their home also have afternoon and evening rooms? Maybe she should refer to her parents' kitchen as the all-day room. She swallowed a giggle and eased into the hall. "Is Champagne for breakfast a typical Sunday-morning indulgence?"

"When we entertain important visitors."

What did he mean by important? One of the firm's rising stars or a woman Michael found intriguing?

"What about your family? Mimosas for guests or a more southern drink?"

After her grandmother, Rose, disappeared all those years ago, no adult outside her immediate family had ever set foot in her parents' home. "We tend to opt for piping hot coffee, scrambled eggs, bacon, grits, and fresh-from-the-oven biscuits smothered with homemade jam or honey."

"Grits?" He held her arm while they descended the grand staircase.

"Slathered with butter."

"I've never noticed that option on a menu." They walked through the foyer to a hall.

"You obviously haven't spent much time in the south."

"A situation I plan to correct."

Her bottom lip caught between her teeth. If he was fishing for an invitation, forget it. No way she'd invite him to her parents' humble home. At least not until their relationship became far more serious.

They reached the end of the hall and walked under an arched opening into a space flooded with sunlight streaming through floor-to-ceiling windows. Plants and potted trees set in pots on the stone-tile floor swayed beneath whirling ceiling fans shaped like palm fronds.

Mrs. Warner, wearing black slacks, a white, long-sleeved, silk shirt, and gold sandals wandered over and kissed Michael's cheek "Good morning."

"Morning, Mother."

She touched Daisy's arm. "I trust you slept well."

"Yes, thank you."

"Excellent." She swept her arm toward a wrought-iron buffet laden with serving platters. "I hope you're hungry."

Daisy struggled to maintain a casual demeanor as she eyed the array of choices. Fruit. Smoked salmon. Eggs Benedict. Was that caviar? For breakfast? "It looks scrumptious."

"A special buffet for a special guest." Mr. Warner approached carrying two Champagne flutes. He handed one to Michael and offered the other to Daisy. "If you prefer, I'll ask our chef to bring you a Bellini."

Their chef? How could she ever relate to these people? She released Michael's arm and accepted the drink. "Mimosas always hit the spot."

Michael set his flute on a glass-topped, wrought-iron table before sauntering to the buffet and spooning caviar onto his plate. "Know what's missing? Grits."

Heat surged up Daisy's neck. Was he mocking her? "Shrimp and grits are served in the finest southern restaurants."

Mrs. Warner linked her arm around Daisy's elbow. "My college roommate was a southern girl from a prominent, South Carolina family. Such a sweet accent. I'm wondering why you choose to attend a Georgia university rather than Princeton, your grandfather's alma mater?"

Daisy's jaw clenched. Had the entire Warner family boned up on Curtis Butler?

"Give her a break, dear." Mr. Warner approached. "Our guest hasn't enjoyed the first bite of breakfast, and you're already grilling her."

"Please forgive me, Daisy. I'm always eager to become better acquainted with Michael's lady friends."

How many lady friends had his mother met?

"My mother's inquisitive nature is one of the traits we find most endearing." Michael set his plate on the table.

"And sometimes irritating." Mr. Warner laughed. "Fortunately, her beauty and grace make up for her overzealous curiosity." He reached for Daisy's glass. "I'll set your drink on the table while you fix yourself a plate. I suggest you try the smoked salmon with caviar and a dollop of sour cream. One of my all-time favorites."

So much for shrimp and grits. "Mine too." At least it could be. After filling her plate with what she hoped was the appropriate amount of food, Daisy settled between Michael and his father, across from his mother. Unlike meals at her home where everyone waited for her mom to bless the meal, Michael and his father dug right in. She tasted the salmon and caviar first, followed by a swallow of mimosa. Interesting breakfast choices.

Mrs. Warner wrapped her fingers around her flute while eyeing Daisy. "How does it feel to become the firm's newest rising star?"

Was this some sort of test? How did the two law-firm partners expect her to respond? With confidence or gratitude? "Encouraging."

"I find it interesting how women of means choose high-powered, lucrative careers."

Daisy's eyes shifted from Mrs. Warner to Michael.

He winked, as if they savored a shared secret.

Daisy smiled at Mrs. Warner. "Mom always encouraged me to forge my own course."

"Speaking of courses." Mr. Warner turned to Michael and engaged in a conversation about a high-powered legal case.

While Mrs. Warner speared a kiwi with a gold fork, Daisy's mind drifted to last night. Walking on the beach with Michael. The warmth cascading through her the moment he wrapped his arm around her, pulled her close, and kissed her. Were his feelings driven by passion? Or had she become a pawn in a grand scheme to secure an inside track to Curtis Butler's business empire?

Daisy reached for her mimosa as images of the law firm's conference room skated across her mind. She imagined taking a seat at the long table as the newest partner—one of a handful of women to reach that pinnacle. A huge salary. Tons of prestige. Fulfilling her mom's wishes to make a name for herself. Maybe the path leading to that level of success didn't matter. Or did it? She tuned into the men's conversation. How long would it take to learn the real reason she'd been invited to the Warner's home?

Chapter 8

Dark clouds drifting from the west cast a gray pall in the greenhouse as Poppy finished watering a row of petunias. She turned off the spigot and spotted Danny standing at the end of the building with his back turned toward her. Over the years, she had learned that every once in a while, gloomy weather sent him into a reflective mood and unleashed his silence. She strolled to his side, ready to listen if today turned out to be one of those days.

He stood with his arms folded tight across his chest, his thumbs thrust in his armpits.

Should she start a conversation or exercise patience? She removed her gloves and stuffed them into her jeans pocket.

Minutes passed.

Impatience won out. "Looks like a storm coming."

Danny remained silent.

"We can use the rain."

Lightning flashed in the distance. Another flash, followed by a long, low rumble. A chipmunk scampered across the path between rows of potted trees filling the space behind the greenhouse. Scattered raindrops struck the glass roof. How many times had she waited for Danny to talk, only to face another disappointment. Maybe she should walk away and leave him alone.

The rain intensified. Another lightning flash, closer this time.

Poppy remained by his side. "Could be a real gully washer."

More silence.

A thunderclap shook the glass.

Poppy inched closer to Danny as memories of their years together played in her mind. Despite his physical strength, he was a gentle man who had never spanked his children. Instead, he disciplined with a stern look and a few well-chosen words.

"She married him for his wealth and position."

Poppy startled at Danny's sudden comment. Somehow she understood he spoke about his mother.

"Which was all Curtis Butler had to offer."

Her heart jumped to her throat at his tone's bitter edge.

Danny scoffed. "He chose her for her social status. A marriage of convenience and opportunity."

Poppy pressed her lips tight to prevent her mouth from falling open. He had never before uttered a word about his parents' relationship.

"His wife's penchant for entertaining along with her insane efforts to prepare my sisters for their place in Savannah's high society consumed every bit of her time and energy." Danny stared straight ahead. "She didn't have much use for a son or my old man."

Thunder shook the building again.

"He stayed away from our Savannah house for weeks, sometimes months at a time."

The rain escalated to a downpour and released sheets of water cascading down the glass and obscuring the view. "My poor excuse for parents hired a string of nannies to raise me." Danny turned away from the window and trudged down the center aisle.

Poppy fell in step beside him.

He stopped to pluck a dried leaf off the concrete walkway. "The day I turned eleven, Curtis didn't bother to show up for my birthday. That's the day mother told me he managed his business empire from his ranch and couldn't afford to take any time off." Danny crushed the leaf. "Two more years passed before we set foot on his ranch for the first time. Things might've turned out different if that day had never happened." After the pieces of leaf fell between his fingers, his lips tightened.

What did he mean by *we*? Did a nanny or a friend go to the ranch with him? She yearned to ask yet knew it was best to listen without revealing a hint of emotion. The last thing he needed from her was pity. She remained beside him as he meandered back toward the glass.

Danny thrust his hands in his pocket, an indication his revelations had come to an end.

As they watched the storm intensify, Poppy's mind drifted back to her own childhood. The way adults stared at her and Pansy amid whispers. Children's cruel taunts about her birthmark and her sister's simple ways. How much more painful were Danny's memories?

"Is Daisy dating someone?"

Poppy's brows raised. Where did that question come from? She hadn't mentioned Michael, and as far as she knew, Pansy didn't know about him. There was no way she could lie and say no. Maybe she could pretend ignorance. Better to come clean. "She's dated a young man a few times. Casually."

"Another attorney?"

She nodded. "One of the partners."

Danny pulled his hands from his pockets and plucked a twig off the walkway. "I don't want her getting mixed up with a man who isn't good enough for her."

Poppy placed her hand on his arm. "Will you ever consider any man suitable for your firstborn?"

"A man like Andy. Down to earth. Loyal to his wife and family."

"You mean not rich."

Danny's jaw tensed. "Money is a curse."

"Maybe not if used for good. Besides, Daisy won't fall for a man who doesn't live up to her standards."

"Something needs to bring her closer to home."

"I miss her too, sweetheart."

A long moment of silence.

"You're a good mother."

"And you're a good father."

He snapped the twig in half, then turned and strode away.

Poppy remained by the window as images of the day she met Danny played in her mind. Months after her mama disappeared, she'd responded to a knock on the front door. He stood there dressed in jeans and a tee shirt. His stare lasted for a brief moment before he explained that his car had broken down a half mile away. Her delight when he accepted her invitation to sit on the porch after using their phone to call a tow service. The shock mingled with joy when he showed up at her door two days later, and afterwards twice a week for two months. Each time he stayed for dinner. Then...the trip to the ranch to meet his father.

The rain slowed to a drizzle. The greenhouse cat slinked around Poppy's leg. She stooped, gathered the feline in her arms, and stroked its back. Despite Danny's initial interest in her as a knife to thrust into his father's heart, he was the best thing that had ever happened to her. She would do anything within her power to help him move beyond his past and continue to live life on his terms.

Chapter 9

Tuesday morning after the weekend visit to Southampton, Daisy exited the elevator on the floor dedicated to the law firm's senior associates and entered the long, narrow space occupied by administrative assistants. Was it her imagination or were admins staring at her as she passed their desks? Perhaps a stab of guilt about spending the weekend at the senior partner's home played havoc with her emotions. Or more likely an adrenaline rush muddled her brain after her mad dash to work forced by sleeping a half hour past her normal wake-up time.

She walked into her new office, the same size as her previous spot but less crowded, with two instead of three associates. "Happy Tuesday, Walter."

"Morning." Her office mate, a young international-law attorney, spoke without looking up from his work.

"How early did you show up?"

"Couple of hours ago." Although the guy wasn't big on talking, he normally exchanged a few pleasantries. Maybe today he found his work far too engrossing to bother with conversation. Daisy hung her purse on a hook, then exchanged her sneakers for high heels. Desperate for a caffeine jolt, she walked out of the office at the same moment her assistant arrived carrying a cup from the ground-level coffee shop. "Hey, Shannon."

"Good morning, Ms. Butler."

Despite Daisy's insistence she drop the formal title, Shannon refused to veer from the firm's directive that underlings address all attorneys by their surnames. Which in Daisy's opinion created an environment akin to a class system rather than a healthy-working partnership. "Pretty suit. Blue is a great color for you."

Shannon's cheeks pinkened, as if shocked by a compliment from a superior. "Thank you."

Daisy leaned close. "You know, not every attorney in the building suffers from stuffed-shirt syndrome. Truth is, we'd all be up a creek without administrative expertise and support."

Shannon aimed her thumb over her shoulder. "You treat me with more respect than every other lawyer who ever occupied that office."

"Perhaps because I'm the first southerner. I'm heading to the break room for a cup of coffee."

Shannon bolted from her chair. "I'll go for you."

"Why? Is it off limits for lawyers?"

"We...um...always bring coffee to our bosses."

"Maybe it's time attorneys fetch their own caffeine. I assume the break room is in the same place as the one on the junior-associate floor?"

Shannon nodded while lowering to her chair. "Except bigger."

"Higher floor, more prestige." As Daisy neared the open door, she tuned into chatter drifting into the hallway. Eager to prove her self-sufficiency, she barged in, made her way to the coffee station, and popped in a pod.

Conversation abruptly stopped.

One glance at the mass exodus made it clear she had broken protocol and stepped way over the line. The instant her coffee cup filled, she grabbed sugar and creamer packets and headed back to her office.

Three admins huddled around Shannon, seemingly deep in conversation. Had her ill-planned trip to the break room put her assistant in an awkward position? What if the partners heard about her brazen move? Would they tag her as a troublemaker? A rebel?

When she came closer, the admins scattered as if someone had yelled fire. She stopped beside Shannon's desk. "I apologize if I created problems for you."

She kept her head down. "You didn't."

Questioning whether her assistant's comment was accurate, Daisy walked into her office and settled at her desk. While booting her laptop, the admins' bizarre behavior troubled her. By noon the urge to clear the air had tensed every muscle in her body. She shouldered her purse, strode from her office, and stopped beside her assistant's desk. "I want to treat you to lunch."

"I uh…" Shannon hesitated as if debating whether or not to beg off.

Tension crawled down Daisy's spine. She leaned close. "Name the place and I'll meet you there."

Shannon scribbled an address on a sticky note and handed it over.

Daisy nodded, then headed toward the elevator bank, keenly aware that eyes followed her. Fifteen minutes later, she stood on the sidewalk in front of a café eight blocks from the office. Too far for a typical forty-five-minute lunch break. Her foot tapped the pavement until Shannon rounded the corner and closed the distance. Daisy smiled. "I'm famished. Hope you're hungry."

Inside the fifties-style diner, a hostess escorted them to a table toward the back. They settled across from each other. After a waiter delivered menus and water, Daisy sensed Shannon's uneasiness. The way she laser-focused on the menu while seemingly avoiding eye contact. Somehow, she had to create a safe atmosphere before addressing the three-hundred-pound gorilla in the room.

After ordering, Daisy crossed her arms on the table and summoned her best smile. "How long have you worked for the firm?"

"Going on twelve years."

"Wow." Daisy noticed her wedding ring. "Does your family live in the city?"

"Bronx." Shannon reached for her water and took a sip. "My husband's a police officer."

"One of New York's finest. Do you have children?"

Shannon's eyes lit. "Two little girls. Eight and ten. My mother's a widow. She lives with us and helps take care of them."

"My sister, Lilly, is pregnant. Her first."

"Babies are God's gifts to the world." Shannon's eyes finally met Daisy's. "Sometimes we talk about having another, until we consider how much it costs to raise a child." As they continued talking about family, Shannon's shoulders seemed to relax. During lunch they engaged in idle chatter about growing up in the city and even managed a few laughs. By the time the waiter delivered dessert menus, Daisy sensed the time had come to broach the subject. "About this morning and my visit to the break room, I had no idea an attorney getting her own coffee would cause such a stir."

Shannon broke eye contact and fidgeted with her napkin.

Daisy's brows furrowed. "If there's something else going on, please don't keep me in the dark."

Shannon released a heavy sigh. "The thing is...another admin saw you and Michael Warner in his car Saturday morning."

With millions of people living in the city, how was that possible? And why would it matter? Except that she was considered an underling in the firm's hierarchy. Reality released a sensation akin to a swarm of butterflies invading her chest. "Is everyone assuming I'm using more than skills to work my way to partnership?"

Shannon's eyes widened. "Not me. I know you're smart and kind. Personally, I think some of the busybodies are jealous." She glanced around, then leaned forward. "I doubt there's one single woman in the firm who hasn't dreamed of capturing Michael Warner's heart."

Should she tell Shannon about her dinners with the law firm's heart-throb? Best to keep that bit of news private.

"Do you want me to tell everyone they're full of baloney?"

"I've already put you in a difficult position. It's best to let the rumor die down. In a few days, it'll be old news." Daisy tapped her fingers on the menu. "For now, how about we order the most decadent dessert on the menu?"

"Something chocolate?"

"Insanely rich and loaded with calories."

After strengthening their bond over ganache chocolate cake, Shannon headed back to the office. Daisy strolled south on Fifth Avenue, avoiding eye contact with passersby. How could anyone believe she would use feminine wiles to achieve success?

She stopped and faced a display window fronting an upscale men's store. Her reflection mingled with the headless male mannequin outfitted in designer jeans and a button-down shirt. Had the rumor reached Michael's ears? She pulled her phone from her purse. Maybe she should wait before calling him and find out if the rumor would die down. What if it didn't? He deserved a heads-up. She pressed his private number.

He answered after the second ring. "What a nice surprise."

"We need to talk."

"Business?"

"Personal."

"Come on up—"

"Not at the office."

"What's going on, Daisy?"

She explained.

"Are you serious? In my car?"

"Afraid so. Now speculation about us...me...is running amok."

"Hold on a sec." He placed the call on hold.

Daisy swallowed hard while staring at her reflection. A tainted woman. A prostitute's granddaughter. Why did people tend to assume the worse?

Michael returned. "Don't worry about the rumor. I'll take care of it."

"Sorry to burden you with this nonsense."

"It's not a big deal. Gotta run. We'll talk later." He ended the call.

How would he take care of it? Start a new rumor? Find out who started it and fire that person? Why should she wait for him to rescue her? She had to take control and act like a smart, educated woman. Strong. Confident. Capable of making it to the top on merit.

She dropped her phone in her purse, spun away from the window, and headed north to Nine West. During the elevator ride to her floor, she laced her fingers and tapped her thumbs. As the door slid open, Daisy squared her shoulders. She walked into the office, making eye contact and speaking to every admin she passed. If nothing else, she'd win them over with good old southern charm.

Chapter 10

T hree days after the rumor about Daisy sleeping her way to a partnership spread through the office like a swarm of starving mosquitoes, a new story emerged. That Michael had driven the firm's newest senior associate out of town to help calm a ticked-off corporate client. From *femme fatale* to the most admired woman in the firm in fewer than forty-eight hours.

"Looks like a storm coming." Her office mate glanced up as thunder rumbled, followed by a distant lightning flash.

"Thankfully today the storm is weather-related."

"What?"

Apparently Walter hadn't heard either rumor. "I hope it passes before time to leave. Hailing a cab in a rainstorm is a nightmare. Especially late Friday."

"Good reason to keep raingear handy."

"Wise words from a native New Yorker." Like Michael. Even though she suspected he had circulated the new rumor, he hadn't reached out to her since she'd called him with the news. Had he decided their personal relationship had run its course, or that she wasn't worth the effort? One good point if they had parted ways—it would prove her promotion was based on talent and potential rather than her connection to Curtis Butler.

For the remainder of the afternoon and early evening, Daisy remained focused on her current project. By eight, the storm had passed and her anxiety over hailing a cab abated. She changed from heels to sneakers, shouldered her purse, and rode the elevator to the ground floor. Outside she pulled her coat tight and breathed deeply, hoping the rain-washed air would revive her energy.

She walked up 57th toward 6th Avenue. At the corner she turned right, made her way to the end of the block, and crossed Central Park South. Horse hooves clopped from behind. She peered over her shoulder and cringed at the sight of the magnificent animal wearing blinders and pulling a buggy through crowded streets. Nothing like Curtis Butler's thoroughbreds she'd read about—prize-winning horses living on a ranch hidden from view by acres of trees and shrouds of mystery.

At the roundabout, Daisy turned up Broadway. The trees planted along the sidewalk and in the median softened the buildings' hard edges but did little to diminish the street noise too often punctuated by blaring horns and screaming sirens. Like night and day—different from the quiet back home. Except this was home now. A bustling city with millions of strangers and never-ending traffic snarls.

At the next corner, her eyes drifted to a figure crouched at the curb. The woman digging through a big black trash bag looked up. Daisy flinched at the sight of burn scars distorting the left side of her face. Curiosity mingled with heartfelt compassion compelled her to move closer. She breathed through her mouth to avoid the stench emanating from the woman's body and soiled clothing. The moment their eyes met, she detected profound sadness. Defeat. A deep sense of hopelessness. "If you're hungry, I'd be happy to buy you a meal."

The woman eyed Daisy from head to toe, before wiping her hands on her pants. She brushed nicotine-stained fingers through her matted hair. "A sandwich?"

"Sure. What kind would you like?"

She shrugged. "Dunno. Maybe chicken?"

"Perfect choice. Wait here." Daisy dashed toward the deli two doors down. She paused at the door and glanced over her shoulder. Of all the homeless people she passed every day on her way to and from work, why had she been drawn to that particular woman? Was it her scarred cheek? The woman opened another trash bag. Maybe she didn't trust a stranger to follow through.

Ten minutes after entering the deli line, Daisy rushed back to the curb and handed the woman a paper sack filled with two sandwiches, three apples, and four bottles of water. "What's your name?"

The woman's eyes narrowed as she removed an apple from the sack. "Why do you wanna know?"

"If our paths cross again, I want to address you by name."

She bit into the apple. Juice dribbled down her chin. "Ruby."

"Like the gem. My name's Daisy."

"Like the flower." The woman grinned, revealing teeth in desperate need of a dentist. "You're a good lady." She clutched the deli bag to her side, then scooted around the corner and out of sight.

Daisy suppressed the urge to follow Ruby and discover what bench or doorway she called home. What if her grandmother had ended up on the street? Desperate and alone. Michael's ringtone startled her. She pulled her phone from her purse. "Hey."

"Sorry I haven't called. Tough court case."

Nearly nine p.m., and he was likely still at work. "I hope everything turned out okay."

"We're back in session Monday. In the meantime, I'm treating you to dinner at my apartment tomorrow night."

"Another fundraiser?"

"Strictly a private event. I'll send a car to pick you up at seven. Be sure to bring a big appetite." He ended the call without waiting for a response.

Did anyone in the Warner family ever bother to ask before demanding an appearance? Maybe their personal relationship wasn't on the skids after all. A pigeon bobbed across Daisy's path and plucked a crumb off the pavement. What if someone spied her walking into Michael's building? In a city teeming with millions of residents, what were the odds of that happening? Besides, her personal time was her own business.

Reality hit home as Daisy caught sight of her image in a storefront window. She had become a rising star in a prestigious law firm. Maybe the time had come to start acting the part of a charming woman who was capable of attracting a handsome, rich northeasterner.

She headed straight to an upscale women's clothing store she had passed every day but had never entered. Until today. Why not treat herself to an outfit not relegated to a discount rack? After all, she might have moved one step closer to becoming one half of an admired New York-power couple.

Chapter 11

Poppy buttoned her sweater and stepped out to the backyard. A morning breeze rustled leaves, displaying the autumn colors in the overhead canopy. A squirrel clawed the ground at the base of a tall oak tree—a hint that cooler weather was fast approaching.

Pansy scurried from the greenhouse. Her cheeks flushed beneath her US Army ball cap, a gift from Basil. "Danny said I can shop at the thrift store while he delivers flowers."

He followed close behind Pansy. "If your sister has time to go with you."

"She does."

Danny planted his hands on his hips and shot Pansy a playful look. "Have you asked her?"

"Why?" Pansy's head tilted. "She always says yes."

"One of these days, she might say no."

"Not today." Pansy dashed to the delivery truck and climbed onto the back seat.

Danny shook his head. "Are you sure you don't mind me dropping you off? You'll be stuck in that old building for a couple hours."

"How can I deny my sister a trip to one of her happy places."

"Okay then."

Poppy slid onto the front seat and peered over her shoulder. "Did you remember to bring your money?"

Pansy patted her fanny pack. "Fifteen dollars. Remember how sometimes Mama gave us money she'd saved in her tin and took us shopping after we finished our lessons?"

"I do."

"Maybe today I'll find the perfect gift for her."

Danny climbed in and backed from the parking space.

Pansy clicked her seatbelt. "Safety first." During the ride, she ticked off a long list of thrift-store treasures she had discovered over the years.

Poppy smiled at her mental image of shelved random items covering an entire wall in Pansy's bedroom. The way she reorganized her display every time she brought home a new find, and the stories she created about each piece.

By the time Danny braked at the curb in front of the ancient brick building, Pansy's face flushed with excitement. She jumped to the curb and dashed up the walkway. The overhead bell jangled as she rushed inside. Pansy waved at the woman sitting behind the checkout counter while scurrying toward the aisle on the far left.

Poppy approached the counter. "Hey, Maddie."

"Two of my favorite customers." The widow who owned the shop and lived upstairs with her elderly mother smiled from her stool.

"How's everything going?"

"Slower than a turtle on tranquillizers. What's happening with the Butler clan, and how's Daisy doing way up there in New York?"

Poppy shared the news about her daughter's promotion.

"I always knew she'd make it big, and it's good to have a successful lawyer in the family. You never know when you might need one." Maddie aimed her thumb over her shoulder toward the window. "Have you heard the latest about old Agnes?"

"What's she up to now?"

"Nobody's seen hide nor hair of her for weeks. Her oldest son visited a few days ago. I hadn't seen either one of those boys in years. Anyway, a rumor's spreading like a grass fire on a windy day that Agnes is sick. If you ask me, she's too ornery to up and die."

Poppy stared across the road at the elaborate stone and iron fence guarding Agnes's Victorian-style home set atop a hill, surrounded by trees. "If she is on her way out, what do you suppose her sons will do with her house and all her land?"

"They'd be crazy not to sell. I mean, what would they do with thousands of acres? If I had the money, I'd scarf up a bunch and hold onto to it 'til the value skyrocketed."

"Around here?"

Maddie sighed. "I know it's a long shot. Besides, wishful thinking won't buy a bag of donuts, much less a parcel of land."

A squeal resonated through the building.

"Sounds like your sister found another treasure."

"Maybe more than one."

Poppy scooted to the last aisle and found Pansy crouched beside an ancient brown suitcase featuring thick leather straps and buckles.

"How did Mama's suitcase end up here? Did you bring it down from the attic?" Pansy unbuckled the straps and lifted the top. "Why's it empty? Where's all her fancy clothes?"

Poppy squatted and ran her fingers along the mottled leather top. How many years had passed since she'd last ventured into the overhead space? "It only looks like Mama's, sweetie."

"Is hers still in the attic?"

"Buried under mounds of dust."

Pansy straightened. "Dust makes me sneeze." She skipped to a display cabinet and lifted a figurine dressed in a red gown. "Maybe Mama ran away from home because she didn't love us anymore."

"Impossible." Poppy stretched her arm across her sister's shoulders. "Do you remember what she said every night before she tucked you in?"

"That I was her special girl sent straight from heaven."

"Exactly." Poppy squeezed her sister's shoulder. "Because she loved you with all her heart."

"This is pretty, like Mama." Pansy tilted the figurine and tapped the sticker on the bottom. "Twenty-five dollars. Come on." She raced to the front, set her new treasure on the counter, and removed three five-dollar bills from her fanny pack. "Fifteen isn't enough. Danny always says people go to thrift stores to negotiate."

"He's right." Maddie propped her elbows on the counter and laced her fingers. "What are you willing to pay?"

Pansy pinched her chin between her thumb and forefinger. "Fifteen dollars?"

"How about we split the difference." Poppy fished a five from her purse and set it beside Pansy's bills.

"Deal." Maddie scooped the cash off the counter. "Twenty dollars is a fair price for a treasure this special."

Pansy hugged the figurine to her chest. "When Mama comes home, I'll give this to her for her birthday."

Maddie, who had always treated Rose and her daughters with respect, eyed Poppy then Pansy. "Your sweet mother would like that."

Pansy's head tilted. "Do you remember her?"

"We were best friends, honey. She was an elegant lady who never spoke ill of anyone."

"A lot of people didn't like her." Pansy's brow pinched. "Maybe that's why she ran away. Is it okay if I look around some more?"

"Take all the time you want, sweetie. I'll keep Maddie company."

Pansy set her treasure on the counter and scurried to the second aisle.

"Your sister still believes Rose will show up one day. It's sad no one ever found out what happened to her."

A distant wailing siren perked Poppy's ears. "We don't often hear sirens in these parts." It grew louder.

Maddie spun toward the window. "Maybe the sheriff's chasing a stolen car or an escaped convict. We could use a little excitement around here. You know I keep a gun close by. But, if shooting breaks out, I'll duck behind the counter faster than a chipmunk skittering away from a cat."

Poppy peered out the window as an ambulance slowed in front of the shop and turned onto Agnes's driveway. "Looks like a medical emergency."

"Oh my goodness. Watch the store while I find out what's going on." Maddie raced outside, dashed across the street, and headed up the steep driveway.

Poppy refused to wish old Agnes ill, especially if she was near death and facing eternity. She lifted Pansy's figurine from the counter and gazed at the delicate features and long dark hair. A knot gripped her stomach. Would she ever discover what happened to her mother? Maybe it was best to continue holding tight to a glimmer of hope. For Pansy's sake.

Ten minutes after pulling onto the driveway, the ambulance turned onto the street and sped away with lights flashing and siren screaming.

Maddie returned and climbed onto her stool. "Agnes looks as pale as a bleached-out ghost, but she's still breathing."

"Any idea what happened to her?"

"EMT's wouldn't say. Like I said, she's too cantankerous to kick that ole bucket. Know what I think?"

By the time Danny returned, Poppy and Maddie had dreamed up a long list of possible maladies inflicting Agnes. Every one of their speculations had her returning to her roost in as unpleasant a mood as ever.

Chapter 12

Saturday after supper, Poppy settled beside Danny on their date-night arbor swing. She tucked her foot under her thigh, fingered a jasmine-vine leaf, and gazed at multiple shades of pink and orange painting the western sky. "Gorgeous sunset. Almost as pretty as one of Pansy's drawings."

Danny set the swing in motion and sipped his once-a-week bourbon. "Find anything interesting at the thrift store?"

Poppy clung to the possibility that a complete sentence meant he might talk about his past. "Pansy found a treasure for her collection." She described the figurine. "I suspect it will inspire her to write another story about Mama. Hopefully a happy tale."

She waited.

Danny remained silent.

"An ambulance showed up at Agnes's place today and carried her off. According to Maddie, she was still alive. It's a shame that mean old woman owns all the land around here except for ours and the Butler ranch."

Danny clutched his drink in both hands. His features grew rigid.

Tension enfolded the moment as a knot of regret settled in Poppy's chest. Why had she mentioned the ranch? Should she apologize or let Danny work through his emotions?

Minutes passed.

He stared at his drink, as if expecting the liquid to reveal answers to long-held questions.

"I didn't mean to upset you. I thought you'd want to know about Agnes."

Danny polished off his bourbon and swiped the back of his hand across his mouth. "To keep up the façade my old man called a marriage after he moved to the ranch, he showed up at the Savannah house for social events."

Maybe mentioning Agnes wasn't a mistake after all. She laid her hand on his thigh as newspaper clippings of Butler parties cascaded through her mind like a fast-paced slideshow. Photos abounded of Curtis posing with VIPs, but not a single picture of him standing beside his wife. "What happened to drive them apart?"

"Other than the fact they're both self-centered, heartless human beings?"

Poppy's chest tightened at the picture he'd painted of his parents. The opposite of her mom who loved and cared for her children the best she knew how.

Danny refilled his glass and swallowed another mouthful. "I was thirteen the first time my old man beat me. At the ranch after we'd slept in the stables with the horses."

"You and your sisters?'

"Me and my kid brother."

A gasp escaped as Poppy stared wide-eyed at her husband's profile and flared nostrils. All the years they'd lived together and shared the same bed, he had never mentioned any siblings other than his two sisters. "You have a brother?"

"Bobby was the sweetest boy." His voice was barely above a whisper. "He liked to draw and watch cartoons. And he loved those horses." Danny fell silent.

Why had he kept his brother a secret? She gripped the swing's arm, and prayed for Danny to continue talking.

"My parents yanked him out of private school after he failed first grade. Mother made sure nannies kept him hidden from her society friends." Bitterness laced his tone. "Other than me, nannies were his only companions. That Sunday at the ranch Bobby begged me to ask our old man if he could ride one of the horses. I knew it was a bad idea. At the same time, I didn't want to let my brother down. We found Curtis in his study.

Drinking. When I asked about Bobby taking a ride, he said his horses were too valuable to let an idiot saddle up."

His eyes narrowed to a slit. "Something inside me snapped. I accused him of treating his youngest son worse than any real man would ever treat a rabid dog, much less another human being." Danny's neck veins pulsated like poisonous snakes coiled to strike. "He slugged me. Knocked me off my feet. Blood poured from my nose. He planted his foot on my chest. Spittle spewed while he screamed that a kid as stupid as my half-wit brother couldn't possibly have come from him."

A shudder ripped through Poppy.

"Bobby crept to him and wrapped his arms around his waist. He said, 'I love you Papa.' I'm sorry I'm not smart like Danny.' The man who controlled a fiscal empire peeled his son's arms away and shoved him to the floor." His voice faltered. "That night I discovered what it meant to hate with an intensity I didn't know existed."

Confusion mingling with compassion muddled Poppy's brain. "I don't understand. Where is Bobby, and why haven't you talked about him before now?"

Danny bolted from the swing. The last of his drink spilled on the ground. He hurled the empty glass at a massive oak tree, shattering it on impact.

She recoiled. A sense of trepidation heightened as she watched the man she loved charge to the greenhouse and disappear into the dark interior. Tears pooled and tracked down her cheeks. Torn between aching to know more and fearing what she might learn, Poppy peered at the sun as it sank below the horizon. Long after darkness enveloped her and cold air penetrated to her bones, she trudged to the house and peeked into Pansy's room. Her night-light created a soft glow on her sister's face, her arm wrapped around her favorite teddy bear. Boots looked up from beside her bed and wagged his tail.

Poppy backed away and tiptoed to the master bedroom. She dropped onto the bed, laid her head on her pillow, and stared at the dark ceiling. Why had Danny kept Bobby's existence a secret? Had something tragic happened to him? Her eyelids grew heavy. At some point she succumbed to sleep disrupted by nightmares and the empty space beside her.

Chapter 13

Daisy checked her makeup in the bathroom mirror, then stood on her toes to catch a glimpse of her new form-fitting red sweater dress. Tonight, she aimed to discover where she stood with Michael. Serious lady friend or Butler family connection? She spritzed cologne behind each ear and stole one more glance before her phone pinged a text from a limo driver.

She slipped into her one winter coat, locked her apartment, and rode the elevator to the ground floor. Outside, a uniformed driver stood beside a black sedan. The moment she arrived at the curb, he opened the rear passenger door. "Good evening, Ms. Butler."

"Good evening." Grateful Michael hadn't sent a stretch limo, she slid in and breathed in the scent of leather and air freshener. Undeniably better than a taxi reeking of sweat and stale food. She willed her shoulders to relax as the driver pulled away from the curb and eased into traffic. Before she had time to relax, he stopped in front of a luxury apartment building across from Central Park, within easy-walking distance to the law office.

A doorman dashed to the curb and opened the door. "Ms. Butler?

She nodded.

"Mr. Warner is waiting for you." The doorman escorted her through a well-appointed lobby to an open elevator and inserted a key into a slot marked penthouse. "Have a nice evening." He tipped his cap then stepped out.

Daisy's pulse accelerated as her ride rose past each floor. How would Michael expect her to act? The elevator eased to a stop and opened to a luxurious private foyer illuminated by a contemporary chandelier. A massive double door eased open, revealing a living room featuring floor-to-ceiling windows along one wall and glass doors leading to a wide terrace. An elaborate oriental rug and a massive glass coffee table anchored three cream-colored contemporary couches. Her entire apartment would fit in half this space with room to spare.

"Welcome to my home." Michael approached, wearing dark slacks and a pullover sweater. He slipped her coat off her shoulders and tossed it over the back of a couch. "Gorgeous dress."

"Beautiful apartment. How many rooms?" Why had she asked a question that made her come across like a real-estate broker clamoring for a listing?

"Counting bathrooms, seven or eight if you consider the terrace a room."

How many hours for how many years would she need to bill top dollar to afford such luxury in prime Manhattan real estate?

"What would you like to drink? A cocktail? Glass of wine?"

She had to stay focused. "Wine. White."

"Good choice." He strolled away and returned within minutes carrying an uncorked bottle and two half-filled glasses.

Daisy tasted. "Domestic or French?"

"Napa Valley. Are you ready to enjoy one of the city's best views?"

"Absolutely."

Michael led her out to the terrace and over to the waist-high wall facing Central Park.

Daisy peered down at the remaining vestiges of fall color illuminated by streetlights placed throughout the massive space. "I imagine you spend a lot of time drinking in this scenery."

He pointed to the end of the wide space which offered a stunning view of downtown Manhattan. "Next Sunday we'll watch the sun set over the city."

Did he assume she was available or expect her to cancel her plans to suit his whims? "I'll need to take a raincheck. I'm taking a week off and flying home to celebrate Thanksgiving with my family."

"In that case, after you return."

Her focus returned to the park and a horse-drawn buggy meandering under the lights. She imagined lovers snuggling beneath a blanket as the horse clopped along the path.

Michael slid his arm around Daisy's waist. "Horses and carriages, one of the city's shameless tourist magnets." He pulled her close. "Are you hungry?"

For a shameless buggy ride cuddling beside Michael or dinner? "Starving."

"You're in for a treat." He pivoted away from the railing and nodded toward four silver dome plate covers on a round table set beside a fireplace.

"Did you spend all day cooking?"

"Why waste time working up a sweat in the kitchen when some of the most talented chefs in the world are a phone call away?"

"Spoken by a man with unlimited cash flow."

"Thanks to a well-paid profession and plenty of family money." He pressed his hand to Daisy's back and led her to the table. After pulling out her chair, he settled across from her. Candlelight and the gas-fueled blaze cast a warm glow as he lifted the two smaller domes. "Lobster bisque. Best in the city."

Of course, why else would Michael Warner order it? Daisy spread a napkin across her lap and dipped her spoon into the thick, creamy soup. She tasted. "Delicious."

He stared at her, smiling. "Beautiful women like you should always dine in candlelight."

"Including breakfast?" Heat inched up Daisy's neck to her earlobes. What possessed her to make such a suggestive comment?

"Especially in the glow of a magnificent sunrise."

She broke eye contact, hoping the dim light hid the blush she knew had pinkened her cheeks. "I bought lunch for a homeless woman today."

"Abrupt change of subject." He chuckled. "Are you planning to solicit pro-bono clients eager to sue the city?"

"Maybe one day I'll provide free help to a small upstart company. But not Ruby. That's the woman's name. There was something about the way she looked—lost and hopeless."

"If you intend to feed every homeless derelict roaming the streets, you'll need to bill a lot more hours. Or earn one gigantic bonus."

"I doubt I'll ever see her again." She dipped her spoon in the bisque. "Although I wouldn't scoff at a financial windfall."

"Another reason the partners tagged you for a promotion."

"A southern-educated lawyer making it good in a New York law firm."

He refilled her wineglass. "At the moment, you're a brilliant woman who looks stunning in red."

"I'm glad you approve." Especially since she had spent way more than she could afford on a dress she hoped would please him. After finishing her bisque and listening to Michael describe his favorite chefs, Daisy wrapped her fingers around the wineglass stem. "What entrée did you order for the lady in red?"

He lifted domes off the two remaining plates. "Dover sole flown fresh from the Mediterranean."

"First class or coach?"

"Definitely first class." He winked. "Sautéed with butter and capers."

She savored the delicate taste. "Oh my gosh, this is incredible."

"One of my favorites. Right up there with smoked salmon and caviar."

"And now one of mine." While continuing to savor the meal, their conversation centered on the firm's most important clients and the newest Broadway play—the only one Daisy had seen, thanks to a half-price ticket. After swallowing her last drop of wine, she set down her glass. "Dinner was amazing."

"One more treat." Michael pulled her chair away from the table and guided her to a wicker love seat facing the park. He settled beside her and poured two drinks from a fancy bottle with an ornate glass stopper. "Remy Martin cognac."

More name-dropping. The drink most likely cost more than her new dress.

He tapped his glass to hers. "To a bright future."

Whose? His, hers, theirs? Daisy's first sip added to the buzz from three glasses of wine. She cradled her glass and imagined falling in love with Michael and embracing his wealthy lifestyle. Would his family accept her if they knew the truth about her family?

"You're deep in thought."

Daisy blinked. "I was wondering if you dine out here often."

"When the weather permits, and when I entertain special guests."

Like his parents' sunroom. "I'll take that as a compliment."

"You and I are good together."

Somehow his tone seemed more appropriate for a closing statement to a jury. A siren and a blasting horn conjured images of a fire engine racing up Fifth avenue toward some unknown mayhem.

"When do you leave for Georgia?"

"Tomorrow afternoon."

Michael swirled his brandy. "I assume you're aware of your grandfather's alleged failing health."

She didn't have a clue. "Of course."

"Rumor is he fired the law firm representing his business empire and is in the market for a new one."

Was this the real reason behind the invitation, expensive brandy, and pricey dinner?

"We want you to bring him onboard. In case you're wondering, landing his business account would come with a sizable bonus."

Daisy fumbled with her earring while peering around the terrace and mentally comparing his expensive décor to her furnished apartment. "How sizable?"

"Enough to buy a Ferrari and a closet full of designer clothes."

"Is that what tonight is about?"

"Mixing pleasure with business isn't a new concept." He reached for her hand and kissed her fingers. "You're an amazing woman, Daisy."

She retrieved her brandy and stared at the amber liquid. How long would the heir to his father's law firm find her amazing if she failed to deliver Curtis Butler? Only one way to find out.

Chapter 14

S unday afternoon Poppy smoothed the spread on Daisy's twin bed while breathing the scent of freshly-washed sheets mingling with chocolate aromas wafting from the kitchen. She pressed her fingers to her lower back, straightened, and eyed the space her daughters had shared from the time Lilly outgrew her cradle. The same room where years ago her mother entertained men. Her eyes drifted to the brown stuffed bear on Lilly's bed—Daisy's gift to her sister the day she left for college. She lifted a photo off the dresser—her three children sitting on the back porch with their daddy. The man who harbored secrets. Had anyone ever taken a picture of Danny and his mysterious brother?

Pansy swept into the room, her cheeks flushed. "Daisy's favorite cookies are on the cooling rack. How come Danny slept on the couch last night?"

Guilty conscience or regret over his shocking revelations? "I suppose he didn't want to wake me."

"Oh." Pansy plopped on Lilly's bed and lifted the bear. "How long before Daisy comes home."

"About three hours, if her plane lands on time."

"Is Danny picking her up?"

"She's renting a car."

"When's Basil coming? Is his room all fixed up?"

"Wednesday afternoon, and yes, your nephew's room is freshened up and ready." Poppy placed the photo back on the dresser. "This is the first time in three years we'll all celebrate Thanksgiving together."

"All 'cept for Mama. I wish I was pretty like you and her."

"You're way beyond pretty, sweetie. You're one of God's most special creations. Beautiful inside and out."

Pansy hugged Lilly's bear to her chest. "Maybe God will send a man to love me like Danny loves you. Someone special like me."

Poppy choked back tears while stroking her sister's arm. Would the woman with a heart of gold and the mind of a child ever experience romantic love? "Someone extra special."

The front doorbell chimed prompting Pansy to toss the bear aside and bolt to her feet. "Maybe Basil's home early." She dashed from the room.

Poppy caught up with her sister the moment she flung open the front door and faced a handsome young man with a worn leather satchel slung over his shoulder.

"Good afternoon." He handed over a business card. "My name is David Lambert. Are you Pansy Fowler?"

"Uh-huh." She tilted her head. "You have pretty blue eyes. Did God send you?"

He brushed his fingers through light brown hair. "Not exactly."

Poppy's eyes narrowed as she spread her palm across her birthmark and stepped beside Pansy. "I'm Mrs. Butler. How do you know my sister's name?"

"Good question." He removed a stapled document from his satchel and handed it over. "From this."

Poppy read the words above a drawing of their front porch with Boots sprawled on the steps, *Where Did Rose Fowler Go?* Pansy's name and address were scribed beneath. "I don't understand. How did you end up with this?"

"Your sister mailed it to me. If you'll grant me a few minutes, I'll explain why I drove down from Atlanta to talk to you."

He looked safe enough. Besides, she knew where Danny kept his guns and how to use them. Poppy lowered her hand, relieved he didn't flinch or gasp. "We'll give you ten minutes." She led him to the front room and pointed to a pair of mismatched wingback chairs before settling on the sofa beside Pansy. "Okay, what's your story?"

"Interesting you asked that question. I'm a freelance investigator and journalist specializing in unsolved missing-person cold cases."

"Our mama went missing a long time ago." Pansy's eyes widened as she scooted to the edge of her seat. "Do you know what happened to her?"

"Not yet, but I'm confident I can find out. That is, if you're willing to work with me."

Poppy's brows pinched. "Work with you how?"

"Let me interview you both about Rose Fowler up until the day she disappeared."

"And do what with the information?" Poppy's brows released.

"Put the pieces together like a giant jigsaw puzzle and write a book about your mother."

"Like one of my stories." Pansy pressed her palms together. "'cept this one'll be real."

"Not so fast." Poppy crossed her leg over her knee and pumped her foot. "Why would we let a stranger dig into our past, much less write a book about it?"

"I understand your hesitation—"

"How could you possibly understand? You don't know anything about my family."

"Actually, I do." He leaned forward. "Pansy's story intrigued me enough to do a little research. I know your mother entertained men for money and that the investigation into her disappearance was slipshod at best. Despite her occupation, she deserved better, and you two deserve to know what happened to her."

Poppy stilled her pumping foot and stared at the stranger for a long moment. What was it about him? She pointed to a framed drawing on the wall beside her bedroom door. "See that picture over there? Pansy drew it. Mama hung it in that very spot the day after my sister turned eight. Five more of her drawings are displayed around the house. I can't draw, but I fancied myself as a poet."

She uncrossed her leg, scooted forward, and tapped her fingers on the scrapbook lying on the coffee table. "Even though my poems were amateurish, Mama proudly pasted them in here for everyone to see. Despite our flaws, she loved us unconditionally. Until the day she disappeared."

"That's the mystery I want to solve. The story I want to write." David planted his forearms across his thighs. "About the mother who vanished in her prime and left two daughters to fend for themselves."

"See?" Pansy's face beamed. "God did send David to us."

Poppy's gaze shifted from Pansy to the man sitting across from her. Maybe Pansy was on to something. "How long would you take?"

"Couple of weeks. Maybe more."

"There's no place to stay close by."

"Not a problem. My camper's parked in your driveway."

Pansy jumped up and raced to the front porch. She returned, her face beaming. "David brought his house with him. We can't let him go away."

"Hold onto your chickens, sweetie." Poppy faced David. "Come back tomorrow morning at nine, and we'll give you an answer."

"Fair enough." He removed a sheet of paper from his satchel and handed it to her. "My credentials and phone number in case you need some questions answered before tomorrow." He shouldered his satchel and walked out.

Poppy pushed off the sofa and placed her hands on Pansy's shoulders. "Where did you find David, and when did you send him your story?"

"Lilly told me 'bout a month ago. He's gonna find out what happened to Mama and bring her home."

"You know she disappeared a long time ago." Poppy released a heavy sigh. "Which makes unraveling the mystery difficult at best. Maybe impossible."

Pansy twisted away from her sister's grip and planted her hands on her hips. "He's gonna find her for us. You'll see."

If he somehow managed to discover that something bad had happened to their mother, he'd break Pansy's heart. Could she bear to steal her sister's hope and dash her story-writing mission? On the other hand, their mama deserved to have the truth revealed, no matter how painful. "We'll only agree to his request if Danny gives us his okay."

"Come on." Pansy pulled her sister's arm. "We'll go talk to him now."

"We can't. He's out on a delivery."

"Oh yeah, I forgot." Her shoulders slumped as she ambled away from the window and dropped onto the sofa.

Poppy sat beside her and read David's credentials. The man seemed legitimate, with plenty of articles and three books to his credit. "We'll talk to Danny and Daisy during supper."

"Promise you'll make him say yes?"

Poppy traced an X across her chest. "With all my heart."

Chapter 15

Daisy glimpsed the road from her rental car's rearview mirror. No one behind her. She slowed to a crawl as her eyes fixed on the driveway leading to Curtis Butler's ranch. Before her trip back to New York, she'd need to drive onto that stretch of pavement and meet her grandfather for the first time.

A car approached from the opposite direction. Her pulse quickened. She gripped the steering wheel and accelerated. How could she confront the man, much less convince him to hire her law firm if the prospect of someone seeing her enter his property made her heart pound against her ribs? An eagle soared overhead, circling to detect unexpected prey. Was that what her grandfather had become? A target to enrich a law firm and pad her bank account?

Daisy dismissed the notion and drove past familiar places until she turned onto her family's driveway. She eased along the gravel through the dense woods to the paved section and parked beside her childhood home.

Moments after she popped the trunk and climbed out, Pansy dashed across the manicured front lawn with Boots matching her pace. She pulled Daisy into a bear-hug. "I baked chocolate chip cookies for you."

"You're the best cookie baker in the whole world, Aunt Pansy. I can't wait to taste them."

Pansy released her niece. "David's gonna find Mama."

Daisy's brow arched as she scratched Boot's ears. "Who's David?"

"I'll explain later." Her mom embraced her. "For now, we're happy you're home for a whole week."

"We'll have lots of time to catch up."

"Your room's all sparkly clean." Pansy scooted to the back of the car and hoisted Daisy's suitcase from the trunk. "Did you bring me a present?"

"Something extra special."

"Goodie. I'll help you unpack." She released the handle, pulled the suitcase across the grass, and lugged it up the porch steps.

Daisy linked arms with her mom. "I love her enthusiasm."

"You'd best catch up with her before she opens your bag and digs through your clothes."

"Not to worry, Mom." She pulled a key from her purse. "Unless Aunt Pansy learned how to pick a lock, she'll have to wait."

"As far as I know, she hasn't mastered that talent." They made their way into the house and then on to Daisy's bedroom. Pansy knelt beside Lilly's bed jiggling the suitcase lock.

"Looks like you'll need this." Daisy handed over the key.

After releasing the lock, Pansy unzipped the bag and flipped it open. A gift-wrapped package lay atop the clothes. Her eyes sparkled. "Can I open it now?"

"Of course."

Pansy peeled back the wrapping paper and squealed with delight as she lifted a denim ball cap inscribed with sparkly NYC letters that featured a bill encased with rhinestones. "This is the fanciest hat ever." She popped it on her head and scooted to the mirror over the dresser.

Daisy slipped behind her aunt, wrapped her arms around her waist, and rested her chin on her shoulder. "You look beautiful."

"Like Mama?"

"Even prettier."

"What's all the squealing about?"

Daisy turned toward her dad's voice. "Your sister-in-law's new hat is a big hit."

"So I see." He strode into the room.

Daisy released Pansy and embraced her dad.

"Glad you made it home."

The kitchen timer pinged prompting her mom to scoot from the room.

"Supper's 'bout ready." Pansy stole one more glance in the mirror before dashing into the hall.

"Shall we?" Daisy looped her hand around her father's arm.

He patted her fingers. "Are you hungry?"

"Starving." As they entered the hallway, she eyed two framed pictures displayed opposite the door—one drawn by Pansy, the other by Lilly. Her family's treasured art. In the kitchen six more framed drawings created by Pansy and the three Butler children filled the wall separating the space from the front room. Nothing like the Warner's art collection worth untold millions. She choked back the lump forming in her throat. Yet priceless and far more meaningful.

Daisy lowered onto the ladderback chair her father held out while breathing in mouthwatering aromas wafting from bowls and platters placed in the center of the table. "Black-eyed peas, mashed potatoes, fried chicken, and homemade biscuits. My all-time favorite comfort foods."

Pansy settled on her chair at one end of the table. Boots sprawled on the floor at her feet. "I baked sweet potato pie for dessert."

Fat chance Michael would ever see that dish in any of his favorite New York restaurants. She giggled.

Daisy's mom sat across from her. "What tickled your funny bone?"

"I doubt my New York friends have a clue what their tastebuds are missing." Anticipating a blessing, Daisy folded her hands in her lap and closed her eyes. While her mom blessed the meal and gave thanks for her daughter arriving home safe and sound, mental images of her visit to the Warner mansion raced through her mind. Mrs. Warner sipping a mimosa and dining on a chef-prepared breakfast while firing questions about the Butler family. When the prayer ended, Daisy opened her eyes and found her mom staring at her.

"Are you happy, honey?"

Daisy blinked. What prompted that question? "Of course, I'm happy. Why are you asking?"

"You seem a bit tense."

So much for masking her anxiety over the Curtis Butler drama. "It takes more than a few hours and a plane ride to unplug from a demanding workload." Daisy reached for the mashed potatoes. "What's new with you, Dad?"

He spooned black-eyed peas onto his plate. "Picked up a couple new landscape clients."

"We're gonna open a flower shop when Danny wins the lottery." Pansy slipped a chunk of chicken to Boots. "Tomorrow, David's gonna park his house in our driveway. Right next to Danny's truck."

"Who's David?" Daisy and her father asked in unison.

Her mom's fork froze halfway to her mouth. She eyed Daisy, then her husband. "I'd planned to wait until dessert to bring up the subject. Might as well jump in now." She set her fork on her plate. "He's an investigative journalist and a writer—"

"He has blue eyes, and he liked my story about Mama." Pansy's tone exuded excitement.

Daisy's mom stretched toward her sister and patted her arm. "Give me a few minutes to explain, sweetie."

"Okay?"

"He's a young man who showed up earlier today." After relaying the encounter, she read David's credentials aloud. "He expects an answer tomorrow morning." She handed the paper to her husband.

Silence enveloped the room as Daisy's dad pursed his lips and laser-focused on the document.

Pansy chewed her fingernail, her expression wide-eyed.

Daisy's mom laced her fingers and tapped her thumbs.

Minutes passed.

He laid the paper on the table and faced Daisy. "What's your opinion?"

"As your daughter or as an attorney?"

"Both."

Conflicting thoughts collided in Daisy's head. Delving into the past could lead to profound disappointment or painful discoveries. What would she want if her mom, rather than her grandmother, had gone missing? "All these years we've wondered what happened to Rose, so maybe Pansy's story finding its way to David was more than a fluke."

Her mom unlaced her fingers. "Then you're okay if we let him stay?"

"We'd need a written agreement that spells out his intentions as well as our expectations."

Daisy's dad held eye contact with her for a long moment before turning to her mom. "You deserve to know what happened to Rose."

"Are you giving us the go-ahead?"

"If the man signs a legal agreement and Daisy approves it."

Pansy's eyes danced. "David's a nice man. He's gonna find Mama for us, and Danny's gonna win the lottery."

Daisy's lips twitched to a grin. At least the first of Pansy's predictions had a slim chance of becoming reality.

After she helped with kitchen cleanup and strolled through the greenhouse with her dad, Daisy changed into pajamas and sat on her twin bed. She set her phone alarm for six a.m. Time enough to write an agreement in the event the mysterious investigator slash journalist showed up unprepared.

A faint knock. The door creaked open. "I noticed the light under the door," her mom whispered. "Are you too tired for a chat?"

"I'm never too tired to talk to you. Especially since we missed our conversation this morning."

"Mothers are born with the unique ability to recognize their children's emotions." She closed the door and settled beside her daughter. "You put on a good front, honey, but I know something's eating at you."

The moment she had dreaded since she first arrived home. Daisy scooted back and leaned against the wall. "It's Michael."

"You're in love with him, aren't you?"

"I have feelings for him, but that's not the issue." Daisy breathed deeply and slowly released the air. "Michael and his father expect me to recruit Curtis Butler's business empire for the law firm."

"Oh my, I didn't see that coming. Do they understand that you've never met the man?"

Daisy pulled her knees to her chest and wrapped her arms around her shins. "They don't have a clue."

"That kind of puts you smack-dab in the middle of one big mess."

"Tell me about it."

"What are you going to do?"

Daisy stared at her sister's bed across from hers. "Lilly and I often talked late into the night. Sometimes about our mysterious grandfather, and why no one in our family dared mention his name in front of Dad. The fact that he hated the man with such bitterness somehow escaped us."

"None of us understood."

"There's no way I can back out. Not after I committed to represent my law firm."

Her mom fingered her wedding band. "You need to break the news to your dad."

"That's the hardest part. How do you suppose he'll react?"

"That depends."

"On what?"

"How much more he loves you than he hates his father."

Chapter 16

Daisy's eyes eased open ten minutes before her alarm. She stretched her arms over her head, swung her legs to the floor, and trudged to the bathroom. After indulging in a long hot shower and dressing in jeans and a sweatshirt, she carried her laptop to the kitchen table and found her mom clearing the breakfast dishes. "The empty plates tell me Dad's still an early riser."

"He's always wide awake and in the greenhouse before dawn." She poured a cup of coffee and set it in front Daisy. "Did you bring work with you?"

Daisy set down her computer. "Other than the pitch to you know who and writing an agreement for the mysterious investigator, no."

"It's good to have a smart lawyer in the family."

"We'll see how smart after I confront the infamous business tycoon."

Pansy wandered in wearing her new sparkly cap. Boots padded behind her. "What's a tycoon?"

Relieved she hadn't uttered Curtis Butler's name, Daisy stirred creamer and sugar into her coffee. "Someone who owns a business."

"Like Danny."

"Exactly."

Pansy let her dog out before pulling a box of cereal and a bowl from the cabinet and milk from the fridge. She plopped onto her chair and pointed to Daisy's computer. "Are you gonna write a story?"

"You're the family's storyteller, not me."

Daisy's mom filled her coffee mug and carried it to the table. "She's fixing to write a contract for David."

"I like him. He's nice." Pansy poured cereal into her bowl and drowned the flakes with milk. "How long will it take David to find out what happened to Mama?"

"She's been gone a long time, sweetie." Daisy's mom pulled her chair beside her sister.

"David liked the story I wrote about her. He's gonna find her."

Daisy's heart swelled with admiration for her mom and aunt. Two amazing women whose love for each other exemplified everything good and noble about family. "I've missed you both more than you can imagine."

Pansy dipped her spoon into her bowl. "Poppy and me are gonna visit you in New York. Maybe on a big airplane." Boots barked, prompting Pansy to open the door. After he padded in, she plopped back on her chair. "Airplanes fly like birds." She giggled. "'cept their wings don't flap."

Daisy's mom patted her sister's hand. "We'd best stay quiet for a spell and let Daisy finish typing David's agreement before he shows up."

"Okay." Pansy zipped her thumb and forefinger across her lips. "Quiet as a spider."

Daisy stifled a laugh while opening her laptop. An hour and a half after she began typing, she placed a printed copy on the front-room coffee table beside a plate of cookies. "All set." She settled on the sofa beside her mom while Pansy and Boots stood watch at the front door.

"Never in a hundred years would I have anticipated an investigative journalist showing up at our front door." Her mom held her hand in front of her mouth, her voice low. "You've read Pansy's stories. They're sweet, but simple."

"Something she wrote obviously captured his attention."

"He's here." Pansy dashed out to the porch. Boots loped beside her.

Daisy and her mom strode to the front porch as Pansy bounded across the yard. "Should we rescue our guest from my over-zealous aunt?"

"If he's worth a shaker of salt, he'll welcome her enthusiasm."

A man dressed in jeans, a button-down shirt, and sport jacket slung a leather satchel over his shoulder and followed Pansy to the front porch. "Good morning, Mrs. Butler."

"Welcome back. David Lambert, I'd like you to meet my daughter Daisy."

Daisy offered her hand. "It's a pleasure to meet you."

A smile lit his face and sent a twinkle to his eyes. "The pleasure's all mine."

The moment his hand touched hers, a spark cascaded through her limbs. Was it static electricity? Or something else?

His gaze remained fixed on her. "You favor your mother."

Daisy swallowed past the tightness in her throat and clamored for an appropriate response. "She's my best friend."

"My mom and I were close."

"Were?"

"Fatal heart attack." His smile faded. "Two years ago, tomorrow. Spending Thanksgiving alone is still painful."

"You're welcome to celebrate with our family."

"We'd best discuss his proposal before inviting him to supper." Daisy's mom swept her arm toward the front room. "Come in and take a seat, Mr. Lambert."

"Please, call me David." He released Daisy's hand, then strolled into the front room, settled on the wingback chair, and set his satchel on the floor.

Daisy remained standing beside the front door, her eyes fixed on the alluring stranger. What was it about David that prompted her to extend an invitation without a moment's hesitation? His gorgeous blue eyes? His warm smile? His touch? Floorboards creaked, jolting her from her reverie. She blinked.

Her dad hastened from the kitchen and strolled into the front room.

David stood. "Mr. Butler."

"Mr. Lambert." He planted his feet shoulder-width apart and crossed his arms. "Before you go digging into the past, you need my wife and my daughter's approval. Daisy's a top-notch New York attorney, so she knows her stuff."

"Understood, sir."

Taking her dad's cue, Daisy joined her mom and aunt on the sofa. "Mom explained how you ended up in our home and what you propose. I read your credentials."

"Good." David lowered to the wingback. "What additional information do you need?"

"I'm curious." The same comment Daisy had made to Michael. "What about my grandmother's disappearance intrigues you?"

"To begin, the fact that officials brushed off the incident as inconsequential. There's a mystery that warrants exposure, and a missing woman who deserves to be found."

"You know she disappeared before I was born."

"I specialize in cold cases."

Daisy studied his expression, his handsome face. He seemed trustworthy and was definitely charming. "To protect you and my family, I've taken the liberty of preparing an agreement." She pushed the document across the coffee table.

"I'd expect nothing less from a good attorney." After reading her proposal, he extracted a sheet of paper from his satchel and handed it to Daisy. "My standard contract. It's not as impressive or comprehensive as yours."

Pleased he'd come prepared, Daisy perused the document, which proved his legitimacy. She turned to her mom. "Rose is your mother, which means the final decision about moving forward is up to you and Pansy."

"There's a reason my sister's story ended up in your possession, David." Daisy's mom folded her hands in her lap. "No matter the outcome, we're all eager to find out what happened to Mama."

Daisy faced her dad. He nodded. She scooted forward and locked eyes with David. "If you're willing to sign the contract I prepared, we have a deal."

"Done." He pulled a pen from his satchel and signed.

After Daisy and her mom added their signatures, she leaned back and crossed her leg over her knee. "Now that the legal stuff is out of the way, where do you propose we begin?"

"First, do you mind if I camp out in your driveway?"

"If Dad approves."

He uncrossed his arms. "You can park beside my delivery truck. For now, I'll leave you in the ladies' capable hands." Her dad strode from the room and out the front door.

Pansy's face beamed as she pressed her palms together. "Is there a dog in your house on wheels?"

David chuckled. "Afraid not. The space is barely big enough for me, much less a dog."

"Can Boots visit you sometime?"

"I'd like that."

At the mention of his name, Boots slapped his tail on the floor, inviting Pansy to stroke his back. "Maybe today?"

"Give me a few days to step up my investigation." David removed a notepad from his satchel. "I take notes the old-fashioned way. Although sometimes I have a hard time deciphering what I wrote."

Daisy couldn't help but smile at his easygoing, self-effacing approach. "Now that parking arrangements and canine visits are nailed down, what do want to know?"

"For today, background information, beginning as far back as your mom and aunt can remember."

Pansy grabbed a cookie, then pushed the plate toward David. "Every Sunday me, Poppy, and Mama baked a yummy dessert. Sometimes a cake. I like chocolate best. With fudge icing."

"That's also my favorite." David reached for a cookie. "Did you bake these?"

Pansy's chest puffed. "Uh-huh. They're also Daisy's favorites."

He took a bite. His eyes met Daisy's. "The verdict is you're guilty of excellent taste."

"No deliberation?"

"None needed."

Daisy tilted her head, delighted by his playful banter. "What's my sentence?"

"That's up for discussion. For now, back to my investigative role." He opened his notepad. "I'll start with you, Poppy. What are your earliest memories of your mother?"

She lifted a framed photo off the end table. "This is a picture of Mama her friend, Maddie, took before I was born." She handed it to him.

"She's a beautiful woman, as are her daughters and granddaughter. Do you have other photos of her?"

"A few. Up in the attic."

Pansy's eyes widened. "Do you wanna go up there?"

"Eventually." While David continued to ask questions and make notes, Daisy vacillated between concentrating on her mom and aunt's responses and marveling at the stranger's relaxed demeanor, attentiveness, and sense of humor. By noon the desire to understand why her heart skipped each time an endearing look passed between them consumed her. Somehow she had to find the answer before she returned to New York and to Michael.

Chapter 17

After spending hours summoning childhood memories—some fun, other's bordering on painful—Poppy's stomach protested with an audible grumble. "Answering brain-straining questions stirs up quite an appetite. You're welcome to join us for lunch, David."

"I appreciate the invite, but I don't want to become a burden. Besides, I stocked my camper with plenty of food. One more question. How many structures were on the property when Rose was here?"

"Two. This house and our little retreat."

"This afternoon I'd like a tour of both." David stashed his pad in his satchel. "But first I'll walk your land and see if anything suspicious pops up."

Daisy uncrossed her legs. "I'm guessing you work a case like a well-trained attorney. Thorough to a fault, looking under every rock, and searching every nook and cranny."

"I'll take your comparison as a compliment." He pushed up, grinning. "We should compare notes."

"If you stay around for a couple days."

"Not a problem. Unraveling a mystery this cold could take weeks."

Poppy scooted forward. "Well then, you're for sure invited to join us for Thanksgiving. Unless you plan to celebrate with your family."

"Mom *was* my family, so I accept your invitation. I'll touch base again this afternoon." David shouldered his satchel and sauntered out.

Pansy bit into the last cookie. "David's for sure gonna find Mama." Boots padded after her as she carried the empty tray from the room.

"I hope she's right about the *finding her* part. By the way." Daisy's mom patted her knee. "I noticed the little dance going on between you and our investigator."

Daisy stared wide-eyed at her mom. "What are you talking about?"

"The glances. The compliments. The not-so-subtle attraction."

"Have you taken on the role of amateur psychologist?"

"I'm simply a mother who knows her daughter." Poppy brushed Daisy's hair away from her ear. "I knew it. Pink earlobes."

"It's the heat."

"Last I looked, the temperature's in the sixties. Hardly a heat wave."

Daisy's cheeks warmed to the shade coloring her ears. "No matter what you imagine is going on, I find David interesting from a professional perspective. Nothing more." She pulled her hair back over her ear. "You do realize when he steps inside your retreat, he'll want to know what you keep in the trunk."

"I could tell him it's empty."

"An empty trunk in your private space? Do you honestly think he'd believe you?"

"I suppose not. How can I tell a stranger about my scrapbook when your father doesn't know it exists?" Poppy swept crumbs off the coffee table into her hand. "I'll ignore his question. Change the subject."

"Refusing to respond to an attorney would arouse all kinds of suspicion. You should expect the same reaction from an investigative journalist. Maybe the time has come to stop all the secrets and tell Dad about your clippings."

Her mom stared at the crumbs cradled in her palm before trapping them under her fingers. "After all these years, I have no idea how he'll react."

"As you told me, it depends on how much more he loves you than he despises his parents." Daisy stood and strolled from the room.

"That's the big question," Poppy mumbled as she followed her daughter to the kitchen.

Pansy stood at the counter spreading mayo on bread slices. "Tomato and cheese sandwiches for everyone."

"Perfect." Poppy removed a pitcher of sweet tea from the fridge and filled four glasses.

As if on cue, Danny walked in and settled in his chair. "How'd everything go with Mr. Lambert?"

Pansy wiped her hands with a paper towel. "He asked lots of questions 'bout us when we were little kids."

"Background information," added Daisy.

Poppy set a glass of tea on the table while Pansy plated the sandwiches and added scoops of potato salad. "He asked to tour the house and the retreat."

Danny sipped his tea. "Are you okay with him invading your private space?"

"What do you think?"

"If you want a shot at finding out what happened to Rose, you need to go all in."

A sense of trepidation heightened as Poppy imagined revealing her secret obsession to Danny. Would he consider her scrapbook a betrayal? How could he when he refused to share secrets about his past? She set a plate in front of him while offering a silent blessing and asking for divine guidance. By the time they finished eating, she had come to the only decision that made sense.

"Time to get back to work." Danny pushed away from the table and lumbered to the back porch.

After helping her sister rinse the plates and load the dishwasher, Poppy pulled her daughter aside. "I need you to keep Pansy company while I talk to your dad."

"You're going to tell him, aren't you?"

"Better he finds out from me than from a stranger." She wrapped two cookies in a napkin and walked through the porch to the backyard. Clouds painted gray swatches across the sky while a cool breeze rustled the leaves and triggered a goosebump invasion. A shudder cascaded through Poppy and heightened her anxiety. Maybe she should convince David the retreat wasn't worth seeing. Except Pansy had revealed its history with vivid detail.

Poppy filled her lungs, slowly released the air, and walked into the greenhouse. Fans whirring overhead created white noise and helped ease her rattled nerves. She walked to the middle of the massive space and found Danny bent over, tending a row of miniature boxwoods.

He looked up.

She forced a smile. "I brought you dessert."

"To satisfy my sweet tooth or soften bad news?" He straightened.

She handed him the cookies. "David's out walking our property."

"What does he expect to find?" Danny bit a chunk.

"I don't know. Probably nothing." A twinge of guilt pricked Poppy's conscience. She had to spit it out before losing her nerve. "When I show David inside my retreat, he's gonna ask questions about the trunk."

Danny stood, removed his cap, and swiped his fingers across his brow. "Is that where you keep your Butler-family newspaper clippings."

Poppy's jaw dropped. "How did you find out? How long have you known?"

"Discarded newspapers with stories cut out. Since you were pregnant with Daisy."

She squared her shoulders with all the dignity she could muster. "All these years and you never said a word?"

He shrugged. "I figured if you wanted me to know, you'd come clean."

"Then you're not angry?"

"First time I noticed a hole in the society page, I ripped the newspaper to shreds and considered canceling the paper." He faced Poppy. "Until I realized my refusal to discuss my family couldn't erase your curiosity about where I came from. Your secret clippings were the only way you could connect. I didn't want to take that away from you."

Silence enfolded the moment as she gazed deep into his eyes. "If I had any idea you'd understand, I would've come clean years ago."

"I know life with me falls way short of ideal—"

She opened her mouth to protest.

He pressed his fingers to her lips. "You're the finest woman I've ever known." The man who seldom displayed emotion gathered her in his arms. "Some secrets are okay."

"I love you, Danny Butler." She melted in his arms and prayed he'd come one day closer to sharing his deepest, most painful secrets.

Chapter 18

While savoring the intimate moment with Danny, Poppy strolled from the greenhouse to their front lawn and admired the color explosion of pansies framing the porch. After stooping to lift a dried leaf off a flower, she climbed onto the porch and settled on a rocking chair. Another gift from one of her mama's satisfied clients. She ran her finger along the center vein. Such an intricate pattern created by the master designer.

Daisy strolled out and sat beside her. "Are you admiring nature or contemplating the future?"

"Danny's known about the newspaper clippings since before you were born."

Daisy stared, her jaw slack. "Are you serious?"

"His silence all these years sheds a whole new light on the depth of his love." Poppy opened her palm, blew the leaf, and watched it flutter to the floor. "Why that same man continues to hold his family in such contempt remains a mystery."

Daisy set her rocker in motion. "Relationships are complicated."

Poppy matched her daughter's movement. "When do you plan to tell him about your commitment to contact Curtis?"

"Jury's still out."

"Lawyer talk?"

Daisy tucked her right foot under her knee. "More like gut-wrenching anxiety."

"Over your dad's response or meeting your grandfather?"

"If Michael had any inkling that I've never met the man—" She released a heavy sigh. "My career and relationship with Michael are at stake, Mom. Not to mention how much I'm likely to upset Dad."

"Secrets have plagued our family far too long."

"They've also sheltered us from painful truths."

Poppy caught sight of David springing onto the porch from the side yard. "Looks like our investigator has returned."

"Afternoon, ladies." He approached and leaned against the porch railing.

Daisy lowered her foot. "Did your walk provide any revelations?"

"Afraid not." His eyes shifted to Poppy. "Is this a good time to take a look at your retreat?"

"As good as any. Is it okay if Daisy joins us?"

"More than okay."

His grin confirmed what she had observed earlier. Her daughter captivated or at a minimum intrigued David. And why not? Daisy was a smart, successful, beautiful young woman. "Well then, let's get this adventure under way." She pushed off the rocker and held her hand out to Daisy.

"Are you sure you don't mind if I tag along?"

"Positive," Poppy and David replied in unison.

Daisy wiped her hands on her jeans before accepting Poppy's hand.

Sweaty palms? No doubt David had also charmed her firstborn. Poppy led the way down the porch steps and around the master-bedroom side of the house. She hadn't told David anything about Danny's family. Maybe she should back out and tell him there was nothing to see in her private space. Except Daisy was right. Her refusal would arouse a heap of suspicion. Her shoulders tensed as they arrived at their destination. "It's not much to look at."

David touched the rough-hewn wood. "This has been here for a long time."

Poppy nodded. "Almost as long as Pansy."

"Do you remember who built it?"

She dug deep into her memory and pictured a big, burly man with a black beard hauling lumber from a pickup. "Someone Mama called our uncle. Funny I'd never seen him before or after."

"Probably one of her johns."

Poppy cringed. "You mean client?"

David stared at her for a long moment. "Or maybe she hired a local handyman."

"That's a good explanation." She stepped inside.

David followed and turned in a slow circle. "The curtains add a homey touch."

Daisy sauntered in and sat on the bench. "Mom and I have shared a lot of special moments in here."

"I suspect these walls hold a lot of secrets." David remained standing.

More than he could imagine. Poppy settled beside her daughter. "Mama always had a pitcher of lemonade ready when she sent me and Pansy out here. We kept a little battery-operated radio in the corner." She pressed her hand to her birthmark. "For a long time, I believed Mama didn't want anyone to see my face or discover that Pansy's kind of slow."

"Did your assumptions eventually change?"

"When I was eleven." Poppy's eyes drifted to a spiderweb strung between two overhead rafters. "One day at school during recess, an older boy pulled up my skirt. I took a swing at him and missed. He laughed and said if I wanted to become a prostitute like my mom, I'd need to hire a doctor to fix my ugly face. All the other kids stared at me, like I was some kind of freak." Her voice faltered. "When I asked my teacher what the word prostitute meant, she told me to look it up in the dictionary."

Daisy reached for her hand.

"That night I confronted Mama. She held me in her arms and explained that the men who visited her paid for companionship and conversation." Poppy swallowed the lump forming in her throat. "The next day she took Pansy and me out of school and hired a tutor to come to our house twice a week. The kitchen doubled as our classroom and the table as our desk."

David leaned back against the wall. "Did you accept your mother's explanation about the men?"

"For a while. Until the day Pansy got sick and threw up over there in the corner. I left her here and ran back to the house. Strange noises came from Mama's bedroom. The door was cracked open. I peeked in and found her in bed...with a man. I watched. Horrified. My stomach heaved. I ran out the back door and vomited. That's the night I understood that she sent us here to protect us from the truth, not because she was ashamed of us."

Daisy stroked her mother's hand.

"Except for Danny and Daisy, I've never told anyone about that day."

David pushed off the wall and sat beside her. "That's a heavy burden for a young girl to shoulder."

"Somehow I managed to shield Pansy from the truth until two months before Mama disappeared. After we'd finished shopping at the thrift store, I drove Mama's car to gas up at Willy's. I gave my sister money to buy ice cream. If I'd known she'd run into Agnes Watkins, I would've made her stay in the car. That woman had no business shooting her mouth off to a vulnerable young girl." Poppy's hands fisted. "When Pansy came back to the car, she said Agnes told her Mama liked to use her body to make lots of men happy."

"Was Pansy upset?"

"She asked me if being a prostitute was bad. I told her Mama had a special way of entertaining clients." Poppy's fingers uncurled. "In her childlike mind, she didn't want to believe anything bad about our mama."

"We all want to believe our mothers are without flaws." David pointed to the trunk. "What do you keep in there?"

"When we were little, it held toys and later books, paper, and colored pencils. Things to keep us busy while we listened to music and waited for Mama to take us back in the house." Decision time. Dodge the question or reveal the truth? Like Danny said, if she wanted to find out what happened to Rose, she needed to go all in.

"Now it hides a secret collection I discovered isn't as secret as I imagined." She scooted forward, removed her scrapbook from the trunk, and placed it on David's lap. "Stories about a father-in-law who despises me and has never met his grandchildren. A mother-in-law I've never met, and Danny's sisters who don't know or care that my family exists."

David pulled back the cover. "*The Butler Family Legacy*." He turned to the first page, and tapped his finger on a newspaper photo of Curtis Butler poised beside a stall with his hand on a horse's muzzle. "Is there a story behind this picture?"

"Reminder of the first and last time I came face-to-face with my husband's father."

David flipped through more pages. "What prompted you to collect all these clippings?"

Poppy couldn't admit how many hours she'd imagined living in her in-laws' world. "In part because I wanted my children to know where they came from." Poppy slid off the bench and knelt beside the trunk. She pulled out a thin manila envelope and removed a yellowed newspaper clipping—a document she'd kept hidden from everyone. She traced her finger over the headline above a front page photo of her mother. *Prostitute Disappears without a Trace.* "I wanted to believe the Butlers would one day accept us, or if nothing else, at least acknowledge our existence." She handed the article to David.

"Your mother was a stunning woman."

"She never uttered an unkind word about anyone." Poppy laid the envelope on the floor and returned to the bench. "Not even about people who treated her like she was a bad person."

Daisy squeezed her mother's hand. "You are the smartest, kindest, most beautiful woman I know, Mom, and I'm proud Rose Fowler is my grandmother."

Poppy sniffled while twining her fingers with her daughter's. "She'd be proud of you, honey."

David reached into his pocket and withdrew his phone. "I'd like to capture this mother-daughter moment."

"You want to take a picture?" Poppy fanned her fingers across her left cheek.

He nodded. "Rose Fowler's daughter and granddaughter, like her are both beautiful."

"How about it, Mom? Should we let David play photographer?"

Poppy filled her lungs and slowly released the air. Except for her birthmark, maybe she did resemble her mother. She forced her hand to slide down her cheek to her neck. "Do you have some kind of fancy program to fix the picture?"

"I can't improve on perfection."

Daisy elbowed her mom. "Our investigator is a charmer."

"I'm simply stating the facts, ladies." David set the scrapbook and newspaper clipping aside. "Do I have your permission, Poppy?"

"I suppose it's okay." Poppy leaned close to Daisy and turned to expose her unmarred cheek.

David lifted off the bench and aimed his phone.

Would she ever find the courage to face a camera head-on?

Chapter 19

Sun streaming into Daisy's bedroom nudged her eyes open. She yawned, eased out of bed, and lifted her phone off the nightstand. Seven-forty. The latest she'd slept in months. Eager for a cup of coffee, she opened the door, took two steps, and halted. Her ears perked at David's voice drifting in from the kitchen. Had his house tour begun an hour ahead of schedule, or had her mom invited him for breakfast? Whatever the reason, she had no intention of facing him without looking her best.

She backed into her room, grabbed her phone, a pair of jeans and a sweater, then tiptoed to the bathroom. While showering, dressing, and drying her hair, images of David played in her mind. The way his eyes lit with a smile when he caught her staring at him. His habit of clicking his pen before he jotted notes. His attentiveness when he listened to Aunt Pansy prattle on about mundane topics. The way he treated her mom with respect.

Her phone vibrated on the sink. She eyed the screen. Michael. "Good morning."

"How's everything going in Georgia?"

What did he mean by everything? "I'm winding down. What about you? Are you still working or taking time off?"

"I leave for Southampton at noon."

"Big family celebration tomorrow?"

"Three days on my grandfather's yacht. Thanksgiving tradition."

Of course, why would the Warner clan celebrate their blessings gathered around a dining-room table feasting on a family-prepared meal? "Sounds like fun."

"I'd enjoy the time a lot more if you were joining us. What about your family? How are you celebrating?"

Not even a snack on a fishing boat. "Intimate gathering at home." With one intriguing stranger.

"Is your grandfather hosting?"

Uh-oh. How could she respond without revealing the truth or telling a lie? "Not this year."

"I trust you've arranged a business meeting with him."

Another moral dilemma. Sweat popped out on Daisy's upper lip. "It's on my schedule."

"Don't wait too long."

Why the big rush? Was Curtis Butler standing at death's door?

"We're not the only firm pursuing his business."

That's why. "I'm on it, Michael."

"Good. Give my regards to your family, and happy Thanksgiving."

Following a sharp rap, the door swung open. Pansy, wearing her pajamas, rushed into the bathroom. Daisy retreated to the hall. "Same to you, Michael."

"We'll talk in a few days."

The moment he ended the call, Daisy switched her phone to silent and sauntered into the kitchen. "Good morning."

David stood. "Indeed, it is." His eyes met hers. "Your mom's been enlightening me with descriptions of Pansy's *Rose Fowler* series."

"Stories straight from my aunt's creative imagination."

Her mom placed a cup of hot coffee on the table in front of Daisy's chair. "You had a nice long sleep."

"It took a couple of nights to adjust to the quiet. No traffic or late-night sirens bouncing between the buildings." Daisy dropped a slice of bread in the toaster.

"I know what you mean." David lowered to his chair. "Last year I spent three weeks in a Manhattan hotel."

"Business or pleasure?"

"Chasing a cold case."

"Did you solve it?"

"With help from a local detective. Turns out the missing hooker had fled to Canada to escape a crazed stalker. After the guy was shot during a drug bust, she returned to New York with a new identity."

Daisy's toast popped up. "Do all your projects involve women like my grandmother."

"If you mean missing people who were shunned or easily dismissed by authorities, yes. Otherwise, no."

Had he interpreted her query as snippy? She plated her toast, carried it to the table, and sat across from David. "I wasn't questioning your motives."

"Mind if I ask you a question?"

"Not at all."

He leaned forward and planted his forearms on the table. "What do attorneys and investigative journalists have in common?"

Was this a trick question? "They're the butt of not-so-hilarious jokes?"

He grinned. "Besides that."

"I give. What do they have in common?"

His eyes remained focused on hers. "They both thrive on uncovering the truth."

"No matter where it leads?"

"Exactly."

Pansy wandered in, still wearing pajamas. "Who were you talking to on the phone in the bathroom?"

"A friend." Daisy broke eye contact with David and spread jam on her toast. "When do we begin today's fact-finding mission?"

Her mom swallowed a sip of coffee. "As soon as Pansy eats breakfast and changes out of her PJ's."

"If I make my bed, can we start in my room? I wanna show David my collection."

"That's his decision, sweetie."

Pansy eyed David. "Can we? Please?"

He smiled. "Your room is the perfect place to begin."

"Goody." Pansy bolted from her seat, plucked a cookie from the canister, and dashed to the hall.

David chuckled. "I love her enthusiasm."

An involuntary smile curved Daisy's lips. "What do you hope to discover today?"

He eyed her while tapping the corner of his mouth. "Jelly."

She wiped the smudge with a napkin. "Thanks."

"You're welcome. To answer your question, insignificant details often provide unexpected clues."

Poppy snapped her fingers. "Like NCIS."

"One of Mom's favorite television series."

He nodded. "Appropriate comparison."

While David revealed clues he had uncovered in previous cases, Daisy's mind drifted to subtleties she'd noticed. The way the skin around his eyes crinkled when he smiled. How his animated hand gestures punctuated his enthusiasm. The scents of soap and shampoo drifting around him.

"...right, Daisy?"

"What?" She flinched. "Sorry Mom, mental vacation."

"I understand."

What did her mom understand? That she yearned to know more about David? Or that more than once, she found herself mentally comparing him to Michael?

Pansy scurried in from the hall and grabbed David's hand. "My room's all ready."

"Well then, pretty lady, let's get this tour under way." He lifted his notepad off the table and followed Pansy.

Daisy's mom leaned close. "Is Michael as handsome and charming as David?"

Had she read her mind? "I'm not comparing the two." The moment the comment rolled off her tongue, she questioned if the words sounded as insincere to her mom as they did to her own ears?

"I didn't say you were."

Yeah, you did. "Michael's as handsome."

Her mom rose to her feet. "Is he as charming?"

"He's a highly sought-after defense attorney." Daisy looped her arm around her mom's elbow. "Charm isn't his most important attribute."

"What about when he schmoozes juries into returning not-guilty verdicts?"

Daisy rolled her eyes. "Are you still watching old *Law and Order* reruns?"

"One of the programs your dad and I enjoy." She patted her daughter's hand.

They made their way to Pansy's room. David nodded while listening to Pansy describe her thrift-store treasures and ball-cap collection. Would Michael treat her aunt with the same amount of respect?

"This one's my favorite." Pansy plucked her new ball cap off the shelf and plopped it on her head.

"I can see why." David tapped the rhinestone-studded bill. "Fanciest hat I've ever seen."

"Daisy gave it to me."

"Your niece has excellent taste." He lifted a scrapbook off a shelf and set it on the dresser. "Is it okay if I look inside?"

"Uh-huh."

David flipped it open, revealing a sheet of construction paper folded in half. A cake topped with candles was drawn on the front.

"It's from Mama."

He opened the card. Dozens of tiny stickers decorated the inside, but not a single hand-written word. "I see where your artistic talent comes from." He turned pages and opened more hand-drawn cards, all devoid of words. "Did your mother ever read to you?"

"She said reading made her dizzy." Pansy grabbed her newest treasure and stroked the figurine's red dress. "She told us lots of stories about castles and princesses and their fun adventures."

David flipped through more pages, then turned to Poppy. "Did your mother write checks to pay bills?"

She shook her head. "Once a month we'd drive around and pay with cash."

"Do you know if she graduated from high school?"

"Mama never talked about her growing-up years."

Pansy set her figurine back on the shelf. "A lady came over to teach me how to read and write."

David closed the scrapbook and set it back in place. "I remember one of my college buddies telling me it took him years of training to learn how to unscramble letters enough to read. Maybe Rose suffered from the same challenge."

Poppy's brow furrowed. "I remember when I brought my first report card home from school and asked Mama to read my teacher's note. She said the letters were too messed up to make out."

"Oh my gosh." Daisy pressed her hand to her chest. "Is it possible my grandmother entertained men because she was too proud to let anyone know she couldn't read?"

David's eyes met hers. "As an investigative journalist, I've witnessed the devastation caused by circumstances that affected one's self-image."

His words collided with memories of her first law-firm interview. Comments made about Curtis Butler. Her evasive denial. Had ambition coupled with unreasonable self-image forced her to skirt the truth? The reason didn't matter. She'd chosen her path. Now she had find a way to control the outcome. No matter the consequences.

"Mama believed invisible angels watched over us." Poppy lifted a ceramic angel off Pansy's dresser. "We bought this for her last birthday before she disappeared."

Pansy pulled off her ball cap and fingered the sparkly bill. "Maybe Mama's angels are with her now."

Poppy drew her sister close. "So many angels she can't count them all."

"Maybe one of 'em sent David to us."

"I believe you're right." David snapped his fingers. "In fact, I'm positive I heard wings fluttering the first time I read the story you sent me."

"Do angels fly like birds or airplanes?"

"Hmm." David pinched his chin between his thumb and forefinger. "More like butterflies."

"Butterflies are pretty. They like our flowers." Pansy popped her NYC ball cap on her head. "Do you want me to show you Mama's bedroom? It's Daisy's room now."

"Lead the way."

Pansy clutched David's hand and led him out to the hall.

"Don't you love how David treats my sister?" Poppy looped her hand around Daisy's elbow.

"What do you expect? He's an investigative journalist looking for a credible story."

"He's also a sensitive man who needs a family."

"Do you want me to draw up adoption papers?" Daisy nudged her mom's arm. "Or are you planning to hold him captive after he finishes his investigation?"

"I'm just saying, we're lucky to have him on our team. I have a question. Did you invite Michael to spend Thanksgiving with us?"

"We've only been dating for a few months. Besides, he's spending the holiday with his family on his grandfather's yacht." Daisy scooted to her bedroom door.

Poppy followed and leaned on the doorframe. "Lifestyles of the rich and famous?"

"Something like that."

Pansy sat on Lilly's bed hugging the bear her niece had left behind. "Mama slept in a fancy gold bed right over there under the window."

"Before she left, our house had two bedrooms." Poppy ambled into the room. "After we married, Danny and I slept in here."

David faced her. "In your mother's bed?"

Poppy folded her arms tight across her torso. Why had he asked such a personal question?

"Sorry, I didn't mean to pry."

Daisy touched her arm. "He's an investigative journalist, Mom. He asks a lot of questions."

"I understand. After we drove to Savannah to buy a marriage license, Danny hauled the mattress to a dump and the headboard and footboard up to the attic."

"Lots of Mama's things are up there." Pansy tapped the bear's nose. "Wanna see them?"

"If your sister and aunt give me the go-ahead."

Daisy shrugged. "Doesn't matter to me."

"How about Friday?" Poppy unfolded her arms. "After we celebrate Thanksgiving?"

David nodded. "Works for me."

The front door creaked, followed by footsteps striking the hall floor.

"Hey, I'm home." The male voice boomed.

"Basil." Pansy bolted to her feet, tossed Lilly's bear on the bed, and dashed out.

Poppy scurried behind her.

"The best aunt in the whole wide world." Basil dropped his duffle, lifted Pansy off her feet, and whirled her in a circle before setting her down. "Fancy hat." He pulled off her ball cap and popped it on his head. "Mind if I borrow it?"

"It's a girl's hat, silly."

"Not to mention it's too small for my little brother's fat head." Daisy stood on her toes and kissed Basil's cheek. "Glad you made it home safe and sound, knucklehead."

"Good to see you, noodle-noggin."

Poppy smiled at the childhood nicknames and wrapped her arms around her son. "Welcome home, honey."

"You're as beautiful as ever, Mom."

Daisy straightened his shirt collar. "We didn't expect you 'til noon."

"I caught an earlier flight." He returned Pansy's ball cap and nodded toward David. "Is he your new boyfriend or Pansy's?"

"I'd find it difficult to choose between them." David stepped forward with his hand extended. "David Lambert. Investigative journalist."

"Basil Butler." He grasped David's hand. "Ex-marine as of yesterday." Their hands released. "Did my lawyer sister hire you to work on a murder case?"

Daisy knuckle-thumped her brother's arm. "My brother doesn't know the difference between a corporate and a criminal-defense attorney."

"And my brilliant sister has a hard time remembering who ranks higher. A master or a first sergeant."

"Logic dictates first comes before master."

"Just like old times. My oldest and youngest swapping playful jabs." Poppy grinned as she grasped Basil's hand. "Come on in the kitchen, and Pansy will pour you a glass of fresh-squeezed lemonade."

"After I give Dad a hug."

"He'll be thrilled to see you." Poppy peered over her shoulder. "Finish the tour, Daisy, while Pansy and I take your brother to the greenhouse and give him the real scoop about David."

"The real scoop?" Basil chuckled as they walked toward the front door. "Sounds like journalism talk."

"I'm learning a thing or two from our guest."

Slick move, Mom. Daisy pushed her hands into her jeans pocket. "You've seen the front room and kitchen. Other than the attic, I don't know what else to show you."

"Mind if we talk out on the front porch?"

"Suits me."

David held the front door open. "After you."

She strolled out and stopped at the railing facing the front yard.

He sidled beside her. "Your brother seems like a fun guy."

"He's a treasure. We all missed him like crazy. Especially Mom."

"A special bond exists between mothers and sons." His arm brushed her shoulder as he turned and leaned back against the railing. "Do you have any idea what caused the rift between your dad and his family?"

"Why are you asking?"

"Journalistic curiosity."

Michael's demand skated across Daisy's conscience as she flicked an ant off the railing. "I promised to confront him."

"Your dad?"

"My grandfather." She pushed away and dropped onto a rocking chair. What insane trigger had prompted her to reveal that secret? Her confusing attraction to David or a guilty conscience?

He settled beside her. "Do you want to talk about it?"

"Not now." She set her rocker in motion. "Have you formed any theories about my grandmother's disappearance?"

"She didn't run away."

"I've always suspected foul play."

"Does your mom hold the same opinion?"

"Probably. Although for Pansy's sake, she goes along with her stories about finding Rose and bringing her home."

"How will your family protect your aunt if I uncover devastating details?"

"She's strong enough to handle the truth." Daisy fell silent as their chairs rocked in sync, creating a calming rhythm. Her eyes drifted to David's ring-free hand resting on the chair's arm. No symbol of wealth or status. Only tanned skin and neatly-trimmed nails. "You're welcome to join us for dinner and help us celebrate my brother's safe return."

"I was hoping you'd invite me."

Another involuntary smile curled her lips as she gazed across the front lawn. For the first time since she'd laid eyes on David, she wondered which man might become part of her future. The wealthy attorney who treated her to fancy dinners on his Manhattan terrace? The man who could become one half of a sought-after power couple? Or the stranger who had drifted into their lives out of nowhere?

Chapter 20

Poppy hummed an upbeat country tune as the first hint of dawn shone through the kitchen window. She donned her special-occasion, lace-bordered apron and removed a turkey from the fridge. Today her family would celebrate Thanksgiving together for the first time in three years. Along with one special guest.

Danny wandered in and poured a cup of coffee. Thanksgiving and Christmas were the two days he allowed himself to sleep late. If one could call six-thirty late. "It's good to have our son home."

"The best reason to give thanks." Poppy relished the close bond between her son and her husband—a miracle considering Danny's toxic relationship with his father.

"He managed to survive the Marines unscathed physically *and* mentally."

"I imagine my daily prayers helped, or as Mama would've said, his angels worked overtime to keep him safe." Poppy studied her husband's expression, anticipating a scoff. To her surprise and delight, his expression remained unchanged. "I'm breathing a whole lot easier knowing he's no longer in danger."

The back porch light illuminated, revealing their son stretching his arms over his head outside the bedroom Danny had built on one end of the porch. "Our boy's awake."

Basil sauntered in and planted a kiss on his mother's cheek. "Morning, Mom."

"You're up early."

"Force of habit."

She washed her hands and poured him a cup of coffee. "Do you still take it black?"

"The stronger the better." He set the cup on the table and reached for her hand. "Come sit with me. There's something I need to tell you before the rest of the household wanders in."

"Sounds serious." Poppy pressed her hand to her chest. "Oh my gosh, you've met a girl. You're in love, aren't you?"

"Wishful thinking, but no." He pulled a chair out for her.

"What's the big secret?"

Basil settled beside her. "Do you remember the first time I said I wanted to be a Marine?"

She nodded. "The day you turned six. You marched right in here, saluted your dad, and asked where you could sign up."

"Yep." Basil faced his dad. "You told me I had to grow taller. It took twelve more years before I was tall enough to walk into an enlistment office. Best decision I ever made." He paused and took a drink of coffee. "During the past few years, I've been trying to figure out the best way to continue doing what I love. Serving our country."

Poppy's pulse accelerated. She grabbed her son's hand. "Please tell me you didn't reenlist."

"I'm out for good."

"Thank heaven. You should go to college like Daisy. Maybe study law to defend innocent people and keep them from going to jail."

David chuckled. "One lawyer in the family is more than enough."

"How about a business tycoon or a doctor?"

"Thanks for the vote of confidence, Mom. But you know academics aren't my thing. I want to help people by doing what I can to keep communities safe."

Poppy sensed the color draining from her face. "What are you saying?"

"I plan to enroll at Savannah's police academy in January. I told Dad last night."

She jerked her head toward Danny. "Did you try to talk him out of it?"

"It's his decision. Besides, law enforcement is a noble profession."

"Because it won't make him rich?" She faced her son, her eyes pleading. "Do you know how much danger policemen face every day? How many are killed every year?"

"The entire time we were growing, up you urged me and my sisters to follow our hearts. This is what I'm meant to do, Mom." He pressed his hand over hers. "I want—no, I need you to support me and accept my choice."

How could she support a decision that could cost Basil his life? And yet, he was right. She had always encouraged her children to trust their instincts. Was it fair to deny him his passion because he'd chosen a path she considered too dangerous? She swallowed the argument begging to race across her tongue. "It seems I'll need to keep counting on angels to keep you safe."

"An entire platoon of angels." Basil kissed her cheek. "When's the last time I told you how much I love you and what an incredible mom you are?"

"If any bad guys lay a hand on you, they'll be forced to deal with me."

"You *are* handy with a pistol. Maybe you should consider law enforcement."

"One police officer in the family is more than enough. When are you going to tell the rest of the family?"

"At an appropriate time during our Thanksgiving feast."

"Well then." Poppy pulled her hand away. "I'd best start fixing the turkey if we plan to eat at two." She pushed up, dropped a stick of butter in a measuring cup, and placed it in the microwave. Somehow she had to put on a happy face and trust God to keep her only son free from harm.

At one-thirty Daisy slipped out of the kitchen and peeked in the front room. She smiled at David's animated gestures as he described one of his investigations to her dad, brother, and brother-in-law. He fit right in with the men in her family. Easygoing. Unpretentious. How would Michael fit in? She imagined him sitting on a luxury yacht's rear deck, discussing law-firm business or the family's latest million-dollar art investment. Drinking outrageously expensive Champagne while waiting for a staff of chefs to put the final touches on an extravagant meal.

If their relationship escalated, her family would expect to meet him—the sophisticated man accustomed to the best money could buy. If that day came, how would she explain her family's lifestyle? At least she didn't have to face that dilemma any time soon. Daisy returned to the kitchen and breathed in the mouthwatering mix of aromas.

Lilly transferred their mom's thrift-store wine glasses from the hutch to the table. "Do you suppose Dad will want his grandson to call him Granddad or Grandpa, or something more creative, like Pop or Papa? And what do you want him to call you, Mom?"

"Hmm. Maybe Grammy."

"I like that." Lilly patted her swelling tummy. "I'm glad our baby will be blessed with grandparents to love on him. Something Daisy, Basil, and I missed."

A scrapbook photo of the grandfather she'd never met accepting an award for a sizable contribution to a hospital flashed across Daisy's mind like a lightning bolt. The man she'd committed to recruiting. She couldn't avoid the inevitable conversation with her dad much longer. Tomorrow she'd find the right time to broach the subject.

Pansy pushed Basil's formal Marine hat higher up her forehead, then set a sweet-potato casserole on the table between bowls of brussels sprouts and cornbread dressing. She pointed to the chair around the corner from her seat. "Can David sit there?"

"Of course." Daisy's mom transferred the turkey platter to a spot in front of her husband's place at the table.

"Just think." Lilly pressed her palms together. "If David discovers what happened to Grandmother Rose and writes a book, our family will become celebrities."

Her mom set down a bowl of cranberry sauce. "I hope that never happens."

"The book or the fame?"

"The celebrity part."

Daisy removed a carving knife from a drawer and laid it beside the turkey. "Which makes David's book idea a challenge. You know Dad would balk at the idea of strangers reading about our family's business."

Lilly's brow scrunched. "Are you saying you don't want David to find Rose?"

"I'm saying if he finds her—"

Pansy planted her hands on her hips. "He's gonna find her."

"Of course, he is." Daisy patted her aunt's hand. "What I mean is, if David writes a book, readers will consider him the celebrity. Not us."

Heavy footsteps struck the hall floor. The floorboards creaked. Daisy's dad accompanied the men into the kitchen. "All these delicious smells are making our stomachs grumble."

Basil pulled a corkscrew from a drawer and uncorked two bottles of wine. "Sure beats the heck out of last year's Thanksgiving dinner."

Lilly elbowed Basil. "Even though you're still my irritating little brother, I'm thrilled you're finally on this side of the Atlantic."

He grinned. "Sounds like Mom's and Dad's middle child missed the pestering."

"Yeah. Especially these." Lilly knuckle-thumped her brother's arm.

Andy gripped Basil's shoulder. "We're all glad you're out of danger."

Daisy noted her mom's clenched her jaw while exchanging glances with her dad. Did they know something the rest of the family didn't? Had Basil reenlisted? If he had, he would've told her last night. Wouldn't he?

Pansy directed David to sit to one side of her place and Basil on the other. Daisy sat between her mom and David, ignoring Lilly's raised eyebrow, her *I know what's going on* expression.

After everyone was seated, David leaned forward and turned toward Daisy's dad. "I know it's a bit brazen, me being a guest. But sharing today with your family means a lot to me, so do you mind if I say grace?"

He shrugged. "Why not."

Daisy closed her eyes, delighting in David's presence. Was she falling for this man who showed up unexpectedly at her parents' door just as her dad had shown up on the porch all those years ago? Or was she simply caught up in the moment?

Surprised by David's request as well as Danny's approval, Poppy laced her fingers and listened to his heartfelt words about her family and God's blessings. Perhaps the first guest she and Danny had welcomed into their home since they married, was destined to do far more than solve her mother's disappearance.

"Amen." Pansy's acclimation punctuated the end of David's prayer. "Danny's the best turkey carver ever. I always take one leg and Basil takes the other."

"Who ate my share while I was away, Aunt Pansy?"

"Me." She leaned across the corner and thumped Basil's arm. "I ate it for breakfast."

"Well now, I'd call that a gobbling good way to start the day. In fact, it's so good I'm gonna donate my leg for your breakfast tomorrow."

"Really?" Pansy's eyes widened. "You sure?"

"Yep. Besides, after I load up on all this food I won't have room in my belly for anything more than a little slab of dark meat."

Danny sliced a leg off the bird and placed it on a platter. "Pass this to the world's best sister-in-law."

A deep, satisfying breath filled Poppy's lungs as she scanned the faces around the table. Her beautiful family enjoying each other's company. Three children who thrived despite her and Danny's troubled backgrounds. Her eyes landed on Basil. When would he announce his career decision? And how would his sisters and Andy react? Maybe they'd talk some sense into him.

Danny continued carving the turkey while the rest of the family passed the sides and reminisced about other Thanksgivings they'd celebrated together. The same fun stories Poppy had heard before and never tired of hearing again. She caught Lilly's smile and made a mental note to pull her children's highchair from the attic and fix it up before next year's celebration.

After everyone's plate was filled, Lilly pointed her fork at David. "Did you solve every cold case you tackled?"

"All except one. It still bugs me."

"I'd call that an impressive record." Lilly slid her fork into the stuffing. "How does our grandmother Rose's case stack up?"

Basil laughed. "I forgot how nosy my sisters are."

"Hey." Lilly pointed her finger at Basil. "How do you suppose Daisy and I always knew a whole lot more than you?"

"Ouch. Ganging up on me again."

"One more thing, little brother, I suggested Aunt Pansy send her story to David. Even though I only half expected him to show up, or maybe less than half...the fact is, he's here." Lilly eyed David. "So, what's your answer?"

"Your grandmother's disappearance promises to be one of the more challenging and interesting cases I've taken on."

"What made you choose investigative journalism?"

"Good open-ended question." David set his fork down. "It all started on my twelfth birthday. Somehow, Mom scraped together enough money to take me and a friend to Washington DC. Hands down the best part of the trip was the Spy Museum. That experience hooked me on digging up clues. Afterwards I began reading spy mysteries."

Lilly's eyes remained glued on David. "Then why didn't you become a cop or an FBI agent?"

A mischievous grin lit Basil's face. "See what I mean? Nosy."

"Ignore my brother. He can't help himself. Back to my question."

"Either of those careers would seem logical. Except facing some lunatic brandishing a gun isn't my idea of fun."

Poppy stole a glance at her son.

Basil winked. "Tracking down old cases takes more than courage."

"My brother's right," added Daisy. "It requires keen puzzle-solving skills."

David turned toward her. "Same as an attorney."

"Seems you and my big sister have a lot in common, David." Lilly's head tilted. "How many famous people have you investigated?"

Andy laughed. "My wife is fascinated with celebrities."

Basil shook his head. "And she's never met a single one."

"Hey, little brother, our dinner guest comes close to qualifying."

"Not quite." David chuckled. "To answer Lilly's question, I prefer cold cases involving people local law enforcement ignored or considered too insignificant to pursue."

"David's gonna find Mama and bring her home." Pansy plucked the turkey leg off her plate. "Daisy is David's girlfriend."

Poppy choked.

Daisy's ears turned three shades of pink.

Basil guffawed.

Lilly's brows shot up.

"Know what, Pansy?" David's tone hinted of playfulness. "Everyone at this table is a friend. Especially you."

Pansy's eyes widened. "Do you wanna live with us?"

"Did you forget that I brought my house with me?"

"Oh yeah. It's too little for a dog."

Basil lifted his wine glass. "Now that living arrangements are figured out, how about a toast to the four beautiful ladies who prepared this feast."

The men raised their glasses amid a flurry of compliments.

Lilly lifted her apple juice-filled wine glass. "Mom and Pansy deserve most of the credit." She took a sip and set her glass down. "So, Daisy, when do you return to New York?"

"Sunday night. I'm taking a week off and coming back home to celebrate Christmas and New Year's with y'all."

"Christmas is my favorite holiday." Pansy slipped Boots a piece of turkey. "Me and Poppy make sugar cookies in lots of fancy shapes, like Mama used to do. We sent a big box to Basil last year. Lots of soldiers sent us thank-you notes."

"Your cookies were a big hit with all the guys, Aunt Pansy—tasty reminders of home."

"Speaking of home." Lilly wiped her mouth with a napkin. "Now that you're here, what are your plans, Basil? Are you moving back in with Mom and Dad?"

Poppy caught her son's eye. Was this the moment he'd give another family member the chance to talk him out of his career choice?

"I suppose this is as good a time as any. I've already told Mom and Dad." Basil set down his fork. "I've given a lot of thought to how I can use my skills, even if I'm not as smart as my inquisitive sisters. Is that better than nosy?"

"Definitely," Lilly and Daisy responded together.

"Fact is—" Basil grinned. "I've made the decision to become a police officer and protect citizens here at home."

Andy snapped his fingers. "A cop *and* a lawyer in the family. We'll have all the bases covered."

"One thing I've learned as a journalist," added David. "This country needs more dedicated policemen."

"He's right." Daisy stretched and touched Basil's arm. "You'll make one fine officer, knucklehead."

"My little brother, a police officer." Lilly smiled. "Who'd have guessed?"

Pansy speared a brussels sprout. "Will you wear a badge and carry a gun?"

"You bet I will."

"Will bad guys shoot at you?"

"They wouldn't dare."

"'Cause no one messes with Marines?"

"I couldn't have said it better, Aunt Pansy."

Poppy clenched her jaw. Why hadn't at least one person tried to talk Basil out of putting his life on the line? Didn't anyone understand the risk? Especially since he'd managed to survive military service without being shot.

"One thing I know about sons—they want their father's respect." Danny lifted his wineglass. "A toast to my son, who makes me proud and honored to be his dad."

"Thanks, Dad." Basil's eyes reddened. "I couldn't ask for a better father."

Poppy choked back tears while joining her family and lifting her glass. After swallowing a sip of wine, she reached across the corner of the table and squeezed her husband's hand. When his eyes met hers, she understood a profound truth—one she had suspected for years. Despite Danny's confessed hatred for Curtis Butler, deep down he'd spent a lifetime craving the man's approval. Maybe one day he would find it in his heart to forgive his father for whatever evil drove them apart.

Chapter 21

S unlight streamed into Daisy's bedroom as memories of yesterday's family celebration played in her mind and warmed her heart. The way they shared stories and playfully teased each other. Pansy gathering them on the back porch to watch the setting sun paint brilliant colors across the western sky. Returning to the table to enjoy one more slice of pumpkin pie before Lilly and Andy hugged everyone and drove home.

She stretched her arms over her head and caught sight of her phone, facedown on the dresser. Twenty-four hours had passed since she'd last checked for messages. She could wait another day or until the holiday weekend ended before turning her phone back on? What if Michael called to wish her a happy Thanksgiving? If she didn't respond, would she set off alarm bells? Unwilling to test that theory, she turned her phone on and found a text from Michael.

Hope you're having a wonderful day. Talked to Dad about Curtis. He expects an update Monday morning. See you then.

Did the Warner men ever take a break from work? Daisy's stomach churned as she tossed the phone on her bed. She couldn't continue delaying the inevitable another hour, much less another day. As soon as she showered and dressed, she'd find her dad and break the news.

Thirty minutes later she walked into the kitchen. Pansy was relishing the turkey leg Basil had donated. "Am I the last one up?"

Her mom set her coffee cup on the table. "By more than an hour."

"I assume Dad's in the greenhouse."

"You missed him by twenty minutes. He and Basil are delivering a big order to Tybee Island."

She released a sigh. "I forgot he always works the day after Thanksgiving. Any idea when they'll return?"

"Sometime late this afternoon."

Daisy poured herself a cup. Why hadn't she broached the subject days ago? Because she dreaded her dad's anger. Even worse, his disappointment. Time was not on her side. She had no choice but to face the consequences head-on tonight and confront her grandfather tomorrow morning.

"David's coming back at eight."

Daisy carried her cup to the table and dropped onto the chair beside her mom. "Coming back?"

"He joined us for breakfast."

Pansy pointed her turkey leg at Daisy. "We're gonna go up to the attic to look at all of Mama's things. Wanna go with us?"

"Of course she does."

"Because she's David's girlfriend?"

Daisy released a long sigh. "I love you tons, Aunt Pansy. But you have to stop calling me his girlfriend."

"Okay." Pansy wiped her fingers with a napkin.

A knock followed footsteps striking the back-porch floorboards.

Poppy faced the door. "Come on in."

Boots padded over and welcomed David with a tail wag. He stooped and petted his greeter. "My best-ever canine friend."

"He wants to visit your house on wheels." Pansy set her turkey leg down. "Me too."

"After we explore the attic."

"Daisy says I can't call her your girlfriend anymore."

Sensing her ears were seconds from coloring beyond pink to fire-engine red, Daisy cradled her coffee in both hands and stepped back. "Sorry, David."

"No apologies needed." He pulled a chair close to Pansy. "Do you want to know a secret?"

"Uh-huh?"

"Daisy's a real smart lawyer. Know what that means?"

Pansy shook her head.

"We'd best pay attention when she tells us something. How about we call her my special friend?"

"Okay."

David caught Daisy's eye and winked. "Now that we've settled the most important matter of the day, is everyone ready to explore the attic?"

Pansy tapped David's arm. "Do you want a piece of pie first?"

"What do you say we wait until after our adventure."

"Then we'll eat two pieces." Pansy popped off her chair and grabbed David's hand. "I'm too short to reach the rope. You can pull the ladder down."

"Now you're talking."

As they disappeared around the corner, Poppy's face lit up with a grin. "You've gotta love that man."

"In less than a week, he's managed to worm his way into Pansy's heart as well as yours."

"I'm just saying he has a good heart, and he called you his *special* friend."

Daisy rolled her eyes. "To keep Pansy from embarrassing the dickens out of both of us. And when did you switch from being a Michael fan to a David enthusiast?"

"I can't compare the two when I've only met one. That doesn't keep me from wondering. Like what Michael calls you and how he'd treat Pansy."

"Good grief, Mom. He calls me Daisy, and I have no idea how he'd react to her or anyone else in our family."

"You should find out."

"Maybe I will."

Pansy peered around the corner. "Come on, you two slow pokes. David's already up there."

"We're on our way." Poppy pulled a bottle of window cleaner and a roll of paper towels from under the sink.

Daisy scooted into the hall and followed Pansy as she scrambled up and over the edge of the opening. The floorboards flexed under her feet as she moved away from the stairs. Her mom climbed up and headed straight to the first of two dirt-encrusted windows while David pushed aside a cobweb curtain and pulled a chain to illuminate the single bulb hanging from the rafters. Pansy sat cross-legged beside a suitcase, unhooked the leather straps, and lifted the top.

David knelt beside her. "Your mother's clothes?"

"Some of 'em." She removed a red dress. "This is my favorite. Mama's dresses always smelled like flowers." Pansy held the garment to her nose and sniffed, triggering a sneeze. "They don't smell so pretty anymore."

After wiping the glass dry and opening the window, Poppy scooted to the opposing window.

Pansy removed a pair of pink slippers from the suitcase. "Daisy wore theses when she and Lilly played dress-up."

"That's better." Poppy opened the second window, sending a breeze wafting through the attic and releasing sneeze-triggering clouds of dust. She moseyed to the brass headboard leaning against the wall and wiped a layer of dirt off the curved top. "This belonged to her parents before Mama claimed it."

David pushed up and approached Poppy. "Do you remember anything about your grandparents?"

"All I know is they died in a car wreck when Mama was a teenager." Poppy coughed. "That terrible accident left her all alone in this house. I was born a year later."

David swatted a fly. "What about your father?"

"I don't know anything about him." She swept her arm around the space. "Most everything up here belonged to my grandparents."

"Including those?" David pointed to cardboard boxes stacked along the wall.

"Some of them."

Daisy lifted a tall wooden jewelry box off the floor and set it on a card table. "When Lilly and I were little, we called this Grandmother Rose's treasure chest." She blew dust off the front and opened the double doors. A row of drawers filled the box from top to bottom. Necklaces dangled from hooks attached to the doors.

Pansy placed the red dress and slippers back in the suitcase and ambled over. "Sometimes when me and Poppy played dress-up, Mama let us wear her fancy jewelry." She removed three strands of colored beads, slipped them over her head, and twirled in a wide circle.

David opened a drawer lined with crushed purple velvet. He lifted a bumble-bee shaped broach with blue stones embedded in its wings. "Do you know where her jewelry came from?"

"She bought some from the thrift store. Others were gifts from clients." Poppy set the window cleaner and paper towels on the floor. "Like that piece."

David turned it over and held it toward the light. "Twenty-four carat gold. If these gems are real, this is worth some money." He handed it to Daisy. "What's your opinion?"

"It looks real enough."

"I doubt Mama knew the difference between real and costume jewelry." Poppy grasped a drawer pull and tugged. It stuck. She yanked. The drawer popped, slipped from her fingers, and sent earrings tumbling to the floor.

Pansy stooped to gather the jewelry

Daisy retrieved the drawer, its side askew. A slim slit marred the velvet. "Something's under here." She picked at the edge until the lining peeled back. Her fingers gripped a flat metal object. "Feels like some sort of key." She pulled it out and held it up to the light. "A number's etched on the top." She handed it to David.

"No markings other than the number. Looks like a safe-deposit key."

"I don't understand." Poppy's brow scrunched. "If Mama didn't have a bank account, why would she have a safe-deposit box?"

"A million-dollar question, and one that begs an answer." David turned the key over. "Where did Rose keep the jewelry box?"

"On her dresser. Except it wasn't there after she disappeared. We found it here in the attic weeks later when we packed her clothes in that suitcase and hauled it up."

Daisy examined the broken drawer. "Seems Rose wanted to keep the key hidden from prying eyes."

"Our family is saddled with way too many secrets." Poppy removed a bracelet from a drawer and slipped it on her wrist. "What's your opinion, David? Any chance you'll discover what that key unlocks?"

"It'll take some digging, but yeah, I'll figure it out."

"Good thing we have an investigator *and* a lawyer working the case."

Daisy set the broken drawer on the table. Maybe she should come up with a logical reason to extend her stay beyond Monday and work the case with David. Some kind of excuse Michael and the law firm partners would accept.

Chapter 22

Daisy sat on the back-porch steps with Boots' head laying in her lap. She stroked his muzzle and stared at the empty space beside David's trailer. Maybe she should wait until after dinner to talk to her dad. Except postponing the inevitable would drive her heightened anxiety to intolerable levels. Best to face him the moment he and Basil returned, while her rehearsed approach was still fresh in her mind, not to mention Michael's looming deadline.

Boots lifted his head at an engine's hum and bolted across the yard.

Daisy's mouth went dry at the sight of her dad's delivery truck easing past the house and into its parking space. He stepped out and walked into the greenhouse. Basil headed in her direction. She pushed off the steps, hoping her brother's playful nature would ease her anxiety.

"Hey, noodle-noggin. Did you miss me?"

She thumped her brother's arm. "Like an itch I can't scratch."

"Is that the way to talk to your amazing brother who one day can fix all your parking tickets?"

"Hey, I'm an attorney."

"Oh yeah, you can bribe a judge."

"All day long." She patted his cheek. "Thanks."

"For what?"

"Being the best brother."

"Are you going all sentimental on me?"

"Yeah." Daisy brushed past him. "Get used to it, knucklehead." Daisy filled her lungs, released the air in one long exhale, and closed the distance to the greenhouse. Inside, she eyed the massive space. Her family's livelihood and her dad's sanctuary. She turned right and approached the area designated as his office—a space hidden by a massive potted ficus tree twenty feet from the entrance.

"Hey, Dad. We searched the attic. "

He looked up from his desk—an old door he had rescued from a junkyard stretched across two filing cabinets. "Find anything interesting?"

"A key." She sat in a metal folding chair across from him and relayed the details.

"Could lead to something."

"If David locates whatever box the key unlocks." Daisy reached for a marble paperweight inscribed with the words, Best Dad Ever. "I remember how you choked up when we gave this to you."

"You're not here to talk about Father's Day gifts are you?"

So much for small talk. "I—" She succumbed to a coughing fit.

Her dad rolled his chair back, extracted a bottle of water from a miniature fridge, twisted off the cap, and handed it to her.

She sipped until the cold liquid relieved her parched throat and stopped her cough. "Sorry."

"Something more than attics and keys is on your mind."

Here goes. "You know my law firm is fast-tracking me to a partnership."

"They'd be fools not to."

"The thing is...the position comes with certain expectations."

"Such as?"

"Securing new business." She returned the paperweight to the desk. "In my case, corporate clients."

He propped his forearms on the desk. "What are you trying to tell me?"

She took another sip of water, then set it down and crossed her leg over her knee. "They're counting on me to recruit the Butler empire."

His eyes narrowed to a slit. "You're not talking about my greenhouse, are you?"

She shook her head.

His eyes locked on hers, his glare fierce. "Is your law firm aware the you've never met Curtis Butler?"

"They never asked."

"Did you lie or let them draw their own conclusions?"

She pumped her foot. "It simply happened."

His nostrils flared. "Nothing ever *simply* happens."

"I know I shouldn't have—"

"What? Agreed to do business with the devil?"

Sweat invaded Daisy's armpits. She had never seen such anger in her father's eyes.

"You don't know what evil lives in that man's heart." He spat the words as if they were acid stripping the flesh from his tongue. "Or what he's done."

She diverted her eyes from his pointed stare, grabbed the water bottle, and swallowed another mouthful. "Maybe if I understood."

"Understood what? That he rejected his sons—"

"You mean son."

"I meant what I said."

Daisy's mouth fell open. "You have a brother?"

"Had." He leaned back and remained silent for a long moment.

Daisy pressed her hand to her chest. Did her mom know? "Is he the reason—"

"That I loathe the man? Or that I'd just as soon see him dead?"

"That might happen sooner than you realize."

"Why? Did one of your firm's clients hire a hit man?"

"Rumors are circulating about Curtis suffering from some kind of illness." Tears filled Daisy's eyes as she watched her dad's jaw go slack and the anger in his eyes dissolve to profound sadness. "I'll walk away from the assignment if you want me to."

He grabbed the paperweight and trudged toward the aisle cutting through the center of the greenhouse.

Mountains of guilt sent a quiver racing through Daisy's body. She had cut her dad to his core. Maybe she should call Michael and beg him to assign a more experienced attorney to appeal to Curtis. Except, what message would that send? That she didn't possess the competence to recruit her own grandfather? Or that she had deceived the partners? Her hands clenched as she pictured herself standing in the law firm's boardroom.

Stumbling over words while explaining why she had failed her first big assignment—bringing shame to Danny Butler's family.

Desperate to talk to her confidant, she eased off her chair, walked out, and headed straight to the clapboard retreat.

Her mom looked up from the scrapbook lying open across her lap. "You talked to him, didn't you?"

Daisy dropped beside her. "I broke his heart."

"Did he forbid you to contact Curtis?"

"Not verbally." She detailed the confrontation.

"Walking away means he needs time to sort through his emotions." She patted Daisy's arm. "He'll do the right thing."

"At this point I have no idea what the right thing is." She eyed her mom's wedding ring. Should she mention her dad's revelation or keep it to herself? Better to probe like an attorney facing a witness. "How much do you know about Dad's siblings?"

Her mom stared at her for a long moment. "He told you he had a brother, didn't he?"

"How long have you known?"

"Couple of weeks."

"Any idea what happened to him?"

"Not a clue. After your dad told me, I looked at every picture and read every article I'd collected over the years. Twice. Searching for something about a second son. Nothing. It's as if he never existed." She closed the scrapbook and placed it in the trunk. "His name was Bobby."

Daisy leaned back and folded her hands in her lap. "So many secrets."

"Going back a lot of years." Her mom's shoulders slumped. "What are you fixing to do about Curtis?"

"Talk to Dad again. Maybe after supper."

Pansy wandered in. Boots padded behind her and sprawled on the floor. "Are we making meatloaf tonight?"

"We always fix meatloaf on Friday."

She plopped beside Daisy. "Danny says he'll eat supper in the greenhouse."

Daisy exchanged glances with her mom and understood a heart-wrenching truth. Her dad's oldest child had driven a stake through his heart and likely damaged their relationship. Maybe beyond repair.

While her mom set supper on the table, guilt-ridden nausea gripped Daisy's gut, forcing her to beg off and retreat to her room. An hour later she sat on her bed, hugging her pillow to her chest while attempting to ignore her grumbling stomach. How had she let selfish ambition outweigh loyalty to her family, and worse, let a falsehood stand? If only she could rewind today or better yet the last two years.

A knock made her jump. She released her pillow and scooted to the edge of the bed. "Come in."

Basil walked in, his brow furrowed. "Mom's not talking. Dad's eating supper in the greenhouse. You're hiding out in here. What the heck is going on?"

Daisy's shoulders curled forward. "I've made a great big mess of everything."

"What'd you do?" He sat on Lilly's bed across from her. "Shoot someone or rob a bank?"

"Almost as bad." She explained.

"Wow. My big sister actually messed up."

She eyed the photo on the dresser, taken the day she and her siblings had given their dad the paperweight. "Maybe I need to find him and tell him I won't contact Curtis."

"Bad idea."

"Why?"

"Because you'd gut punch him a second time." Basil leaned forward and propped his forearms across his knees. "If you go crawling back to him in defeat, you'll force him to accept blame for undermining your career."

Daisy stared wide-eyed at her brother. "When did you become so smart?"

"I'm a man, which means I understand Dad on a level you can't."

"Guess I should've talked to you before I burdened him with the truth. Since I didn't, what do you suggest I do now?"

"Wait for Dad to make a move. Then decide."

Daisy pulled her knees to her chest. "I have a long night ahead."

"Maybe not." He stood and held out his hand. "You're coming with me."

"Where are we going?"

"To Willy's Convenience Store for ice cream. Or if you prefer, a couple of beers."

"Better yet, Pepto with a beer chaser." She straightened her legs and accepted his hand.

"Add a bag of chips and we'll call it a party." He pulled her to her feet.

"A pity party?"

"A pity every brother isn't saddled with a sister as smart as you."

"Is that your convoluted make-Daisy-feel-good comment?"

"Yeah. How am I doing?"

"Hmm. This jury of one is handing down a feel-good guilty verdict for effort."

Basil shook his head. "My sister the big-city lawyer."

"Are you complaining?"

"All I have to say is whatever man you end up marrying is in for one interesting ride."

Daisy halted and stared at her brother. Why had he made that comment?

"What? Did you change your mind about Willy's?"

His confused expression made it clear he didn't have a clue about her Michael v. David dilemma. "I'm wondering who's going to drive. The attorney in a rental car or the Marine in his cool Jeep?"

"The cool jeep."

"With a former Marine and future law-enforcement officer as your chauffeur?"

"Definitely." Daisy linked arms with Basil. "This future law-firm partner knows how to ride in style."

Chapter 23

Poppy closed the dishwasher and pressed start. If only she could push a button, restart today, and talk to Danny before Daisy broke the news. Maybe she could have said something to ease the blow and save her husband and daughter from pain and heartache.

She switched off the kitchen light and walked out to the back porch. As the last remnants of sunset faded and turned the sky dark gray, rivers of regret washed over her. Why had she spent all those years urging her daughter to embrace the Butler legacy—encouraging her to admire the strangers who had driven her husband away and carved a deep scar on his soul? How often had she dismissed the life Danny made possible, while daydreaming about living in his parents' world, unmarred by a birthmark. Mingling with well-educated, important people while enjoying the luxuries vast sums of cash could provide.

Poppy closed her eyes and relived yesterday's gathering around the kitchen table in the only home she'd ever known. Surrounded by all the people she loved. Deep down she knew the family she and Danny created offered far more than wealth and status. Their home provided security, comfort, and a place where she and Pansy could live without ridicule. Why hadn't she realized that was enough?

She opened her eyes and squared her shoulders. Although she couldn't go back and undo what she had done, she could find the courage to accept the blame for Daisy's actions. She descended the stairs and made her way to the greenhouse. Inside, she scanned the vast space lit by overhead lights. No sign of Danny. She walked to his office space and found his cell phone lying on the desk beside his untouched supper. She called out to him. No response.

Tension in her neck crept down her spine as she rushed outside. As her eyes adjusted to the dark, she confirmed that his delivery truck remained parked beside David's camper. At least he hadn't driven off. Poppy dashed to the front porch, hoping to find him sitting on a rocking chair. No such luck.

Struggling to tamp down her escalating anxiety, Poppy circled around the house and headed toward their private space. As the arbor swing came into view, Danny's head and shoulders were barely visible in the dim moonlight. She inched closer. Maybe she should walk away and give him space. Not tonight. Not when his heart was broken. "I hoped I'd find you here." She plucked a leaf off the jasmine vine and sat beside him.

His silence spoke volumes.

Seconds turned into minutes. Stars brightened as the dark gray sky morphed to inky black. An owl's hoot followed by a screech shattered the silence as cold fingers of regret gripped Poppy's soul. She couldn't let the silence stand. "Daisy didn't mean to hurt you."

He gripped the swing's arm. "The infamous Curtis Butler legacy lives on. Failure as fathers." His tone hinted of despair. "If I had told Daisy the truth about my old man." His neck muscles protruded. "Instead I refused to utter his name and let her form her own opinion." He fell silent.

Poppy glanced skyward and prayed for strength. "Daisy's failure to reveal the truth isn't your fault."

"Then whose fault is it?"

"Mine. I'm the one who showed her all those pictures of your mother's fancy parties and articles publicizing Curtis's success." Tears spilled as the confession tumbled off her tongue and left a bitter taste in her mouth. "I led her to believe your family was important to her future. That the Butler name would open doors to big opportunities." She lowered her voice to a whisper. "That she deserved far more than what we could give her."

"The Butler name opened doors all right. Straight into the devil's snake pit." He bolted from his seat and kicked at a clump of grass.

Poppy sat paralyzed as she wrestled to summon the courage to continue. She opened her palm and let the jasmine leaf fall to the ground while lifting off the swing. "I should have talked her out of taking the job in New York instead of—" She pressed her lips tight, fearing she'd made a terrible mistake.

Danny turned and gripped her shoulders—his face inches from hers. "Instead of what?"

Poppy swallowed the bile rising in her throat. Why had she let it slip out? Especially now?

The look of disdain in his eyes frightened her. Not because she expected a physical reaction. He had never struck her or their children and she knew he never would. She feared the truth would drive a wedge in their relationship.

"Instead...of...what?"

Whatever the consequences, she couldn't lie. "She had another offer. From a small firm that in my mind wasn't prestigious enough."

His grip tightened. "Where?"

She swallowed. "In Savannah. I begged her not to tell you because I didn't want you to talk her into accepting it instead of the New York offer."

His glare bore into her soul.

She quivered.

He released her shoulders, turned, and strode away.

"Danny, I—"

He thrust his palm above his shoulder without turning around.

Poppy's breath came in shallow spurts. Her eyes followed him until he disappeared into the greenhouse. The lights switched off, plunging the space into darkness. She trudged to the back porch and forced her legs to carry her up the stairs, then plodded through the kitchen and paused in the front room. How many nights since their children had grown had she and Danny sat side by side watching TV after Pansy had gone to bed? Would he forgive her enough to sit on the sofa with her sometime in the future? Or would he spend every waking hour in the greenhouse? Alone.

Mountains of angst kindled inside as she sought refuge in their bedroom. Had she damaged their marriage beyond repair? She collapsed onto the bed, buried her face in her pillow, and sobbed. By the time her tears ran dry, she understood one undeniable fact. When she awoke in the morning, she would not find the man she loved, the man whose children she bore lying beside her.

Chapter 24

Daisy stepped out of the shower, wrapped a towel around her, and stood in front of the bathroom mirror. She didn't look too bad considering she and Basil shared a six-pack of beer and snuck into the house way past midnight. Thankfully she didn't face an early-morning meeting or a long walk to work. After drying her hair and pulling on jeans and a sweatshirt, she traipsed to the kitchen, grateful to find her mom alone. "Sorry I missed breakfast."

"I saved you some."

Daisy peered at her mom's puffy eyes. "Are you okay?"

"A little tired." She removed a plate from the oven, peeled off the foil, and placed it in front of Daisy's chair.

Daisy poured a cup of coffee and carried it to the table. "How did Dad act this morning?"

"He skipped breakfast."

Not a good sign. "Did he say anything about yesterday?"

"He wants to talk to you."

"Where's Basil?"

"With your dad."

Daisy pushed her plate away.

"Too nervous to eat?"

"Yeah." She swallowed another sip of coffee and walked out to the backyard. Her sweatshirt failed to prevent the cool-morning breeze from sending a crop of goose bumps popping out.

Basil rushed out of the greenhouse. "After you talk to Dad, meet me in the kitchen." He swept past her without making eye contact.

"Hold on."

Basil turned and held up his palm. "He's waiting at his desk. We'll talk after."

She snuffed the spark of angst burning inside and made her way to her dad's office space.

He motioned her to sit.

She complied. Keeping her back straight, she folded her hands in her lap.

Her dad's eyes locked on hers. "Yesterday you said you'd walk away from your firm's assignment if I asked you to. Does your offer still stand?"

Daisy swallowed. "In a heartbeat."

He broke eye contact and lifted his paperweight off the desk. "The simple things are what make life worth living." He traced his finger over the curved top. "Love of family. A home filled with laughter and respect. An honest day's work." He set the gift beside a picture of his three children. "What would a refusal do to your career?"

"Our relationship is far more important than my job."

His eyes met hers before he pushed up and strode to the center aisle.

She followed him while envisioning Michael's reaction to her failure. There were plenty of law firms in Savannah. Maybe the one she had turned down would extend another offer. After all, who wouldn't want to hire an attorney with a prestigious New York firm on her resume? Daisy stopped beside her dad. "I'll call my firm today and tell them the truth."

He stooped and plucked a leaf off the concrete. "I'd be a poor excuse for a father if I let my past jeopardize your career."

Daisy stared at her father. "Are you giving me the go-ahead?" Her voice faltered.

"With a warning and two demands."

"Whatever you want."

"First, don't trust Curtis, and second, don't go to the ranch without Basil."

Gratitude mingled with heart-wrenching regret released a stream of tears. "I'm sorry I let this happen."

"What's done is done. I love you, Daisy, and I don't need an apology."

"I love you, Dad." She swiped her hand across her cheeks. "And I promise something good will come from this."

"Don't make promises you can't keep." He dropped the leaf, turned away from her, and trudged back to his office.

Daisy swallowed the lump gripping her throat as she trekked back to the house and into the kitchen.

"Your brother filled me in." Her mom handed Daisy a hot cup of coffee. "You know it wasn't easy for your dad to give his okay."

"Maybe I should abandon the idea. Call it quits."

Basil, wearing his dress uniform, leaned back against the counter. "No way you're backing out after Dad swallowed his pride and gave you the go-ahead." He crossed his arms and shoved his hands in his armpits. "Are you going to wear that outfit or change into something more suitable for a New York lawyer?"

"Your brother's right, honey." Her mom touched Daisy's cheek. "Whatever the outcome, you need to follow through."

Daisy's eyes shifted from her mom to her brother. "Dad insisted you go with me."

"Why do you think I'm wearing this getup?"

"Intimidation?"

"Bingo."

Daisy took one sip of coffee, then set the cup on the counter and headed straight to her room.

An hour later, dressed in a suit and heels, she steered onto the driveway leading to the Curtis ranch. "I'm sorry I pulled you into this." She braked.

"Don't you know Marines and cops always run toward mayhem? At least a locked gate isn't guarding the entrance." Basil aimed his thumb toward a small clearing off to the right. "Did I ever tell you about the time back in high school when a couple of buddies and I snuck over there to smoke pot?"

"My little brother, a juvenile delinquent? Did you get caught?"

"No, but I ended up sick as an old hound dog. Never touched the stuff again."

"Strange how none of my high school friends ever questioned if I was related to Curtis."

"One of the girls I dated asked if he was my uncle." Basil lowered his window to let a fly escape. "Her brother was one of my pot buddies."

Daisy gripped the steering wheel and eyed the stretch of pavement bordered on both sides by dense woods. "Yesterday Dad told me he had a brother."

Basil stared at her. "You're kidding."

"His name's Bobby."

"Does Mom know?"

"Yeah. We don't know if he's missing or dead."

"Missing grandmother. Dead or missing uncle. No telling what we'll find at the end of this driveway."

"Only one way to find out." Daisy eased the car forward. She drove a half mile and turned left, then drove another quarter mile to a cleared swath of land. The driveway split. One section formed a circle in front of an elaborate stone ranch-style house. The other led to a stable. "Impressive spread."

"What'd you expect? The man's worth millions."

"I always imagined he lived in some gothic monstrosity flanked by giant gargoyles and a gator-infested moat." She drove toward the house and parked behind a black Tesla. "Maybe we should back out."

"Too late." Basil nodded toward his right. "We've been spotted."

Daisy peered around her brother at a tall, muscular man standing at the edge of a three-foot-high stone wall. His sport-coat sleeves stretched tight across bulging biceps. "I'd prefer a moat and a gator to facing that guy. No wonder Dad insisted you come with me." She stepped out.

Basil joined her in front of the car. "Take it slow." His voice was barely above a whisper. "Odds are he's packing."

"Is this a fortress or a home?"

"Looks like both."

They climbed the curved steps to an enclosed, stone patio.

The man stood his ground. "Can I help you?"

Daisy forced a smile. "I represent the Warner Law Firm and I'm here to speak with Mr. Butler."

The man eyed Basil. "And you are?"

"Her associate."

"Follow me." The man opened a glass-inlaid door and led them into a tall foyer lit by a rustic chandelier. "Wait here." He ambled back to the door, unclipped a phone from his belt, and made a call.

Sweat popped out between Daisy's shoulder blades. Was her grandfather a wealthy man in need of protection or some kind of monster? She forced her eyes to focus on the living room's floor-to-ceiling windows flanking a massive stone fireplace. Had her dad spent time in this house? In this room? What happened to Bobby?

Heels clicked across the wood floor. An attractive sixty-something woman approached with an air of authority. "I'm Mr. Butler's assistant." Her stern expression matched her tailored gray suit and single strand of pearls.

Was she the gate keeper, or did she provide more personal service? "Is Mr. Curtis available?"

"Mr. Curtis doesn't see *anyone* without an appointment." Her tone made it clear that any lawyer with half a brain would know not to show up out of the blue and expect an audience with someone as important as Curtis Butler.

Daisy struggled to keep her shoulders squared. What made her believe a wealthy business mogul would drop everything and invite a stranger into his office? On a Saturday no less. She pulled a business card from her purse and handed it over. "Please tell Mr. Butler I traveled from New York to present our firm's credentials."

The woman read the card. "Daisy Butler. Any relationship?"

Should she reveal her identity? Not yet. "A coincidence."

"I'll contact you by the end of next week if he agrees to see you."

Why would he need a week to decide? Was he even on the property? "Do you mind giving me a business card? In the event I miss your call?"

The woman stared at Daisy for a long moment. "Wait here." She spun around and disappeared around a corner.

"We're spending a lot of time waiting," whispered Basil.

"At least no one has shot at us."

"Not yet, anyway."

The woman returned and handed Daisy a card.

She read the name. Cynthia Evans. "Thank you, Ms. Evans."

"Mr. Butler's bodyguard will show you out."

Why did he need a bodyguard? Sensing the woman wouldn't tolerate one more word of conversation, Daisy slid her hand around to Basil's bicep. They passed Mr. Bulging Muscles and hastened out to the front patio. As they made their way to the steps, she peered over her shoulder. The burly man stood at the window with his arms crossed. "Why do you suppose he's watching us?"

"To protect a criminal, a recluse, or an old man who's laid up."

At the bottom of the steps, Daisy pulled her hand away from Basil's bicep. "Chances of that woman granting me an audience with Curtis are slim to none. Maybe I need to fabricate a logical reason why my firm should abandon the idea."

"Are you kidding me?" Basil gripped her shoulders and turned her toward him. "After Dad swallowed every ounce of pride to give you the go-ahead you want to turn tail and run away after one try?"

"It's not that I want to."

"Then finish what you started."

"What if I'm right about Curtis refusing to meet me?"

He released his grip. "Keep showing up until he gives in."

"Do you believe he'll cave?"

"If he's curious enough about your name."

"I suppose you're right."

"You're not the only smart sibling in this family."

As they headed to the car, Daisy's quest to meet her grandfather shifted from lawyer to investigator. If she did manage to meet the man, she'd have a chance to discover what tore her dad's family apart. Maybe even have a hand in reuniting father and son before it was too late. "You know Dad doesn't want me coming here without you."

"Which means you're stuck with me."

She settled on the driver's seat and buckled her seatbelt while Basil slid in beside her. "You're a good brother, knucklehead."

"At your service, noodle-noggin." He set his cap on the dashboard.

Daisy circled the driveway and returned to the main road. During the drive home she mentally calculated two different strategies. One if Curtis agreed to a meeting. The other if he refused. Moments after parking in her parents' driveway, she climbed out and pulled her phone from her purse.

Basil stood beside her. "Give it a couple days before you go hounding his assistant."

"I'm texting Michael."

"Your boyfriend?"

"Jury's still out." She typed the message. *Curtis unavailable until next week. Extending my stay.*

"When are you planning to tell Dad about our adventure?"

"I'm guessing he doesn't want to know anything about it." She headed toward the front porch.

Basil fell in step beside her. "I can tell you've devised some sort of strategy in that brilliant-lawyer brain of yours."

"Are Marines always suspicious?"

"More like alert and ready to take action."

They walked inside. Their mom and aunt sat side by side on the front room sofa. David sat on a chair on the other side of the coffee table.

"You're back sooner than expected." Daisy's mom motioned them in. "How'd the meeting go?"

"Important men apparently don't conduct business over the weekend." Daisy sat beside her mom. "I'm staying another week."

"Seven more days, and you might as well stay 'til after Christmas." She nudged Daisy's arm. "You'd save a lot of money on plane tickets."

Pansy grabbed a cookie off the platter sitting on the coffee table. "David's gonna ask us more questions. Wanna join us, Basil?"

"Sorry, Aunt Pansy. I promised Dad I'd help him move some plants. I'll catch up at supper."

Daisy leaned back and willed her shoulders to relax. At least she could work remotely for however long it took to accomplish her objective. Her eyes met David's. His smile sent a clear message. He was pleased she planned to stay longer. One huge benefit of Curtis Butler's refusal to grant her a meeting—she had more time to spend with David and discover why he stirred her emotions in a way Michael never had.

Chapter 25

Quashing the urge to ask more questions about Daisy and Basil's trek to the ranch, Poppy turned her attention back to David. "Any luck discovering what the key unlocks?"

"I'm still working on it." He flipped his notepad open. "For now I want to explore your mother's last days in this house. Try to remember everything that happened the week before she disappeared."

"That was a long time ago."

"Take your time."

Poppy leaned back and closed her eyes as fragments surfaced and swirled in her brain like a funnel cloud with no place to land. Images without date and time stamps. She squeezed her eyes tight and plucked memories from the mental cyclone. "It was spring. We'd planted flowers out front. Begonias. Mama's favorite." Another memory formed. She opened her eyes. "Several days before she disappeared, we went on a trip to Tybee Island."

"I remember." Pansy pressed her palms together. "We climbed all the way to the top of a big lighthouse."

"Afterwards we had a picnic on the beach. Mama packed peanut butter and jelly sandwiches for lunch."

"I dropped mine on the sand." Pansy giggled. "A big ole bird ate it after Mama gave me hers." She reached across her sister and tapped Daisy's arm. "Do you remember the time Danny and Poppy took us to the beach for a whole week?"

"I do. We rented a house right on the ocean."

"And built lots of fancy sandcastles. Maybe Mama's living in a big castle with a handsome prince."

David cleared his throat and shifted his focus from Pansy to Poppy. "What else do you remember about that week and more specifically about your mother's behavior?"

"Nothing stands out. I mean she seemed normal enough. Except—" Poppy pinched her brows as a memory shot out of the funnel. "The day before she disappeared, a big black car drove up and parked beside the house. I remember because Mama always sent me and Pansy to our little house *before* clients came around. That day she sent us to our room where we could peek out the window. She walked over to the driver's door. The windows were too dark to see who was inside."

David pulled his pen from behind his ear. "Sounds like Rose wasn't expecting whoever showed up."

"After the car drove away, Mama told us a stranger had turned onto our driveway by mistake."

"So obviously not a client." David clicked his pen. "Do you remember what time of day she normally entertained men?"

"Mostly right before or right after supper." Pansy reached for a cookie.

David made a note. "What happened the day after the stranger showed up?"

Poppy dug deep into her memory. "Mama fixed us a pitcher of lemonade and filled a picnic basket with sandwiches. Like always she sent us to our little house and told us to stay there until she came to get us. We stayed there 'til way after dark."

Daisy's brows lifted. "Why didn't you return earlier?"

"After catching Mama with a man that one time, I didn't want to see her like that again. Hours after we'd finished our sandwiches and lemonade, thirst forced us to ignore her instructions and go back to the house. Mama wasn't there. We took a flashlight and walked out front. Mama's car was still in the carport. We looked everywhere."

Pansy picked a cookie crumb off her lap. "We thought maybe she'd gone to Willy's to buy us some ice cream. 'Cept she didn't come home."

"We waited until the next morning to call the sheriff. The man who answered claimed Mama was probably visiting a friend and not to worry. After one more day, we called again."

David's jaw clenched. "How long did it take for someone to respond?"

"Two more days and a bunch more phone calls." Poppy squeezed her eyes shut and pulled more memories from the funnel. "Two deputies knocked on our door. They walked through the house and asked if anything was missing besides Mama. When I told them we didn't know, the taller officer told us to look in her room. That's when we noticed Mama's jewelry box wasn't on her dresser. They said she probably took it with her."

"Did they examine her room?"

She nodded. "They said nothing looked suspicious."

David tapped his pen on his notepad. "Which is why the deputies wrote her disappearance off as a runaway."

"Even though all her clothes were still here, we wanted to believe them." Poppy trained her eyes on Pansy's drawing displayed on the wall beside her and Danny's bedroom door. "Running away meant she could change her mind and come back home. After a while I stopped believing."

"How old were you when she disappeared?" asked David.

"I was sixteen. Pansy was twelve."

"Two young girls left to fend for themselves." He pulled his ringing phone off his belt clip and eyed the screen. After silencing the ringtone, he snapped it back in place. "How did you manage to survive?"

Pansy tugged on her ear. "Some nice ladies from church brought us food."

"Then a couple days, maybe a week after Mama left, another lady came over and gave us an envelope full of money."

Daisy stared at her mom. "Did you know her? Did she explain where the money came from?"

"We'd never seen her before. She told us she'd read about Mama in the newspaper and wanted to help out."

"Now we're starting to make some headway." David scooted to the edge of his chair. "What kind of car did she drive?"

"A big one," said Pansy. "Black, I think."

He looked from Pansy to Poppy. "Like the one that showed up the day before Rose disappeared?"

"Maybe. I don't know. Anyway, she came back every week and gave us enough money to buy food."

"Probably someone Rose knew." David propped his pen behind his ear. "You and Pansy take some time and write down the names of all your mother's friends. Tomorrow we'll talk to them, and see if we can spark some memories."

"We'll start right after I make us lunch. You're welcome to join us, David."

"Thanks, but I need to transfer my notes while all your comments are still fresh in my mind." He flipped his notepad closed and walked out.

Hoping for a moment alone with her daughter, Poppy turned toward Pansy. "Go ask Danny if he wants lunch in the kitchen or the greenhouse, sweetie."

"Okay."

The moment her sister scooted out the front door, she escorted Daisy to the kitchen. "I'm dying to find out what happened at the ranch."

"Not much." While they prepared sandwiches, Daisy relayed details and answered questions.

"Any idea when Curtis's assistant will call you?"

"You mean if, and your guess is as good as mine."

"What if she doesn't call?"

"I'll pester her until he gives in or has me arrested for harassment."

Pansy breezed in with Boots padding behind her. "Danny wants you to bring his lunch out to the greenhouse."

Basil followed. "I'll keep my aunt and sister company while you eat with Dad."

"Your idea or Danny's?"

"Call it a goodwill gesture."

"Might as well. Things couldn't turn much worse," she mumbled under her breath. After preparing two plates and placing them on a tray, Poppy ambled toward the greenhouse. She hadn't seen Danny since she'd slipped into the front room before dawn and found him lying on the sofa with his feet dangling over the arm. Unsure if he was awake or asleep. she'd tiptoed past while wondering if he would ever forgive her.

When she arrived at the greenhouse, she balanced the tray on her hip and pushed the door open. She found Danny sitting at his desk, writing a check. "Basil suggested I bring lunch for both of us. Hope you don't mind."

He continued writing.

Poppy set the plates and glasses of lemonade on the desk, then leaned the tray against the file cabinet. She pulled up a metal chair.

"Last of the turkey?"

"Almost."

He bit into the sandwich.

"Did you get any sleep last night?"

"Enough." He swallowed. "You?"

"About the same."

"Good sandwich." He sipped his lemonade and caught her eye. "I'm glad you joined me."

In that moment Poppy glimpsed the depth of her husband's love. The man who'd married her to spite his father. The man who'd become her soulmate had in his own way forgiven her. Maybe one day he'd find it in his heart to forgive his father.

Chapter 26

Daisy moved Sunday-lunch leftovers to the fridge and returned to her seat beside David.

Her mom pushed a sheet of paper across the table. "These are all the names we came up with."

David stared at the list. "Four?"

"Mama didn't have a lot of friends."

"'Cept for her clients." Pansy placed a water bowl on the floor for Boots. "And we don't know their names."

"Four is better than zero." David folded the paper and dropped it in his satchel. "If we're lucky, they'll lead us to others. Who do you suggest we contact first?"

"The two women who always treated Mama with respect. They're expecting us, so we'd best get going."

Pansy donned her sparkly New York ball cap and skipped out the back door.

Poppy tucked her purse under her arm and led Daisy and David to the family truck. "Pansy, you sit up front with me. Daisy, you and David can ride in the back seat."

David held the door open for Daisy and leaned close. "Is your mom always this obvious?"

"You noticed?"

"I wouldn't be a first-rate investigative journalist if I'd missed her cue."

She breathed in the fresh scent of soap and shampoo. "Are you bragging?"

"Just stating the facts."

His smile reduced her brain to mush. She stuffed her phone in her jeans pocket and slid across the seat.

He scooted beside her, set his satchel on the floor, and buckled his seatbelt.

During the ride, Daisy tuned out Pansy's patter and stole glances of David. What if she made some kind of subtle move? Would he notice? And if he did, would he consider her too brazen? To heck with caution. She laid her hand flat on the seat between them while gazing out the side window. Her breath caught as his finger brushed hers. Was it happenstance or intentional?

"You two are kind of quiet back there." Her mom's voice seemed distant.

David moved his hand away. "I'm enjoying the view."

Daisy smiled. Intentional.

While Pansy resumed her monologue, Daisy's mind drifted to the evening she and Michael had dined on his terrace. When he slid his arm around her waist, why hadn't his touch stirred her emotions? Perhaps angst over the Curtis fiasco?

When the truck stopped in front of the thrift shop, David nudged Daisy. "Time to put our skills to the test."

She tilted her head. "Ours?"

"I'm counting on your feminine intuition to interpret body language and pick up on unspoken subtleties." He shouldered his satchel and climbed out.

As Daisy scooted across the seat, the desire to please the man she had no idea even existed seven days ago accelerated. Was she reacting to his handsome face and alluring charm? Or something more profound?

David opened the passenger door and held his hand out to Pansy. "Have I told you how pretty you are in your sparkly hat?"

She touched the brim. "Do I look smart?"

"Smart as anyone I know."

Pansy's face beamed.

Daisy pressed her hand to her chest. Who wouldn't love this man? Stunned by the musing, she dropped her hand to her side and stepped onto the sidewalk.

Her mom appeared from behind the truck and eyed David then Daisy. "Are you two ready?"

For what? David to pull her into his arms and kiss her right there on the sidewalk in front of the thrift store?

"I'm ready." David cleared his throat. "How about you, Daisy?"

She blinked. "More than ready." Heat inched up her neck to her ears at the double-entendre. Had he noticed? "Lead the way, Mom."

They headed to the left side of the building and climbed up a steep staircase.

Maddie met them on the landing and invited them in. Cinnamon and apple scents wafted in the air. "Mom's so excited to have visitors she baked a pie."

Daisy took her turn to hug Maddie, then her mother. "You look as young as ever, Miss Betty."

The elderly woman with silver hair squared her shoulders. "You're as pretty as you were before you left for college, and I hear successful to boot." She released Daisy and turned toward David. "And who is this handsome young man?"

He extended his hand. "I'm David, ma'am."

Betty sandwiched his hand. "You can call me Betty. Are you Daisy's friend?"

"Actually, I'm investigating Rose Fowler's case."

"It's about time someone found out what happened to our friend. While you're here, you should also investigate the woman who lives in that fancy house across the street. Chances are you'll dig up a bucketful of dirt on old Agnes."

"One mystery at a time."

Betty released David's hand and faced Poppy. "I suspect you want to talk about your mother. Do you want to begin before or after we have pie?"

"Is before okay?"

"If we start this conversation straightaway." Betty motioned her guests toward the living room anchoring one end of the long space.

The three Butler women sat on the gold velvet sofa while Betty and Maddie opted for straight-backed chairs. David settled on an overstuffed easy chair catercorner to the sofa and set his satchel on the floor. "Why don't we begin with you sharing what you know about Rose Fowler's background, Miss Betty?"

"Excellent idea." Betty crossed her legs at her ankles and smoothed her floral skirt. "To begin, Rose was a pretty little girl—so lively and curious. She was the oldest of four."

Daisy stared at her mom's wide-eyed expression and slack jaw. "Did you know she had siblings?"

"Mama never said beans about her family, except that her parents died in an accident. Pansy and I found a couple of pictures of kids we assumed were her friends. They must have been her siblings."

"So much sadness in that little family." Betty seemed to stare into space. "Rose's baby brother died of what folks called crib death. Her mama was never the same after he passed. Rumor was Rose quit school to help out at home and take care of her younger sisters. I expect Rose didn't talk about them because the memory was too painful. Especially after that horrible wreck. Their car was run off the road by a drunk driver. Fifteen-year-old Rose was the only survivor. Not long after the accident some boy got her pregnant. Rumors floated around about Agnes's oldest son being the culprit."

A gasp escaped from Daisy's mom.

"Oh dear." Betty held up her left hand. "Don't worry, honey. It turned out that boy had gotten himself into some kind of trouble and was serving a sentence in juvenile detention. No one ever found out who got Rose in trouble, which made life extra tough for the poor, uneducated girl with no husband. Fortunately, she had a roof over her head. Although she darn near worked her fingers to the bone to pay the mortgage. Her life became a whole lot harder after Poppy was born. It's sinful how some people say such mean things about innocent babies."

Daisy's heart ached at the sight of her mom's hand pressing her birthmark. She slid her arm around her shoulders while noting David's expression of compassion.

"My late husband and I helped out the best we could, given we'd recently opened the thrift store and had our own baby to take care of." Betty nodded toward Maddie. "That's how far back Rose and my daughter's friendship goes."

A flicker of a frown creased Maddie's forehead. "After the accident, Rose took in laundry and sold vegetables on the sidewalk in front of the store. One day she simply stopped showing up. Weeks went by. Then out of the blue, she came to the store and bought a bagful of clothes and jewelry. She said her customers expected her to look pretty. Agnes got wind of Rose's comment and started the rumor about her being a lady of the evening."

Pansy ran her fingers along her ball cap's rim. "Is an evening lady the same as a prostitute?"

Maddie's cheeks pinkened.

"Not exactly." David smiled. "A lady of the evening is elegant and sophisticated."

"Like Mama?"

"Exactly like your mother."

Daisy caught David's eye and mouthed, *thank you.*

He winked, then faced Maddie. "What happened with your friendship after the rumor spread?"

"Even though we seldom saw each other, I didn't want to believe the gossip."

"You were a good friend." David scribed a note. "What did Rose say about her newfound income or how it came about?"

"Not much. Except one time she told me she'd discovered how far rich men would travel and how much they'd pay for secret companionship." Maddie released a sigh. "That's when I had to accept the fact that the rumors were true."

Betty folded her hands in her lap. "Rose coped with hardship the best way she knew how. Lots of people around here took a notion to shun her. My daddy taught me it's not our place to judge anyone or turn away from the people God places in our lives. So we always treated Rose and her family with respect."

David nodded. "Your father was a wise man. I'd like to shift gears for a moment. Yesterday we found a key hidden in Rose's jewelry box. Did she ever mention a safe-deposit box to either one of you?"

"Hmm." Betty tapped her finger on her cheek. "As far as I remember, she never said a word about it to me."

"Me neither." Maddie's brows drew together. "Why would Rose need a safe-deposit box?"

"That's what we're trying to figure out." David propped his pen behind his ear. "One last question. What do you know about a woman who drove a black car and gave Poppy and Pansy money after Rose left?"

"Nothing. Although one fact's certain. If that woman was from around here, Agnes would have known about her."

"Makes sense." David closed his notepad. "Thanks for taking the time to talk to us."

"I hope Maddie and I helped a little, and that everything turns out for the best."

"You helped way more than a little. In fact you filled in some big blanks." David dropped his notepad in his satchel.

"He's right." Daisy's focus shifted to their hosts. "Plus, you deserve special places in heaven for the way you accepted my grandmother."

"We just treated Rose as everybody around here should have. After we have dessert, you should go talk to Willy. His body's frail, but his mind's sharp and his family is one of the few who also treated Rose with respect."

"He's next on our list."

After serving her guests mouthwatering apple pie and a slice of local gossip, Betty escorted her guests to the door. She hugged Poppy, then Daisy. "It gets mighty lonely around here. Promise me you won't wait so long to come back for a visit."

"We promise." Daisy held her mom's hand as they bid their goodbyes and descended the stairs. At the bottom she leaned close. "Do you want to call it a day?"

"Not a chance. We've ripped the lid off a big box of snakes. We need to find out what else slithers out."

Chapter 27

Poppy moved away from the stairs, squared her shoulders, and marched to the sidewalk. Daisy fell in step beside her.

Pansy and David caught up with them. "Do you need to take a break?"

"My mother was an unwed prostitute. Trust me, I can handle whatever anyone throws at us." Poppy slowed her pace. "Sorry, David. I had no right to snap at you."

"After what you've learned, all I have to say is you're as strong as you are kind."

She stopped and faced him, keeping her hands at her sides. "Your mama raised a fine son. Now, before we meet Willy, what do you need to know about him?"

"Anything you can tell me."

Pansy pointed across the street. "That's his gas station and store. He doesn't work there anymore."

"His son took over after he retired." Poppy resumed walking. "He and his wife raised four boys before she passed on. All but one moved away." They turned right at the corner and approached three abandoned stores—two shuttered with plywood, all in need of serious repairs. "There's not much around here to keep young people from hightailing it out of town. If you can even call this a town."

Halfway up the block, Daisy nodded across the street at a two-story frame house. "Looks like our next contact is waiting for us."

"Howdy, folks," Willy called out from the covered porch that stretched across the front of his home. "Been expecting you."

They crossed the street and strolled up his sidewalk.

"How's it going, Willy?"

"Can't complain. Wouldn't do any good if I did."

"You're a smart man." After climbing onto the porch, Poppy and Pansy opted for two mismatched chairs across from Willy's rocker, leaving the wooden swing for Daisy and David.

A tabby cat purred and curled around Pansy's leg. "Hey, kitty." She lifted the feline onto her lap.

David removed his notepad from his satchel and flipped it open. "Thank you for agreeing to talk to us."

"Even though you're here on official business, I appreciate the company." He massaged his white goatee and set his rocker in motion. "After Poppy called, I got to thinking what an investigative writer might want to hear about Rose. I suspect one thing is how she ended up in her profession."

Poppy's eyes widened. "You know?"

"I always suspected it began the day that brand-spanking new white Cadillac drove into the station for a fill-up. Back then we were still pumping gas for customers. I wanted to take a good look at that beauty, so I left my helper at the register and walked outside. The guy rolled down the window and stretched his forearm across the doorframe. I remember because he was wearing the biggest diamond I'd ever seen. On his pinky finger, mind you."

Pansy stroked the cat's back. "Mama liked pretty rings."

David poised his pen over his notepad. "Did you recognize the man?"

"Never seen him before. As soon as I popped off his gas cap, he climbed out and pointed across the street. He asked if I knew the pretty girl selling produce. When I told him yes, he fired off a bunch of questions. Most were none of his business, so I blew him off. That didn't stop him from driving over after I filled his tank."

Willy pointed his gnarly finger toward the street. "He parked right in front of the thrift store. About that time a couple more customers drove up to the pump, but I kept an eye on the Caddy. That man climbed out and talked to Rose. After a few minutes, he handed something to her and loaded everything she had to sell in his trunk. Needless to say, I had to find out what was going on. So, I walked over and found Rose clutching a hundred-dollar bill—payment for a couple buckets of tomatoes and potatoes. A heap of money back then."

Poppy cringed. "Did she know the man?"

"No, but she claimed he planned to meet at her house to buy more produce. I told her it wasn't safe to let a stranger anywhere near her property. Especially since she lived alone and a good distance from any neighbors. She stared at the hundred and said she'd never seen that much money." Willy raked his fingers through his thinning white hair. "That was the last day she came to town to sell vegetables."

David scribed a note. "Did you ever see the man again?"

"Once a week like clockwork, he stopped for a fill-up. Couple of times I went out to talk to him. He claimed he owned businesses in South Georgia and traveled from Atlanta to check on them." Willy's thin shoulders curled forward. "I should've done more to protect Rose. Truth is, I was too busy earning a living and taking care of my own family."

David looked up from his notepad. "Did the man tell you his name?"

"I never asked. Guess deep down I didn't want to know."

Daisy pulled her phone from her jeans pocket and stared at the screen.

David touched her arm. "Do you need to answer?"

"It's not important." She swiped her finger across the screen and stuffed it back in her pocket. "When did you last see that man, Willy?"

"A week after Rose disappeared, he came in the store and asked if I knew why she'd stopped taking phone calls."

Pansy ran her fingers along the cat's spine. "Mama never let us answer her private phone."

David eyed Poppy. "She had her own line?"

"It was disconnected after the deputies toted off her answering machine."

He made another note. "Back to the white Caddy. When that man asked about the phone, what'd you tell him?"

"That Rose had mysteriously disappeared." Willy paused. "Funny how he looked angry and sad at the same time. Anyway, he walked out without saying another word. Never saw hide nor hair of him again. For a while my wife helped collect food from neighbors for Poppy and Pansy. Guess folks suffered from a big dose of guilt over mistreating Rose all those years."

The cat leapt off Pansy's lap and sprang onto Willy's. "Couple of months later, someone told Agnes about a rich man spending time at Rose's house. Don't know how that woman got away with sticking her nose in everyone's business. She spread a nasty rumor about Rose's daughters following in their mama's footsteps."

Poppy pressed her hand to her throat. "Did people believe her?"

"Not after my sweet wife learned that Danny was the visitor. Agnes wasn't the only woman who could find out what was what. Soon afterwards you and Danny tied the knot."

Pansy nudged her sister's arm. "What knot's he talking 'bout?"

"Not a real knot, sweetie. It's another way of saying Danny and I got married."

"Oh." Pansy adjusted her ball cap. "Maybe someday me and a handsome man will tie a knot."

Poppy patted her sister's arm. "You know God has something special in mind for you."

The cat sprang back onto Pansy's lap.

"Whiskers was my wife's favorite cat." Willy plucked a cat hair off his pants. "Seems she's taking a real liking to you, Pansy."

"Animals are drawn to people with pure hearts." David held up his phone. "Mind if I take a picture of you and Whiskers?"

Poppy pushed her chair back against the railing. "Just Pansy." After David snapped the photo, she scooted back and faced Willy. "Do you remember if other strangers asked about Mama?"

Willy pinched his chin between his thumb and forefinger. "Can't say I do."

David flipped his notepad closed. "Now we know at least one of her clients was an out-of-towner."

"Every one of them. Believe me, if any of the locals visited her, old Agnes would've gotten wind of it and let the whole town know."

Poppy stared at Willy. "You're right about Agnes. Before her health went south, she didn't let one bit of news pass her by. Thank you for talking to us."

"Anything to help you folks figure out what happened to Rose." He gripped the rocker's arms and pushed onto his skinny legs. "She was a strong lady who found a way to survive despite all the terrible things that happened to her family."

"Indeed she was." David slid his notepad into his satchel.

"I hope you find out what happened to her, and y'all come back any time."

Poppy stood. "We'll do that."

"Next time we'll bring you some cookies," added Pansy.

After they made their way back to the sidewalk, Daisy pulled her phone from her pocket. "Y'all go ahead. I'll catch up in a sec."

Poppy eyed her daughter. "We'll wait for you at the at the truck, honey."

Daisy's jaw tensed as she tapped voicemail and pressed the phone to her ear.

"I just read your text. We need to talk. Call me ASAP."

She grimaced at Michael's curt tone. Couldn't he bother to say hello or at least how are you? And what was so urgent on the weekend? Maybe she should return his call. Daisy's eyes drifted to David strolling toward the corner between her mom and aunt with his satchel slung over his shoulder. Much more humble than Michael's monogrammed briefcase.

Daisy released a long sigh. A full day had passed before Michael read her text. If he had good news, it could wait. On the other hand, she wasn't in the mood to deal with any kind of controversy or unreasonable demands. Whatever he had to say could wait until tomorrow. She pocketed her phone, crossed the street, and caught up with the investigative team.

David nudged her arm. "Everything okay?"

"Attorney business."

"Demands of a high-powered career?"

"Yeah." She scooted across the seat and buckled her belt.

David slid in beside her and removed the list of contacts from his satchel. "Last name on the list, Aletha Davis."

"The tutor Mama hired." Daisy's mom buckled her seatbelt. "After a heart attack took her husband, Ginny, her widowed daughter moved in with her. Neither one knows we're coming."

"Sometimes surprise visits are the most productive." David stuffed the list in his pocket and set his satchel on the floor. "How would you describe Aletha's relationship your mother?"

She pulled away from the curb. "Most days after she finished our lessons, Aletha stayed for lunch. Mama liked talking with her."

Pansy peered over her shoulder. "Miss Aletha said my drawings were real pretty. Sometimes she brought us sugar cookies with icing and sprinkles."

David grinned. "Is that your favorite kind of cookie?"

"I like chocolate chip best. Daisy likes them too."

"Does she now." He faced Daisy. "Do you prefer soft and chewy or crunchy?"

The twinkle in his eyes hinted of playfulness. "Definitely soft and chewy."

"One more thing we have in common."

Was he keeping a list? Did it match hers? Did she dare she ask?

"I baked cookies for Daisy before she came home." Pansy's voice drifted from the front. "Want me to bake you some, David?"

"Absolutely. A big batch."

"Mama taught me and Poppy how to bake." Her stories about baking continued until they turned onto a gravel driveway and stopped beside a white cottage adorned with royal blue shutters.

A woman wearing pink overalls, gloves, and a straw hat sat back on her heels at the edge of a flower garden and waved.

"That's Ginny." Daisy's mom unbuckled her belt and climbed out. Pansy followed.

David pulled his notepad and pen from his satchel, then opened the door.

As the foursome closed the distance to the middle-aged woman, Ginny plunged her trowel into the clay and lifted off her knees. "What a pleasant surprise. My goodness, is that you, Daisy?"

"In the flesh."

"I haven't seen you since you were a little girl. Where did all those years go?" She held her hand out to David. "I'm Ginny."

"Pleasure to meet you." She looked from David to Daisy.

"Are you two a couple?"

"Daisy is David's special friend." Pansy stooped to pluck a petal off the grass. "He's an investigator. He's gonna find out what happened to Mama."

"Good for him." Ginny pushed her hat up, releasing wisps of gray hair. "I suppose you drove all the way out here to talk to Mother."

Daisy's mom nodded. "I called earlier, but no one answered."

"I've been working out here since sunup. Come with me and we'll sit a spell." She led them down a gravel path surrounded by rose bushes to a pair of wrought-iron benches. "Mother loved tending flowers. After Daddy passed, her gardens became her refuge. This was her favorite place to pray."

Daisy squeezed onto a bench between her mom and aunt. Why had she referred to her mother in the past tense? "Is Aletha here?"

"Sadly, no." Ginny sat across from them, beside David. "Some folks accused me of being cruel when I moved her into a nursing home." Her voice faltered. "That's because they weren't here to see her mind slip away a little each day."

"I'm so sorry." Daisy's mom pressed her hand to her chest. "Miss Aletha meant a lot to us."

"Every once in a while, something I say sparks a memory. I treasure those moments when she talks about the past." Ginny paused. "Enough sad talk. What do you folks want to know?"

David poised his pen over his notepad. "Anything you can tell us about your mother's relationship with Rose."

Ginny removed her gloves and stuffed them in her overalls pocket. "I was a high-school senior when Rose pulled you and Pansy out of school and hired her as your tutor."

"Did Aletha know about Mama?"

"You mean the rumors about her entertaining men? She'd heard, but it didn't matter. Mother always looked for the best in people. One day after her lessons with you girls, Rose asked her to teach her how to read. It took her six months for Rose to learn how to read simple words. Mother and

I both hoped the new skill would give her enough confidence to find a legitimate way to earn a living. Sadly, she disappeared before she had the chance to finish the lessons."

"Aletha always treated Mama, Pansy, and me with respect."

"You were like family to her." Ginny paused. "After all this time, and given Mother's condition, she'd want me to tell you a secret. When she learned about Rose disappearing, she was heartbroken and wanted to find a way to help out. So, she arranged to pay all your utility bills to keep the lights on. That arrangement continued until you married Danny."

Daisy's mom gasped. "When the bills stopped coming in the mail, I assumed the power and water companies had taken pity on us."

"They would have turned off your electricity and water in a heartbeat if Mother hadn't stepped up. Other than that, there's not much I can tell you."

David penned another note, then looked up. "I'm curious. Did Aletha ever mention Rose renting a safe-deposit box?"

Pansy pulled off her ball cap and scratched her head. "We found a funny-looking key in her jewelry box. We wanna find out what it opens."

"Wish I could help, but I don't remember her saying a word about a key or a safe-deposit box. One thing I can tell you, Mother never believed the rumors about Rose abandoning you and running off with some man."

Pansy picked at her thumbnail. "Do you believe something bad happened to Mama?"

"Oh, sweetie, I meant your mother loved you and Poppy with all her heart."

Daisy stroked Pansy's arm. "What's most important is we find out what happened to her. Right?"

"Mama's in a happy place that has lots of chocolate kisses."

"And dozens of chocolate chip cookies," added David.

Pansy's eyes lit up as she popped off the bench and grabbed David's hand. "I'll bake you some soon as we get home."

He chuckled. "Looks like this interview is over. I'll be around for a while longer, Ginny. If anything comes to mind about the days before Rose disappeared, no matter how minor, please call one of us."

Daisy lifted off the bench. What did David mean by a while? A week? Until Christmas or New Years? On their way back to the truck and during the drive, her attention volleyed between Pansy's pattering, David's glances, and a multitude of questions about Rose. By the time her mom parked in their driveway and David helped her step from the truck, the desire to spend time alone with him consumed her. "Do you mind if we walk for a while?"

"As soon as I drop this off." He pressed his hand to her back and led her to his camper.

She stood at the door and peeked inside. "Compact living space."

"Everything I need except a washer and dryer." He tossed his satchel on a dinette table before stepping out.

A tingle cascaded through Daisy the moment his arm brushed her shoulder. "You're welcome to use ours."

"Thanks. I'll take you up on that offer."

"How long are you planning to stay?"

"As long as it takes."

Dare she ask if he meant more than discovering Rose's fate? What if she had misinterpreted his comment? Best to put on her attorney hat and ask pointed questions. They strolled to the left side of the greenhouse. "What's your takeaway from today's interviews?"

"Sadly Rose Fowler became the victim of circumstances beyond her control."

Desperately needing solitude, Poppy scurried to her private retreat and closed the door. She opened a window, fluttering the curtains and sending a chameleon skittering across the sill—a reptile Pansy called a baby gator and Boots considered fair game. She peered at the bright blue sky peeking through the profusion of autumn leaves. Dozens of seasons had passed during the years she and Pansy had hidden between these walls.

Poppy dropped onto the bench and rocked back and forth. Had her mama kept details about her past hidden because they were too painful?

Or had shame driven her to secrecy? What about the boy who made her pregnant? Her biological father. Did Rose love him, or did he force himself on her? What about all the men she'd entertained? Did she care for any of them, or were they nothing more than meal tickets? Maybe she'd find the answer in the letters she'd kept hidden for years.

She hesitated, then knelt on the floor, opened the trunk, and removed a shoebox filled with envelopes she'd found in her mama's closet a month after she disappeared. Weeks had passed before she'd summoned the courage to open them. Maybe the time had come to read the letters a second time. She carried the box to the bench and retrieved the first envelope. When she finished reading the last letter, she stuffed it back in its envelope. Confusion muddled her mind much as it had the first time she dared read them. Maybe David could make sense of the words and discover a clue about her mother's disappearance.

Poppy closed the trunk and carried the box to the house. Back in the kitchen, her thoughts weighed heavy. If Mama had wanted the letters to remain private, would sharing them dishonor her wishes? Footsteps struck the back-porch floor. She stashed the box in a bottom cabinet. The decision about whether or not to show them to David would have to wait another day.

Chapter 28

The first light of dawn cast a dim glow in Daisy's room as she awoke with images of David dancing in her head. Yesterday afternoon they had strolled among the potted trees behind the greenhouse and beyond to the woods enclosing her family's land. After dinner they sat on the front porch and shared impressions they had formed during the interviews.

She eased out of bed and strode to the window. Light shone from David's camper. How long had he been awake? Was he thinking about her or beginning this glorious Monday morning reviewing his notes?

Oh my gosh. Monday. She yanked her jeans off Lilly's bed, pulled her phone from the pocket, and pressed the on button. Sweat invaded her upper lip as the screen lit and revealed three missed calls from Michael. Two from yesterday. She pressed voicemail and listened to the latest message, recorded twenty minutes earlier.

"Is something wrong? Please call."

Daisy swiped her fingers across her upper lip, then pressed Michael's number.

He answered at the first ring. "Tell me you're okay."

"I'm fine, and I'm sorry I missed your calls." How could she explain without raising red flags? "Cell service is sometimes spotty in rural Georgia."

"I thought you lived close to Savannah."

Tread carefully. "Not that close. You seem stressed. Are *you* okay?"

"In two hours the partners expect an update on the Butler empire, and I need something substantive to report."

"I don't know what to tell you, Michael. Except that Curtis simply hasn't been available."

"He's your grandfather. Why don't you call his personal number?"

A dull ache attacked the back of Daisy's neck and spread to her skull. She couldn't admit the truth and she for doggone sure couldn't afford to end up tangled in a lie. Her only option? Use her brain and go on the offensive. "Believe me, I understand your predicament. But you entrusted me with this endeavor. So, unless you plan to send another attorney down here—one who doesn't know beans about the Butler family—I suggest you trust me to handle this as a professional attorney representing a top-rated, successful law firm and not a relative begging for her granddaddy's business."

Pin-dropping silence.

She held her breath. Was he buying it? Had she gone too far and challenged his authority?

"How much time do you need?"

She released the air. "Give me 'til the end of the week."

"Fair enough. On a personal note, a week from Saturday I'm planning a small dinner party at my apartment with you as my co-host."

Another command performance dictated to an underling or something more personal? "To entertain business associates or clients?"

"A few close friends."

Definitely personal. "I doubt a sophisticated law-firm partner needs a junior associate co-host to pull off the perfect dinner party."

"Need, no. Want? Yes. By the way, Mother insists you attend her New Year's Eve party."

Daisy moseyed to the window and eyed David's profile through the camper window. "I promised my family I'd spend New Year's here in Georgia."

"They enjoyed your company for Thanksgiving and will again for Christmas. They'll understand my family wanting you to spend one of the holidays with us. In the meantime, keep me updated on your progress with Curtis. We'll talk soon."

Daisy tossed her phone on her bed and pressed her fingertips to the base of her skull as the full force of her dilemma struck her like a fifty-pound sledgehammer. In addition to her commitment to deliver a result over which she had little control, she was caught in a relationship triangle—with David in one corner and Michael in the other. One touched her heart. The other offered wealth and status beyond anything she'd ever imagined while holding sway over her career.

Desperate to talk to her confidante, she slipped her robe on and trudged to the kitchen. "Am I the last one up?"

"Pansy's sleeping in, and Basil's working with your dad." Her mom finished wiping the counter. "Are you hungry?"

"Not yet." Daisy meandered to the coffee maker and poured a cup. "I talked to Michael a few minutes ago."

"Business or personal?"

"A little of both." She carried her cup to the table and dropped onto her chair. "The day I flew down from New York, my life and future were on course, headed in one direction."

"Then you met David and faced an unexpected detour." Her mom tossed her dish towel on the counter and sat beside Daisy. "Don't look so surprised. I see the way you two look at each other."

"It isn't logical to feel a strong connection to a man I didn't know existed eight days ago."

"Logic guides the brain, honey, not the heart."

"Michael is smart and ambitious. He lives in a penthouse with a million-dollar view. His grandfather's yacht has a helicopter pad on the bow."

Her mom laced her fingers and steepled her thumbs. "All those years, I carried on about Danny's family because I wanted you to experience everything I couldn't. Independence. A prestigious career. Adventures and accomplishments I considered important."

"As far back as I can remember, you encouraged me to find my own path."

"The important question now—does that path make you happy?"

"I'm good at what I do. If...I mean *when* I land Curtis's account, I'll earn a huge bonus and take a giant leap toward becoming a partner. Everything I've spent years working to achieve."

"You didn't answer my question."

"I believed I was happy."

"Lots of times when I was cleaning up the kitchen or working in the greenhouse, I imagined what sort of life I might have known if Danny had inherited some of his family's money." Her mom unlaced her fingers. "Then I'd watch your dad tending his plants, or Pansy tossing a ball to Boots, or my three beautiful children playing in the front yard. All the special moments we shared. Over the years I've come to understand that making a difference in the lives of those we love and the people who need us is the true measure of happiness."

Daisy traced her finger over a long scratch on the table as memories from her childhood drifted up like bubbles in a glass of Champagne. The hours spent in the kitchen with Lilly and Basil. Playing. Studying. Teasing each other. Michael's phone call surfaced and popped the bubbles. "He's counting on me to deliver Curtis."

"Do you realize that most of what you've said about him has been work-related?"

Daisy mentally replayed the comments she could remember. Her mom was right. She closed her eyes and imagined David with his satchel slung over his shoulder facing Michael clutching his monogrammed briefcase. Each held a scroll inscribed with their characteristics and achievements. She opened her eyes and caught her mom staring at her. "I never expected to come home and meet a man who threw a detour on my path."

"It seems you have a decision to make."

Pansy wandered in with Boots padding behind her. "Decision 'bout what?"

"Daisy and I need to decide whether to scramble up some eggs or indulge in your delicious chocolate chip cookies for breakfast."

Pansy's face beamed. "I vote for milk and cookies."

"Thank you for making the decision for us."

A knock rattled the back door.

Daisy popped up. No way she'd greet David in her pjs without a stitch of makeup. "Plate the cookies, Aunt Pansy, and I'll be back in a jiff." She scooted from the kitchen the moment her mom clutched the door handle.

Poppy opened the back door.

David stepped inside with his pen and notepad in hand.

"You're up early."

"I have a lot on my mind."

Pansy plucked the lid off a cookie jar. "When Daisy comes back, we're gonna drink milk and eat cookies. Do you wanna join us?"

"That's what I call breakfast for champions, so count me in." He meandered to the chair beside Daisy's.

"How about some coffee before you feast on Pansy's sugar-laced breakfast?"

"I'd love some." David laid his notepad and pen on the table. "After we binge on sugar, I want to talk about details from yesterday's interviews."

Poppy filled a cup and handed it to him. "Any new theories?"

"Mostly more questions."

Pansy set glasses of milk, plates, and a platter of cookies on the table, then lowered onto her chair. "I said a blessing in my head so it's okay to eat."

"Well then, I'd say you have us covered." David placed a cookie on his plate.

Daisy strolled in. "I see Aunt Pansy has influenced your breakfast choice."

"Who could resist the best cookies in Georgia?" David stood and pulled her chair out for her.

Poppy couldn't help but notice David's attentiveness. Even though she had never met Michael, she'd begun to lean toward casting her vote for the man sitting across from her.

David bit a chunk out of his cookie. "I'm changing my opinion. This is the best chocolate chip cookie in the whole country."

Poppy peered at her sister's beaming face. Would Michael treat Pansy or her with the same measure of respect as David? It didn't matter, the decision was Daisy's not hers.

After polishing off the rest of his cookie, David tapped his notepad. "I spent the last hour reviewing my notes. My first question, did either of you ever see a white Cadillac or any other car parked in your mom's driveway? Maybe while you were heading out back to your little house?"

Pansy swallowed a bite. "Mama's car was always in the driveway. It was real fancy."

"A white Mustang. After she left I drove it until the engine gave out." Poppy pinched the bridge of her nose. "About her client's cars. The only one I remember is from the day Pansy got sick, and I found Mama with that man. A red car. Sporty. Maybe a two seater, like a Corvette. I'd seen a picture of one in a magazine."

Daisy wiped her fingers with a napkin. "A good indication Rose's clients had money and likely were pillars in their communities."

David clicked his pen. "Men with a lot to lose need to keep prying eyes from discovering their indiscretions."

Poppy leaned forward. "Based on what we learned yesterday, do you believe one of Mama's clients had a hand in her disappearance?"

"That theory isn't out of the question. It would help if we knew how the men she entertained perceived Rose and how they treated her."

Poppy glanced over her shoulder at the bottom cabinet. David needed to read those letters. "I can help." She scooted her chair away from the table and pulled out the shoebox. "Years ago I found this behind a suitcase in Mama's closet." She removed the lid and dumped the contents onto the table. "They're letters from men she knew."

Daisy's brow lifted. "Fan mail?"

"Sort of."

"Perfect." David examined the envelopes and placed them in five separate stacks. "The closest postmark is Atlanta. None have return addresses, which isn't a surprise." He caught Poppy's eye. "I assume you've read them."

"Twice. It's okay if you read them out loud, except those from Memphis."

"All right." David pushed the Memphis envelopes aside, then lifted one from the top of the first stack. He removed a single sheet of paper. "Here goes."

"Dearest Rose,

Your beauty is only surpassed by your skill as a lover. The hours I spend with you are beyond pleasurable. They are filled with intense moments of deep satisfaction that sustain me until we are together again.

Use the extra hundred I left on your dresser to buy yourself lingerie for my eyes only.

Until next time,

Max."

David placed the letter back in the envelope and read the remaining three in the stack. When finished, he nudged Daisy's arm. "What's your impression of Max?"

"He's well educated. Seems he left Rose a lot of extra money which means he's well off, and he adored her. I can't imagine he'd do anything to harm her."

"Neither can I." David removed a single page from the second stack.

"Hey Baby,

Wow, what a night. Thanks for the additional hour. Time with you is worth all the extra money. I bought another present for you. Can't wait to see your expression when you unwrap it.

Stay cool or should I say hot,

Stan the Man."

David handed the letter to Daisy. "What about this guy?"

"He's less sophisticated than Max, but also seems to have money to spare."

"What's your opinion, Poppy?"

"He was crazy about Mama."

Pansy downed her last sip of milk. "Maybe Stan the Man gave Mama one of her pretty necklaces."

"Based on his comment, I'm guessing he gave her lots of presents." David read the rest of Stan's letters and confirmed his assumption. "On to client number three." The next envelope enclosed a birthday card with a folded note inside.

"To My Beautiful Rose,
From the day I first came to your door, I haven't stopped thinking of you.
Your beautiful face. The way you make me feel. I understand I'm not the
only man you spend time with. However, I'm honored you've chosen me as
your favorite. Even though we can only be together in private, I love you more
than I've ever loved any woman. If I wasn't encumbered with obligations,
I'd take you away to a tropical island where we could love each other without
hiding. Since that is only a pipe dream, I must remain satisfied to continue
our relationship as it is.
Yours forever,
KT"

David stared at the letter for a long moment. "These men seem more like lovers than johns."

Pansy giggled. "'Cause their names are Max, Stan the Man, and KT."

"You are one smart investigator, Pansy." David set the letter down. "How about we read one from the fourth stack and find out if his name is John."

"Okay."

David plucked an envelope off stack number four and removed a lined sheet of paper.

"Rose,
On the third you'll receive a call from a man we'll call Grant. He's stuck
in a miserable marriage and needs reassurance about his manhood.
Cad."

David read three more letters from Cad. Each introducing a new client. "Rose obviously worked from referrals."

Daisy's brow pinched. "Maybe Cad was the man driving the white Cadillac."

"Makes sense." David tapped the stack he had pushed aside and eyed Poppy. "Is there a reason you don't want these read out loud?"

She touched Pansy's arm. "Know what, sweetie? Danny and Basil are missing out on our breakfast of champions. How about taking the plate of cookies out to the greenhouse."

"That'll make 'em happy." Pansy scooped the platter off the table and dashed out.

"I didn't want my sister hearing what's in that last stack." After Daisy and David silently read the four letters, Poppy crossed her arms on the table. "Now you know why."

David nodded. "These are more what I'd expect from a john. Lurid and full of inuendoes."

"We know at least one of my grandmother's clients wasn't a gentleman." Daisy sighed. "Although based on his comment about a new Porsche, he also had plenty of money."

David's eyes shifted from Daisy to Poppy. "It's possible these letters are why Rose wanted to learn how to read."

"That's not the reason." Poppy uncrossed her arms. "When I found that shoebox, all the letters were sealed. Mama never opened a single one of them."

David flipped a page in his notepad. "How old was your mother when she disappeared?"

"Thirty-two."

"Based on Ginny's comment, Rose survived as an illiterate for thirty-plus years. Something happened to kindle her desire to read. Can you recall any details, no matter how small, that might give us a clue?"

Poppy closed her eyes and pressed her fingers to her temples. A lot of years had come and gone. Memories faded. Details lost. "Maybe we aren't meant to find out what happened to Mama." Her voice faltered.

Daisy rushed to her mom and wrapped her arms around her. "We need to take a break for a couple days. Is it okay if David takes the letters with him?"

Poppy nodded and sniffled.

"Tell you what." David closed his notepad. "I'll give you gals the afternoon off and fix supper for the family. My way of saying thanks for welcoming me into your home."

Daisy's brows lifted. "Do you know how to cook?"

"I'll let you and your mom be the judge. For now I need to do some serious grocery shopping." He scooped the letters back into the shoebox and carried it out the back door.

"Speaking of shopping." Daisy released her mom. "I'm driving you to the nearest town to buy you a new outfit. Shoes, dress, the works."

"There's no need—"

Daisy pressed her fingers to her mom's lips. "It's non-negotiable."

Poppy pulled her daughter's fingers away. "When did you become so bossy?"

"The day I passed the bar and officially became a lawyer. So, grab your purse and let your firstborn treat you to a well-deserved shopping trip."

Chapter 29

Light from the front room cast a dim glow across the front porch as Daisy sat on the steps holding a glass of wine and gazing at the dark sky.

David strolled out and settled beside her. "Warm night for late November." He set an open wine bottle on the step. "What's your opinion of my menu choice?"

"One fact was more surprising than the delicious meal you prepared."

"Discovering that I can cook?" He topped off his wine. "Or that I know how to select the perfect bottle of Georgia wine to complement sea scallops and angel-hair pasta?"

"Besides the fact that Dad consumed a meal that wasn't simple country cooking, the biggest shock was how you convinced him and my brother to help you clean up the kitchen."

"Doesn't your dad sometimes help your mom?"

"Every once in a while, she lets him."

"Well, there you go. Real men aren't afraid of domestic duties."

The memory of Michael touting his expertise at ordering meals from all the best New York restaurants bubbled up, then morphed to an image of him wearing an apron and standing at a sink full of dirty dishes. Daisy giggled.

"Did my real-men comment tickle your funny bone?"

"I was imagining one of my firm's wealthy defense attorneys trying to figure out what to do in a kitchen."

"That brings up an interesting question." He nudged her arm. "How does a humble investigative journalist stack up against a sophisticated New York lawyer?"

Was he flirting? "Hmm." Daisy swirled the remaining liquid in her wineglass. "Based on your culinary skills, you're definitely the winner."

"Maybe I should quit while I'm ahead."

Daisy tilted her head. "Is your confidence wavering a bit?"

His grin widened. "Not a chance."

He was definitely flirting.

"Are you ready for a refill?"

"A splash." Another difference between the journalist and the big-city lawyer—David poured without touting the wine's label or vintage.

"Your mom looked extra nice in her new outfit."

He noticed. "Dad found her especially appealing."

"How do you know? From what I can tell, displaying emotion isn't one of his strengths."

"The bourbon. He only takes the bottle out of the cabinet for their Saturday-night date. He made an exception tonight." Daisy sipped her wine and fought the desire to touch David's hand.

He sipped his wine. "After growing up surrounded by all this land, how did you adjust to living in New York?"

"My years at the University of Georgia helped with the transition. Although sometimes I miss the quiet, especially nights like tonight. City lights wash out all those magnificent stars."

"Only one vision matches the beauty of a star-studded sky." David paused.

Daisy stole a glance at his profile, willing him to elaborate.

"Is it true that law-firm attorneys work crazy long hours?"

Daisy's shoulders drooped. "Substitute insane for crazy, and you're right on."

"Is it the compensation and prestige or rewarding work that makes that lifestyle appealing?"

Michael's early-morning phone call collided with the Curtis fiasco and hammered Daisy's brain. She had four days to deliver what she'd promised.

"I'm beginning to wonder if anything is worth the demands." The words spilled out before she had a chance to censor them.

"You're fortunate to come home to a loving family."

"I know." Eager to change the subject, she fingered her loop earring. "Any new opinions after reading Rose's letters?"

"Chances are Cad makes his living recruiting desperate young women to service elite clientele."

"At least those men seemed to treat her more like a secret affair than a hired lover." Daisy stared at her wine. "It's possible she told someone, maybe Cad, that she wanted out of the business. The threat of cutting off a pro's lucrative income could lead to repercussions. If he caused her harm, he might have staged his final visit to Willy's as a cover-up. Except no one knew his identity. So, if he was involved in foul play, he'd be foolish to show up and ask questions."

David stared at her. "What type of law did you say you practice?"

"Corporate."

"Maybe you missed your calling. You'd be a dynamite prosecutor or defense attorney."

"I considered criminal law until I realized I didn't want to become emotionally involved in difficult cases. Although my current assignment tops the emotional chart by a mile."

"The businessman who doesn't work on weekends?"

"How'd you know?"

"You mentioned him when you and Basil walked into the front room Saturday. Do you want to talk about it?"

Should she? Maybe his perspective would help. "That businessman is my grandfather."

"The one you've never met?"

"A fact I failed to reveal during my first interview." She highlighted the details. "Now everything's on the line. My career. My reputation. My relationship with Dad." She released a heavy sigh. "It might help if I had more information about Curtis, beyond what's in Mom's scrapbook."

"Do you want me to do a little investigating and see what I can find out?"

"Would you? If I'm not asking too much."

"Compared to solving a thirty-plus-year-old disappearance, piece of cake."

Daisy's eyes drifted to a single cloud hovering close to the moon. "What are the chances you'll solve my grandmother's case?"

"I won't give up until I succeed."

"Inquisitiveness or determination?"

"Takes both."

After finishing the wine and talking for two more hours, Daisy failed to suppress a yawn.

"A good sign it's time to call it a night." David stood and held out his hand.

She accepted and lifted off the step. "Thanks again for offering to dig up information about Curtis."

"Glad to help." His eyes met hers. "Good night, Daisy."

"Pleasant dreams, David."

He released her hand and descended the steps.

Daisy strolled inside and found her mom alone in the front room dressed in a nightgown, her feet propped on the coffee table. "How was your surprise-date night?"

"Sweet." Her voice was low. "Danny mostly enjoyed the quiet. He's asleep. I'll join him after I watch the news."

Daisy yawned again. "I'd stay and watch with you if I wasn't convinced I'd fall asleep."

"Sleep well, honey."

"I will." Daisy blew her mom a kiss then strolled to her room and changed into pajamas. She peeked out the window at David's camper. The shade was drawn. Did he sleep in pajamas? The unexpected mental question sent heat up her neck to her ears. She turned out the light and dropped onto her bed. Her eyelids grew heavy. Within moments she drifted to sleep.

A knock followed by footsteps jolted her awake.

"Please tell me you're awake." Her mom's voice hinted of angst.

Daisy bolted upright. "What's wrong?"

"Never in a million years did I believe it would happen. If I'd had even the slightest notion it could, I would've talked her out of it."

Daisy swung her legs over the side of the bed and switched on the bedside lamp. "What are you talking about?"

Her mom dropped onto the bed beside Daisy. "Pansy's birthday gift to your dad."

"The lottery ticket?"

"Tonight when I watched all those number balls pop up, something told me to check the ticket. They were all there. Every single number."

"What are you trying to tell me, Mom?"

"Even if Danny somehow finds out he won, he'll never take the money."

Daisy's jaw dropped. "Where's the ticket now?"

"Back in the tin with the rest of Pansy's gifts. We need to keep her in the dark. As long as she doesn't find out, we're okay."

"That could be a problem." Daisy's brow pinched. "The ticket came from Willy's, right?"

"Oh my gosh." Her mom clutched her chest. "He'll know someone bought it at his store. But not who, which means I have to keep Pansy away from town until this all blows over."

Daisy slid her arm around her mom. "Do you want Dad to claim the winnings?"

She breathed deeply and slowly released the air. "I'd be telling a fib if I said I'd never dreamed about being rich. Then I think about Curtis. The man inherited millions from his father, and now he's most likely one miserable human being. I don't want the Butler curse to tear my family apart."

"You're taking on a heavy burden, keeping this a secret."

"Given all the stuff you're dealing with, it's not fair to unload on you." She touched her daughter's arm. "The truth is I need your strength to help me through this."

Daisy squeezed her shoulder. "I'd be hurt if you didn't let me share the burden."

"Strange." Poppy trilled her lips. "Any other person who discovered they'd won would wake up the entire family to celebrate. Maybe break out the bourbon to toast their good fortune and make lists of all the goodies they planned to buy. Instead we're trying to figure out how to keep the family from finding out what we consider terrible luck."

"Funny how life presents us with unexpected twists and turns." Daisy fell silent as she drank in the view. The bedroom where her grandmother once entertained men to put food on the table. The same room where she and Lilly said goodnight prayers and slept. And now the space where her mom trusted her to keep a secret that could change her family forever. "Try not to worry, Mom. Everything will work out for the best."

"I hope you're right. For now we both need some serious sleep."

"Five minutes and I'll be out like a light." Daisy embraced her mom. "I love you."

"I love you too, honey."

Poppy sauntered to the front room and dropped onto the sofa. Why of the millions of tickets sold had Pansy's won? Maybe it was a test or punishment for daydreaming about living like Danny's parents. Nonsense. The drawing was random, not orchestrated.

She aimed the remote at the television and clicked through channels until she landed on a mindless sitcom. Halfway through the show, Poppy yawned and turned it off. She crept into bed, comforted by Danny's steady breathing until two questions rocked her brain. Should she tell him about the win? And when, if ever, would she learn what happened to Danny's brother, Bobby?

Chapter 30

Daisy's chest tightened as she stuffed her phone in her pocket and peered out her bedroom window. Heavy clouds darkened the noonday sun and tugged at her conscience. Delaying her return to New York beyond her scheduled vacation hadn't eliminated other work responsibilities. She plucked her laptop off the dresser and carried it to the kitchen table, relieved to find the room empty.

While waiting for her computer to boot, Daisy's eyes drifted to the tin holding all of Pansy's lottery tickets. How much was her dad's ticket worth? A million? Maybe two? She meandered to the hutch and opened the tin. The ticket on top of the pile looked different from the others. What had Pansy called it during her dad's birthday dinner? The big one? It wouldn't hurt to find out how big.

Daisy returned to her chair and logged onto the internet. The instant she found the results, a gasp escaped. Her eyes bulged. How was that possible? She bolted from her chair and grabbed a water bottle from the fridge. After swallowing mouthfuls, she gripped the counter edge to steady her trembling limbs. All those millions. And only one winning ticket sold. How many yachts and Southampton mansions, or expensive paintings and cases of wine could that amount of money buy?

Did her mom know how much her dad's ticket was worth? Of course she knew. Daisy peeled her fingers off the counter and spun toward the table. If her family claimed the ticket and became mega millionaires, would she keep working or tell Michael to forget about her recruiting Curtis, and let the chips fall where they may? If her dad somehow learned his ticket had won and refused to take the money, would Lilly, Andy, or Basil try to convince him to declare the winnings? Would she? Maybe her dad was right. Too much money was a curse.

Daisy meandered to her chair, logged off the internet, and opened a work file. She stared at the screen. How could she focus with everything going on around her? As she slumped back in her seat, her phone pinged. She pulled it from her pocket. Michael's text. *Checking in. What's the status?*

How should she respond? Especially since she had nothing to report. Maybe she could hold him off. *Working on it. I'll update Friday afternoon.*

Another ping. *In court all week. Text me Friday by noon.*

Two and a half days to finish the job. *Will do.* Daisy carried her phone to her room and fished Curtis's assistant's business card from her purse. She added Cynthia Evans' number to her contact list and placed the call. After three rings it kicked to voicemail. She hung up without leaving a message and returned to the kitchen, surprised to find David leaning back against the counter. "Am I interrupting work?"

"Not really." She had to keep her anxiety at bay. "Any new information about Curtis?"

"Still working on it."

"Same thing I texted Michael."

"Is he the guy who can't find his way around a kitchen?"

David's playful tone eased the tension in her shoulders. "I think I'll keep you guessing."

"Since you're not busy, do you want to join me for a little investigative work?"

"What do you have in mind?"

"Another trip to the attic. We might find something interesting in one of those boxes."

Perfect time for a diversion. "I'm game." Daisy closed her laptop, pulled a rag from under the sink, and accompanied David to the hall.

He pulled the ladder down, climbed up, and turned on the overhead light. She followed as he strode toward cardboard boxes lined up along the wall. "Did you ever look through these?"

"Years ago Lilly and I opened them. Nothing interested us enough for a second look."

Daisy wiped layers of dust off the box tops and opened the first of five—filled with old dungarees, flannel shirts, and a worn winter coat. "These most likely belonged to Rose's father."

David sat on the floor and lifted the flaps on a box revealing baby clothes, blankets, and toys. "Painful memories of a baby lost."

A shoebox was filled with photos. Daisy sorted through a handful and pulled out a picture of three girls. "These must be the pictures Mom assumed were Rose and her friends. Now we know they're probably Rose with her sisters."

David lifted another photo and handed it to Daisy.

She stared at a woman holding a baby, then turned it over. "Based on the date, I'm guessing this is Rose's mom and brother." She touched the baby's face. "How much tragedy can one family endure?"

"I've discovered that some people who face tragedy turn bitter while others grow stronger. A lot has to do with their willingness to forgive."

"Examples of both exist in my family." Daisy placed the pictures back in the shoebox and pointed to the two remaining boxes. "If I'm remembering correctly, the larger one is filled with old magazines and the smaller with personal papers and documents."

"That's what I hoped we'd find." David lifted the lid, removed a rubber band from a bundle of bank statements, and handed half to Daisy. "Look through these and give me your opinion."

She read through her pile. "Based on the balances, the Fowlers barely kept their heads above water. Only one deposit a month. Same amount each time."

"Most likely Mr. Fowler's paycheck." David pulled out another stack. "Insurance papers." He flipped through them. "Nothing about life insurance. After the accident, someone had to pay for the funeral. Four caskets and plots don't come cheap."

"Good point." Daisy pulled out a thick document and examined the first two pages. "This is a thirty-year mortgage signed by Rose Fowler three years after her family died." She stared at the document. "What lender would approve a loan for an eighteen-year-old without a job?"

"A satisfied client with clout."

Daisy flipped to the amortization schedule and mentally calculated dates. "Best I can tell, seventeen years remained when she disappeared. How is that possible?"

"Maybe your mom can help answer that question."

After placing every item except the mortgage back in the box, they returned to the main floor and placed the document on the front-room coffee table.

They found Poppy watering miniature-rose bushes in the greenhouse. She looked from one to the other. "I'm guessing you aren't here to help me water plants."

"David and I came across a document we need to ask you about."

"Here?"

Daisy shook her head. "Back at the house."

"Good timing, I'm ready for a break." She turned off the spigot.

They headed to the house and settled in the front room. David showed Daisy's mom the mortgage document.

"I always assumed Mama inherited this house. Wait a sec. If she only paid on the mortgage for thirteen years, seventeen were left when she disappeared." Her eyebrows squished together. "Since I never paid a dime, some mysterious person must have plunked down a heap of money to keep me and Pansy from losing our home."

"That's the most logical explanation." David crossed his ankle over his knee. "Any idea who?"

"Afraid not. Unless—" Poppy tapped her fingers on her forehead. "The mystery money."

Daisy scooted to the edge of the sofa. "Are you talking about the lady who showed up in the black car with an envelope full of cash?"

"After that. About the time that money ran out, we found an envelope in our mailbox with three hundred dollars inside. Then the first of every month, someone left us another envelope. Same place. Same amount of money. It continued until Danny and I were married. That's how Pansy and I survived."

Daisy's eyes trained on her mom. "A mysterious donor inspired by benevolence."

"Or driven by a guilty conscience," added David.

"You still believe one of the men Mama entertained did something to her, don't you?" Poppy slapped her palm on her thigh. "I should've paid more attention, or at least snuck out of our hiding place to see who showed up at her door. If I'd found out what kind of cars her clients drove and written down some of their tag numbers, I could've helped those deputies find her."

"You were an innocent child, Poppy. Nothing would have prompted you to play detective." David propped his elbows on his knees. "Besides, even if you had the men's descriptions, it wouldn't have made any difference."

"How do you know?"

"The lack of evidence of any foul play reinforced the deputies preconceived conclusions about her running away."

"David's right, Mom. They most likely had their minds made up before they showed up."

"Still—" Her voice cracked. "I could have done more."

"You're doing more now when it counts." Daisy stroked her mom's hand. "If the case had been solved back then, David wouldn't be sitting across the coffee table from us."

His eyes met Daisy's. "And I would have missed the opportunity to meet three amazing women and one fine family."

Daisy's heart warmed as her lips involuntarily bloomed into a smile. For the moment Michael and the lottery-ticket dilemma were the furthest thing from her mind.

Chapter 31

P oppy had watched enough Hallmark movies to believe that the twinkle in David's eyes meant the handsome young man sitting across from her was falling for Daisy. Strange how failure and heartache sometimes turned into blessings. Would Danny consider David worthy of his daughter? What if the New York lawyer captured her heart? Her dad would never forgive Michael for conning Daisy into a confrontation with the man he hated. Unless...did she dare hope that something positive could come from her daughter's mission?

An image that had burned into her soul surfaced and sent a shiver skittering up Poppy's spine. Curtis Butler's expression of utter disdain the one time he'd laid eyes on her. There was no doubt that his hatred ran as deep as Danny's. Maybe deeper. All she could do was pray for Daisy to survive any contact with her grandfather unscathed and at the same time keep her relationship with her dad intact.

David pulled his ringing phone from his belt clip. "If you ladies will excuse me, I need to take this." He pressed the phone to his ear and hastened out the front door.

"Ever since you told me about the day you and Dad faced Curtis in his horse barn, a question has been gnawing at me." Daisy leaned back and stretched her arm across the back of the sofa. "When you realized Dad had used you to humiliate his father, why did you keep seeing him?"

How could she explain the depth of her emotions in a way her daughter would understand? Poppy pointed to her poetry scrapbook lying on the coffee table. "What do you remember about the poems I wrote, especially the common themes?"

"It's been awhile since I read them." Daisy scooted toward the coffee table. She opened the scrapbook and glanced through a dozen pages. "Both you and Aunt Pansy have a way with words."

"Mine were simple rhymes."

"But sweet. Best I can tell, you wrote about friendship, love, and romance."

"As far back as I can remember, the kids in school either taunted or ignored me. Except for two girls and one boy. Like me, all three had physical impairments. We became close friends and pretended it didn't matter how the other kids treated us. Truth was, we longed to be part of their inner circles and get invited to their parties."

Poppy's chin dropped. "After Mama pulled me and Pansy out of school, I lost touch with those three kids. My new circle of friends consisted of Mama, Pansy, Miss Aletha, and in summer when school was out, her daughter Ginny. This house and our little retreat became my whole world. Despite the isolation, I had all the normal desires every young girl experiences. I wanted to know what it was like to kiss a boy. To buy pretty party dresses and twirl on a dance floor in a boy's arms."

She paused for a long moment. "My poems became a reflection of the private desires I believed would never happen. Then one day this handsome young man showed up at my door. He didn't cringe when he looked at me. The first time he came back, we sat on the porch and talked. The third time he told me about his Army experiences and what he wanted to do with his life. Most important, he treated Pansy with respect."

Poppy fingered her wedding ring. "After that day at the ranch, I couldn't let him go. Even though I knew Danny didn't love me, he made me feel normal."

"But he did fall in love with you."

Her mom's chin lifted. "The day after I told him I was pregnant with you, he surprised me with a big bouquet of flowers and a box of candy. After supper we stood on the back porch and watched the sunset." Poppy closed her eyes as the memory washed over her like a warm spring shower. "I remember the exact moment he pulled me into his arms and for the first

175

time whispered the words I had longed to hear. 'I love you with all my heart, Poppy. We'll be together forever.'"

"What a beautiful love story."

Poppy opened her eyes. "We were two lost souls who had found each other. All these years I convinced myself that I'd created the Butler scrapbook for you, Lilly, and Basil. But deep down I wanted to feel connected to a family that wasn't scorned by society." Her voice quivered. "If I hadn't made a big deal out of the Butlers, you wouldn't be in the fix you're in with Curtis."

Daisy slid her arm around Poppy's shoulder. "No way you can take one smidgen of blame for my mess. I'm the one who kept from revealing the truth, not you."

"I made such a fuss—"

"Have you forgotten that I'm a big girl now? Besides, you and Dad always taught me what's right. I chose to ignore it."

Poppy patted her daughter's hand. "Sometimes situations get all tangled up with reality and make it hard to know what's right."

"I wonder if Michael will buy that excuse when I fail to deliver?"

"What kind of lawyer is he?"

"Defense attorney." "Based on all the *Law and Order* episodes your dad and I have watched, Michael can't expect to win every case."

"Recruiting Curtis is an assignment not a case, and Michael only takes cases he knows he can win."

"How's that possible? Does he own some kind of future-predicting crystal ball?" "Even better. He has good instincts backed by a hardworking staff and his father's experience and reputation. Which reminds me—I need to do some lawyer work to continue earning my salary." Daisy squeezed her mom's shoulder. "I'm glad we had this talk, Mom."

"Me too, honey." Why all these years had she kept this glimpse into her past hidden from her confidante? Fear of Daisy pitying her? Or shame of secret desires? As Poppy's eyes followed her daughter strolling from the room, the tension gripping her shoulders melted away. Her eyes drifted to her scrapbook and landed on the first verse of one of her poems.

She walked along the winding road beside a field of hay,
In the distance she caught sight of him riding her way.

The friendly boy on a bike who smiled and waved.
Maybe he'd stop and talk to her today.

Poppy pressed her hand to her chest. Danny was her boy on the bike. She closed her scrapbook, pushed off the sofa, and rushed to the greenhouse.

Pansy and Basil busied themselves moving winter annuals onto a flatbed cart for transfer to the delivery truck. At the far end, Danny—the man who'd rescued her from a life of loneliness—loaded shrubs onto a another cart. She ambled down the center aisle and stopped beside him. "Need some help?"

"Sure."

Poppy stooped to lift a plant and eyed her husband's well-worn work boots, one of three pairs he'd purchased over the years. Frugal to a fault. She smiled while transferring the plant to the cart. Even if Danny somehow found out he'd won the lottery and was forced to take the money, he'd most likely give every dollar away. Which reinforced the need to keep him and the family in the dark—at least for a while.

Chapter 32

Daisy sat at the kitchen table as she had thousands of times across the years. Except today she faced a laptop open to a corporate project rather than an open textbook. And without disruptions from Lilly or Basil, which were annoying if her assignment involved civics or English and welcome if her homework was algebra or any other math. Funny how she needed all those skills in her chosen profession.

Even though no one bothered her, she struggled to stay focused on work. Especially after her Mom shared a glimpse into her childhood. The amount of heartache she had overcome escalated Daisy's admiration to a whole new height. Despite her sophistication, Michael's mother could never measure up to Poppy Butler. Daisy blinked. Why had that notion even entered her head? Because she had fewer than forty-eight hours to confront Curtis Butler or risk losing everything she'd worked for.

Daisy yanked her phone off the table and pressed Cynthia Evans' number. Three rings before the call again went to voicemail again. Was the woman screening her calls, or had her grandfather denied her request? This situation called for a serious stress reducing-action. She plunked her phone on the table, plodded to the counter, and yanked the lid off the cookie jar. The rich chocolate aroma made her mouth water. She pulled out one of Pansy's cookies, bit off a mouth-sized chunk, closed her eyes, and relished the rich taste.

The back door creaked.

Daisy's eyes popped open.

"Your mom said you wouldn't mind if I interrupted your work." A grin spread across David's face. "Looks like that cookie already beat me to it."

She swallowed and swiped her fingers across her mouth. "Some projects beg for sweet breaks."

"Always food-related?"

"That depends. What kind of respite do you have in mind?"

"How about a long walk on a sunny afternoon?"

"To work off cookie calories?"

"Call that a bonus."

Daisy popped the other half in her mouth, pulled another cookie from the jar, and pressed it into his hand.

"So we both need to walk off a sugar binge?"

"You bet." She removed two bottles of water from the fridge. "Same path as yesterday?"

"Out front this time."

"New scenery?"

"In part." David escorted her through the house, across the front porch, and onto the driveway.

Daisy glanced over her shoulder at the empty space beside David's camper. "Looks like Dad's out on a delivery."

"He and Basil left a half hour ago."

The gravel crunched beneath their feet as they stepped off the paved portion of driveway. Daisy's shoulder brushed David's arm. She inched away.

"The real reason for the walk is to talk without interruptions." David twisted the cap off his water bottle and swallowed a mouthful. "The phone call I received after we showed the mortgage document to your mom was from one of my go-to contacts. The guy's an expert at digging up hard-to-find details."

She stopped and faced him. "He came through, didn't he?"

"Big time." They resumed walking. "Starting with Curtis Butler's domestic problems. Thirty-six years ago, he filed for divorce. His wife refused to sign. Rumor was she had no intention of giving up even a smidgen of the influence his money gave her. At some point he dropped the suit."

"Talk about a soap opera."

"I haven't even started on his daughters."

"An Emmy-winning melodrama?"

"You tell me. Six months ago his oldest divorced her third husband and moved to Belize with prospect number four—a software genius worth millions. Perhaps the alimony from the first three wasn't enough to support her lifestyle. Then there's the youngest daughter. She's spent the last thirty-plus years in and out of rehab. Alcohol and drugs. For the most part, the family kept her addiction under wraps."

"Anything to protect the family's reputation. What about grandchildren?"

"Neither daughter had kids."

"Which means Lilly, Basil, and I are Curtis's only grandchildren. Talk about irony." Daisy uncapped her water and sipped as they left the gravel driveway and strolled along the edge of the woods. "All those pictures Mom collected hinted that the Butlers led the perfect life. That old cliché, 'money can't buy happiness' definitely applies to their family. Did your contact say anything about Curtis's sons?"

"Did you mean to use the plural?"

Uh-oh. Should she claim a slip of the tongue? What was the point? David knew more about her dad's family than either she or her mom and probably her dad. "Mom and I recently learned that Dad had a brother named Bobby. We don't know where he is or what happened to him."

"Odd nothing came up about him." David's brow furrowed then released. "Is your dad's legal name Danny?"

"Daniel."

"Which means Bobby is likely Robert. I'll ask my contact to dig deeper, see what he can find out. For now, back to Curtis. Every year for decades, he invited business associates and Georgia's elite to a big Labor Day shindig at his ranch."

Daisy envisioned the picture about the event her mom had painted. Big white tent. Tables covered with white cloths. Fancy centerpieces.

"He threw the last party two years ago. About that time—except for occasional weekend visits to his Savannah house—he dropped out of society. Rumors surfaced about his failing health and Cynthia taking over the majority of the business decisions. She was married to Curtis's personal attorney until they divorced."

"Recently?"

"Years ago."

Daisy took another sip of water. "Is there any truth to rumors about Curtis's failing health?"

"He's an old man, so a serious illness is a reasonable assumption. However, since medical records are hard to come by, it's still nothing more than speculation."

"Maybe I need to reconsider my tactic."

They strolled further along the tree line to the end of the grassy area.

"Sorry I couldn't come up with more information. Curtis is one elusive character."

"I know a lot more now than I did an hour ago, so I'd call your efforts a big success." A hawk soared overhead then perched on a limb. "Years ago Lilly, Basil, and I spent hours trekking through the woods searching for buried treasure."

"The country's a good place to grow up."

"Where did you spend your childhood?"

"Not far from downtown Atlanta." David leaned back against a massive tree and propped his foot on the trunk. "Mom spent years paying off our little house."

Daisy's eyes followed the hawk as it took flight. "Is that where you live when you're not chasing down a case?"

"I sold it to a young couple."

"You've mentioned your mom several times, but not your dad."

"He was never in the picture."

A fatherless child, like her mom and aunt. Daisy peeled a piece of bark off the tree trunk. "Did your mother ever talk about him?"

"One time, when I asked what happened to him. What she told me kept me from ever asking again." David pushed off the tree. "Enough talk about my past. What do you say we head back to the house and indulge on a piece of Pansy's chocolate cake?"

"Your reward for digging up details about Curtis?"

"Until I come up with something better."

Chapter 33

Daisy wrapped a blanket around her shoulders to ward off the cool breeze wafting across the front porch and set her rocking chair in motion. The first light of dawn revealed a family of deer grazing near the spot where David had shared a glimpse into his past.

The front door swung open sending a beam of light across the porch floorboards.

"I thought you might need this." Daisy's mom handed her a cup of coffee and settled in the rocking chair beside her. "You've been up awhile."

"It's been a long time since I've watched the sunrise from this spot." A buck raised its head and turned in their direction. "I miss watching deer venture out from the woods. They're such gentle animals. I'm glad Dad doesn't like to hunt."

"His guns are to protect our family. Thank goodness he hasn't had to use them." Her mom pulled her sweater tight. "I noticed you and David talking at the edge of the woods yesterday."

Daisy gripped her cup in both hands. "I'd asked him to find out what he could about Curtis."

"And?"

"He learned way more than I expected." As Daisy relayed the details, her mom's mouth gaped and her brows raised. "All those years we admired Dad's family we had no idea how much turmoil infected their lives."

Her mom blew out a long breath. "You, Lilly, and Basil are the Butler's only grandchildren?"

"Talk about a shocker. I doubt either Curtis or his wife know we exist. Unless his assistant gave him my business card, and he figured it out."

"A decent man who had a heart would want to meet you."

"I'm beginning to believe neither applies to Curtis."

"You'd think he'd possess at least an ounce of curiosity about his granddaughter."

The deer family meandered across the gravel driveway. "Michael's expecting an update in twenty-eight hours, and I haven't heard a peep from Cynthia Evans."

"What are you planning to do?"

"Get dressed and recruit Basil." Daisy pushed off the rocking chair. "It's time to take charge."

A half hour later, she spotted her brother hosing the greenhouse center walkway. She turned off the spigot, pulled him aside, and leaned close. "I need you to come with me."

"Why the fancy getup?"

"You and I are going back to the ranch."

Basil set down the hose. "Want me to wear my uniform?"

"Something more intimidating." She steered him toward the exit. "I'll meet you at my car."

"Who is this take-charge woman who came close to backing out a few days ago?"

"One ticked off, desperate attorney."

"Good going, sis."

After Basil raced across the backyard and bounded up the porch steps, the overwhelming desire to talk to David consumed Daisy. Did she want his advice or simply long to be near him? She eyed his camper. Did the reason matter? She eased beside the door. Should she knock? How long before Basil returned? Long enough.

The door opened seconds before her knuckles made contact. "Based on your outfit, I'm guessing you're on a mission to track down your grandfather."

"I'm down to the wire time-wise. Basil's going with me."

"Marine protection. Smart move." He stepped out. His shoulder brushed her arm.

Daisy's breath caught. "I um...was wondering if you have any words of wisdom or sensible advice."

His smile melted her heart. "Best advice I can give is trust your instincts."

"Like a wise investigator?"

"And a smart attorney." David nodded toward the house. "Your bodyguard is headed our way."

Basil approached, dressed in black from head to toe.

Daisy eyed his tight jeans, tee shirt, leather jacket, and lace-up military boots "You look more like a nightclub bouncer than a Marine."

"Hey, you requested intimidating."

David chuckled. "Anyone with a lick of sense would think twice before giving you a hard time."

Daisy slid her hand around her brother's arm. "It's time to find out if David's assessment applies to Curtis Butler's bodyguard." She waved at David over her shoulder as she and Basil headed to her car.

Hoping to quell her anxiety, during the drive Daisy engaged Basil in playful sibling jabs. By the time she drove up the long driveway and parked behind the Tesla, her confidence had inched up a notch. She peered at the front patio. "I don't see the bodyguard."

"Don't know if that's good news or bad." Basil climbed out and met Daisy in the front of the car. He nodded toward the house. "We spoke too soon."

The burly man was making a beeline to the wall.

Basil leaned close to Daisy as they headed to the stairs. "Our first task is getting in the door, so play it cool."

At the top step, she slid her hand behind her back hoping her crossed fingers would excuse the fib ready to roll off her tongue. "Good morning, sir. I'm with the Warner law firm and am here for my appointment with Curtis Butler."

The muscular bodyguard held his ground.

Basil stood ramrod straight, his feet planted shoulder-length apart. "Ms. Butler is a highly respected attorney whose time is valuable. I suggest you don't keep her or your boss waiting."

The man hesitated.

Daisy flinched. Had her brother engaged them in a standoff?

The bodyguard's eyes shifted from Basil to Daisy. He pivoted and motioned them to follow him.

"Way to go, knucklehead," Daisy whispered.

"Glad to oblige, noodle-noggin."

Inside the foyer, the burly man nodded to his left. "Wait in there."

Basil held his sister's elbow as they stepped into the massive living room.

Daisy eyed the stone fireplace anchoring the rustic, yet extravagant décor. No one could say her grandfather didn't have good taste. She scanned the space. Not a single photograph. At least the Warner family displayed family photos. Heels clicked behind her. Daisy spun and faced her grandfather's assistant. "Hello, Ms. Evans. I believe Mr. Butler is expecting me."

Cynthia raised her chin and moved to the front of the couch. "I didn't return your phone calls for a reason." Her tone broadcasted an air of authority and more than a hint of irritation.

"I understand. However, if you will kindly escort me to Mr. Butler's office, I'll make my visit worth his time."

She crossed her arms and held Daisy's gaze. "I admire your moxie, but your tactic won't work. I know who you are, and Mr. Butler refuses to meet with you."

Daisy glared at the woman threatening her future. "Does he understand that I'm representing a prestigious law firm—"

"You're wasting your time, Ms. Butler, and your law firm's money. I suggest you return to New York and tell your bosses their services aren't needed. Mr. Butler's bodyguard will escort you out." She turned on her heel, headed back to the foyer, and disappeared down the hall.

Daisy released an exasperating sigh.

"There's no point in staying." Basil held her arm while escorting her across the foyer and out the front door.

"She lied to us, Basil."

"I know."

"I'm not going down in defeat until I find a way to speak to my grandfather face-to-face."

"Spoken by a tough, no-nonsense New York lawyer."

"And a Butler on a mission."

Chapter 34

After returning from the frustrating trip to the ranch and changing into jeans and sweater, Daisy carried her laptop to the kitchen table. In fewer than twenty-four hours, she had to come up with a strategy to bypass Curtis's gatekeeper and compose a text to Michael. An explanation he could present to the partners without looking like a fool. Short of telling the truth, she had no idea what would work.

Hoping to find inspiration, she booted her laptop and opened the Warner Law Firm website. One click on the partner tab revealed the senior Warner's photo and impressive bio. Michael's picture and information followed his father's, equally as notable. Maybe she should accept his New Year's Eve invitation and rub elbows with influential people.

Daisy scrolled through the remaining partners—most she'd never laid eyes on. She imagined finding her picture on the page, one of a handful of females granted the honor. Cynthia Evans had put that prospect in serious jeopardy. She returned to the home page and clicked on the firm's mission statement. Her breath hitched as her eyes locked on one word. *Integrity*. Why hadn't she told Michael she couldn't accept the Curtis Butler project? Because her interview omission—a much better word than lie—had boxed her into a corner. Besides, associates never turned down assignments.

Daisy leaned back and peered around the room that functioned as the heart of her family's home. The window leading to the back porch framed by blue gingham curtains her mom had found at the thrift store. The counters, clean and uncluttered. Her eyes drifted to the hutch and Rose

Fowler's tin harboring dozens of losing lottery tickets and one big-time winner.

Pansy bounced into the kitchen wearing her sparkly new cap. Her ever-faithful canine padded behind. She dropped onto her chair and held up stapled sheets of paper featuring a colored-pencil drawing of tall buildings on the front page. "I wrote another story about Mama."

"Awesome picture. What city did you draw?"

"New York. This one's 'bout a man taking Mama to live in a big fancy house with two dogs and a pet raccoon. Like the one Boots chased away from the front porch." At the mention of his name, Boots sat on his haunches and plopped his head in Pansy's lap. "Mama wants to call home, but the man keeps hiding the phones."

"What an interesting and creative story."

"Will David write about me in his book?"

"One of your stories brought him here, so I imagine he'll make you one of the main characters."

Pansy set her latest literary creation on the table. "I wish I was smart like you."

"In lots of ways, you're a whole lot smarter. After all, you're the only person in our family who wrote a story good enough to catch the eye of an important investigative journalist."

"I like David." Pansy stroked Boots' muzzle. "He's nice."

Way better than nice. "Yes he is."

Pansy pointed to the laptop. "Are you working on lawyer stuff?"

"Sort of."

"Will you help me bake a carrot cake for supper?"

Her aunt's wide-eyed expression challenged Daisy's sense of responsibility. The Warner law firm paid her salary and promised a bright future. And technically even though she sat in a kitchen hundreds of miles from the office, she remained on their time.

"Please? Like we used to before you moved away?"

Daisy hesitated for a nanosecond. Work could never overshadow her love for the woman who had brought mountains of joy to their family. "There's nothing I'd like better ."

"Goodie." Pansy popped up and began gathering ingredients. Following two hours of light-hearted conversation and laughter, she placed the cake on the table and slid a Jello mold loaded with strawberries and bananas into the fridge—her response to Daisy's suggestion they prepare an alternative to the sugar-laced dessert.

"This has been the most fun I've had on a Thursday afternoon since I left for college." Daisy swiped a smudge of flour off her aunt's cheek. "Not only are you the best writer in the family, you're also the best baker."

"When Danny wins the lottery, I'll open a flower shop *and* a bakery."

The dreaded word drew Daisy's eyes to the tin. Maybe she should tell Basil about the winning ticket. Too risky, especially if he disagreed with her and her mom's decision to keep the winning ticket a secret from the rest of the family.

Her mom walked in from the back porch and set her straw hat on the counter. "Looks like you two have been as busy as a couple of honeybees."

Pansy grabbed her newest literary creation and handed it to her sister. "Do you wanna read my new story 'bout Mama before I give it to David? Maybe it'll help him find her."

"After we fix supper."

Daisy forced aside the momentary stab of guilt for shirking her professional responsibility. "Seems my afternoon of fun is set to continue." She carried her laptop to her room and set it on the dresser. In fewer than two hours, David would sit beside her at the kitchen table and join in the conversation as if he'd known her family for years rather than days. Hopefully Rose's case would keep him from leaving before Christmas. She returned to the kitchen, eager to help her mom and aunt.

Following supper and clean-up duty, Daisy moseyed to the front room and stood at the entrance. A football game played on the television. Her dad, brother, and David sat on the sofa with their forearms propped across their knees, as if they willed the quarterback to throw a touchdown pass. The family understood that during football season, every Thursday night and Sundays from noon on, their only TV would be tuned to the one sport the man of the house followed, which suited Basil and annoyed her and Lilly. At least with Basil home, she and her mom weren't obligated to keep her dad company.

Cheers from the television and the audience of three sent her dashing to the back porch. She sat on the steps and brooded over another failed attempt to breach Curtis's inner sanctum.

"I hoped I'd find you out here." Her mom settled beside her. "I've been dying to find out what happened at the ranch."

"Basil got us past the body guard." Daisy released a heavy sigh. "Unfortunately, we hit a brick wall with Cynthia Evans. By noon tomorrow I have to decide what to tell Michael. If I don't come up with a noteworthy reason why I haven't met with Curtis, I'll send up all sorts of red flags."

"You're smart, honey." Her mom patted her hand. "You'll come up with a good explanation."

Daisy trilled her lips. "I hope you're right."

Chapter 35

A gentle tap on her door roused Daisy awake. Surprised by sunlight streaming through the window, she swung her legs over the side of the bed. "Come in."

"Good morning, sleepyhead." Her mom sat beside her. "You left your phone on the table last night. It pinged a couple of times."

Daisy blinked. "What time is it?"

"Nine-thirty."

"Oh my gosh." She grabbed her phone and dashed to the bathroom. After splashing cold water on her face, she read a text from Michael.

Change of plans. Need your update by ten.

Cold skittered up Daisy's spine as she raced to the kitchen and poured a cup of coffee.

Her mom moved plates from the dishwasher to the cabinet. "Was the message about work?"

"Twenty-five. That's how many minutes I have to figure out how to tell Michael I haven't connected with Curtis."

"Oh dear. What I can do to help?"

"Pray I'll find the right words to stay employed." Daisy scurried to her room, took one sip of the bitter brew, and set her cup on the dresser. Now what? She paced, racking her brain for some version of the truth. The partners were all attorneys, who at some point in their careers faced unexpected roadblocks and dealt with difficult clients. An idea began to form. She sat on the edge of her bed and typed the first message.

Curtis isn't responding to personal calls. She hesitated. Chances were that statement was true. *His assistant is keeping him in isolation. Possible concern for his health.* At least part of that statement rang true. *Need another week in GA. Taking the weekend off to prepare for head-to-head battle with his gatekeeper. Hope all goes well for you in court today.*

Daisy reread the text. Professional and to the point. She pressed send, muted her phone, and laid it facedown on the dresser. Answers to any questions her explanation might raise could wait until Monday.

Satisfied she had given herself more time, she meandered to the bathroom and turned on the shower. The moment steam billowed into the small space and fogged the mirror, she stepped into the tub and ran her fingers through her hair. As the hot water flowed over her, a stab of guilt for failing to secure a meeting with Curtis lingered for a moment then vanished. If he had agreed to see her and accepted the firm's offer, she'd be on her way back to New York. Funny how Cynthia Evan's roadblock gave her more time to become better acquainted with David. How would he stack up against Michael—the man she had imagined as the other half of a power couple?

Daisy dismissed the question and hummed one of her favorite songs until she stepped out of the shower. She dried her hair and applied a smattering of makeup, then returned to her room and made her bed. Curiosity pulled her to the side window. She peered at David's camper. Today they planned to review notes about Rose's disappearance.

Filled with renewed hope for positive outcomes, at least in her grandmother's case, Daisy carried her cup back to the kitchen. She dropped a slice of bread in the toaster and refilled her cup. Her eyes drifted to the wall clock. A half hour before she and David agreed to meet on the front porch. Had he come over for breakfast this morning or stayed in his camper? Her toast popped up. She slathered it with jam.

The back door flew open. Daisy startled at her mom's panic-stricken expression. "What's wrong?"

"I went to the greenhouse looking for Pansy. Boots was lying on the gravel beside Danny."

Daisy's heart jumped to her throat. "Did something happen to Dad?"

"I couldn't let him see me panic."

"Panic about what?" She gripped her mom's shoulders. "Mom. Talk to me."

She blinked as if coming out of a daze. "Danny sent Basil to pick something up at Willy's. Pansy drove over with him."

"When did they leave?"

"Maybe ten minutes ago."

"Meet me at my car." Daisy released her mom and dashed to her room. She grabbed her purse, then sped across the back porch. As she neared the greenhouse, she slowed her pace and peered through the glass. Her dad was nowhere in sight. She hastened to her car and climbed into the driver's seat beside her mom.

"Why didn't I tell Basil about the lottery ticket?"

"Because we had no idea how he'd react." Daisy eased down the driveway and turned onto the road. She accelerated to twenty miles above the speed limit, praying the county sheriff wouldn't choose today to patrol the remote area. "If Willy's son posted the winning numbers, maybe she won't notice."

"She'd never understand why we don't want to tell Danny he won." Her mom faced the side window as she slid her fingers along her seatbelt.

Silence hung heavy as Daisy sped down the road while keeping her eye out for the law. As the wide spot in the road called a town came into view, she slowed to the speed limit, pulled into the convenience store lot, and parked beside Basil's jeep.

Her mom jumped out and rushed inside. Daisy caught up with her at the counter while scanning the space.

Willy's son grinned. "Must be the Butler family's day to shop. How can I help you, Ms. Poppy?"

"We're looking for Basil."

"He and Pansy left a few minutes ago. Chances are they walked over to the thrift store."

Daisy followed her mom outside and peered down the side street. "They're over there."

They crossed the street and closed the distance to the row of vacant storefronts. Basil stood at the curb while Pansy peered into the first window. Her mom approached Basil. "What brought you over here?"

"Strangest thing. Seems some lucky bum bought that mega lottery ticket at Willy's. Aunt Pansy stared at the sign posting the winning numbers while eating her ice cream bar. When we walked out, she talked about opening a bakery and flower shop, then raced over here."

"She knows," mumbled Daisy.

Basil stared at her. "Who knows what?"

She had to tell him. "Dad's birthday gift is the winning ticket."

He stared wide-eyed at her. "Are you serious?"

Daisy nodded.

"Does Dad know?"

"Not yet."

Pansy scooted to the second storefront and pressed her nose to the window.

Basil leaned close to his mom. "You need to tell him today, before Aunt Pansy breaks the news."

"I know."

"Would it help if I take your sister to Savannah and buy her lunch to give you time alone with Dad?"

"You don't mind?"

"It's the least I can do. Now you and Daisy scoot before I have to explain why you showed up."

"We'll owe you big time, knucklehead." Daisy and her mom returned to her car. During the drive home, her mom fidgeted while staring straight ahead. By the time she parked in her parents' driveway, the tension was palpable.

David sat on the front-porch steps. One glance at the dashboard clock told Daisy how long he'd been waiting for her to show up.

When her mom gripped the door handle, Daisy reached across the console and clutched her arm. "Do you want me to go with you?"

"I need to do this alone. Keep David company while I fix lunch. I'll tell your dad after he eats."

"If you change your mind, you'll find us on the front porch." Daisy released her arm and waited for her to head to the back of the house before joining David. "Sorry to keep you waiting."

"Is everything okay?"

"Not exactly." Daisy dropped beside him and shared everything that had happened since her mom entered her room at nine-thirty.

Chapter 36

Poppy spooned scoops of potato salad on two plates beside ham-and-cheese sandwiches. Why hadn't she told Danny about the lottery the night the winning numbers tumbled out? Now he'd know she kept secrets. Except he already knew, given the scrapbook she'd kept hidden in her retreat.

Footsteps struck the back-porch floor. Her pulse accelerated as she set two plates on the table.

Danny lumbered into the kitchen. Boots followed him and sprawled beneath Pansy's chair.

"Are you hungry?" She rolled her eyes at her lame question. Of course he was hungry. It was lunch time.

He washed his hands and dried them with a paper towel.

"Do you want lemonade or tea?"

"Lemonade." Danny dropped onto his chair.

Poppy filled one glass with lemonade and another with water. "How'd your morning go?"

"Same as usual." He bit into his sandwich.

"Basil and Pansy aren't back from Willy's." How could he not know? Basil's jeep wasn't in the driveway. She toyed with her potato salad while keeping an eye on Danny. Should she dive right in and break the news or wait until he finished eating?

He polished off half the sandwich and downed half the lemonade.

She scurried to the fridge, removed the pitcher, and refilled his glass. "How's the sandwich?"

"Filling."

He was obviously not in the mood for conversation. Best to sit quietly and wait for him to finish. She managed to swallow two bites before he pushed his empty plate away. "Before you go—" She placed her hand on his arm. "How about some dessert? Cake or maybe a slice of sweet-potato pie?"

"No thanks." He pushed up.

"Please, don't leave yet."

He paused halfway off his seat, then dropped back down and locked eyes with her. "What's wrong?"

She breathed deeply to slow her racing pulse. "Basil took Pansy to Savannah to give me time to break the news."

His eyes narrowed. "News about what?"

"The impossible has happened, Danny. Something none of us ever expected." His pointed stare sent beads of sweat to her upper lip. "Your birthday gift from Pansy. It won."

He glared at her as if she'd grown a second head. "What do you mean, it won?"

"The multi-million-dollar lottery. All that cash is yours, if you claim it."

He remained silent for a long moment. "Any chance you're mistaken?"

She shook her head.

Danny downed the rest of his drink, then slammed his glass on the table. "Wealth has cursed the Butlers."

Poppy wiped the sweat off her lip. "Pansy found out today at Willy's."

"Who else knows?"

"Daisy and Basil. Maybe David."

Poppy's skin turned to gooseflesh at the sight of Danny's features growing rigid and his eyes glazing over.

"You know I had a brother. Four years younger than me."

She had to keep him talking. "Tell me about Bobby."

"He was a great kid." Danny's voice came across muted, as if he spoke from a long, narrow tunnel. "Not bright, but sweet and full of love. He had dark wavy hair. Big brown eyes. Bobby loved watching cartoons. *Tom and Jerry* was his favorite. For a while he had a gray cat he called Tom. Until it escaped from his room during one of his mother's parties and pounced on her buffet table. When it disappeared, I told him a ringmaster came to town and took it to star in a cat circus. He liked that.”

Danny stared straight ahead. “*Super Friends* was another one of his favorite cartoons. After the incident at the ranch when Curtis rejected him, Bobby made a list of things he wanted to do to make his old man proud. Number one was getting strong so he could rescue people like Superman. He curled ten-pound dumbbells and did pushups twice a day for years. The second thing he wrote down—*get smart like Danny*. Every day after school I did the best I could to teach him, but he had difficulty.” He slapped his fist on the table.

Poppy jumped.

“I should have taken him away from that evil house.” Danny rubbed the back of his hand with his thumb as if attempting to wipe away an indelible stain. “The night of Bobby’s fourteenth birthday, our parents hosted a big party—for their friends, not their son. I told my brother to wait in his room, and I’d bring him a big surprise. Then I left him alone to go buy a cake and some presents. Most of the time he paid attention to what I told him. That night he didn’t.”

The vein in Danny’s neck pulsed. “When I came back I found him on the main floor telling guests it was his birthday and his dad was throwing him a big party. The woman we called mother turned her back as Curtis approached Bobby. For a second I imagined the man might have a heart.”

Danny’s hands fisted. “I’ll never forget what that heartless old man announced to his guests. ‘You’ll have to excuse this confused boy. Sometimes he wanders away from home. My son will see that he’s returned to where he belongs.’” Danny choked, his face flushed.

Poppy grabbed his glass and filled it with water.

He drank until the choking stopped, then swiped the back of his hand across his mouth. “I guided my brother up the back stairs to the third floor. That’s where Bobby and I lived. He didn’t cry or say a word. He simply curled up on his bed and faced the wall. I lay down on the other bed and tried to keep my eyes open. If I’d stayed awake—”

Poppy froze at the sight of Danny’s eyes spilling tears. Never in all the years she’d known him had she seen him cry. She bolted from her chair and wrapped her arms around his neck.

He swiped his hand across his reddened eyes. "The next morning I found him in the attic hanging from the rafters. A chair tipped over under his body. My parents—" He spat the word. "Told me and my sisters that our brother was dead to the family. They ordered us never to utter his name again. When Curtis refused to have a funeral, I cursed him and called him the devil. He whacked the back of his hand across my face. Knocked me to the floor. He towered over me, glaring as blood poured from my split lip."

Tears erupted and spilled down Poppy's cheeks.

Danny guzzled more water. "When that man turned and walked away, my hatred increased tenfold. It made me detest everything that stunk of wealth and status. I stuffed some clothes in a duffle and walked out of that heartless house for the last time. The next day I enlisted in the Army."

Poppy wiped tears from Danny's chin with her fingertips. "I don't understand how a father could treat his sons with such contempt."

"Because you're a good person with a heart and a soul. You have to understand, if I took the lottery money I'd infect the family I love with the Butler curse."

"When we tell our children about your brother, they'll understand."

"All they need to know is that Bobby is no longer alive."

Poppy pulled her arms away from Danny. "If we tell them why—"

"No!" His tone softened. "Those memories have haunted me for thirty-seven years. I don't want that same poison to infect our family."

"I understand and promise to respect your wishes. But our children deserve to know the truth, just like Pansy and I deserve to know the truth about Mama's disappearance."

Danny released a heavy sigh. "I'll think about it."

Poppy scooted her chair beside his. "Maybe this will help."

As Danny listened to her relay the details David had dug up about his family, a faraway look clouded his eyes. When Poppy finished, silence enfolded the moment. His stoic expression failed to reveal his emotion.

"I didn't know if I should tell you."

"I'm glad you did." He scooted his chair away from the table and stood. "Invite Lilly and Andy to come over tonight. Before supper I'll take the heat for turning down the money."

A wave of mental exhaustion wearied Poppy to her bones as she watched Danny plod across the kitchen and out the back door. She understood the guilt he kept locked in his soul. The haunting question she kept buried deep in her subconscious crept up from the depths. Why hadn't she summoned the courage to disobey her mother and find out why she didn't come for her and Pansy hours before she disappeared? She shoved the guilt she'd struggled to overcome back in its hiding place, grabbed her phone off the counter, and carried it to the front porch.

Daisy turned toward her. "Did you tell Dad?"

Poppy sauntered close and eyed David.

"It's okay, Mom. I told him."

"Tonight Danny will explain to all of us why he can't take the money." She sat on the front steps and pressed Lilly's number.

"Hey, Mom."

"Hi, honey. I hope you and Andy are free tonight."

Chapter 37

Focusing every ounce of energy on cleaning the home she loved failed to keep Poppy's anxiety in check. So many questions raced through her mind. Would Lilly's fascination with celebrities and dreams about traveling to exotic locations prevent her from accepting her dad's decision? What about Andy? His hardworking parents barely qualified as middle class. How would he respond to his father-in-law's rejection of wealth?

While scrubbing the already-clean kitchen sink, Poppy's eyes drifted to the window facing the back porch. She focused on Basil's room, the addition her son helped his dad build. Money never seemed important to her son, but then he'd never faced the prospect of extreme wealth. Poppy forced her attention to wiping down the cabinet doors. How much would an updated kitchen with shiny new appliances cost?

She pivoted to stare at her children and sister's drawings decorating the wall separating the kitchen from the front room. If she had a lot of money, would she be tempted to replace them with expensive paintings?

Daisy strolled in from the hall. "Would you like help fixing supper?"

"Danny's going to break Pansy's heart. All these years she's given us lottery tickets. If one she gave to you, Lilly, Basil, or me won a small amount of money, we could accept it and make her happy. She'll never understand why Danny wants to turn his down."

"She might understand more than you realize."

"You know how long she's dreamed of opening a flower store, and now she has this crazy notion of adding a bakery." Poppy released a resigning sigh. "Her brother-in-law is hours away from dashing her dream."

"Basil knows Dad won't take the money. Maybe he's preparing Aunt Pansy for the news."

"I sent him a text and asked him to bring her home at five, the same time Lilly and Andy plan to show up."

"Try not to worry, Mom. Somehow everything will turn out for the best."

"Turning down millions? Money that could change our lives forever or tear our family apart?"

Daisy fell silent, as if she also understood the threat Danny's decision posed.

Eager to change the subject, Poppy shoved her cleaning supplies under the kitchen sink. "You and David spent a lot of time together this afternoon. Any progress on solving Mama's disappearance?"

"We came up with a couple of theories. Figuring out which theory is accurate depends on us discovering what that mysterious key unlocks."

"Someone, somewhere must know." Poppy opened the fridge.

"The question is who?" Daisy pointed to ingredients her mom set on the counter. "Let me guess. Meatloaf and mashed potatoes for supper."

"Tonight we need lots of comfort food."

For the remainder of the afternoon, they focused on the task at hand while chatting about anything other than lottery tickets and money. By the time five o'clock rolled around, supper was warming in the oven and Poppy—wearing one of her Sunday dresses—stood on the front porch beside Danny. Boots sprawled at her feet. "Have you decided how to break the news?"

"I'm working on it."

Andy's car eased up the driveway

"You'd best work fast. Chances are our daughter will ask about the last-minute invitation before she reaches the front porch."

Moments after Andy parked, Lilly dashed across the lawn. "I'm guessing David discovered what happened to Grandmother Rose." She climbed up the steps and embraced her mom, then her dad.

The front door swung open. Daisy moseyed over. "The inquisitive middle child arrives."

"Since you're the oldest, you probably already know what's happening. So, am I right, or do y'all have other earth-shattering news to share? Is David joining us?"

"A little later. He's still working on the Rose mystery, and whether the news is earth-shattering is questionable." Daisy linked arms with Lilly and Andy and escorted them inside.

Basil's Jeep pulled up and parked behind Andy's car.

Boots bounded off the porch and raced across the lawn. Pansy, wearing a new red ball cap, climbed out and hugged her dog's neck before closing the distance to the porch. "Basil told me 'bout Lilly and Andy coming for supper. We had cheeseburgers for lunch and took a ride in a buggy pulled by a big horse." She brushed past her parents to the front door.

Basil climbed the steps and handed his mom two bottles of wine. "An addition to your comfort food."

Poppy eyed her son. "Your dad knows."

Danny crossed his arms. "What did my sister-in-law say about the lottery?"

"Other than carrying on about a bakery and flower shop, not a word. I doubt she has any idea how much money her ticket is worth."

"Let's get this over with." Danny followed them inside.

Pansy settled on one of the wingback chairs. Poppy set the wine on the floor and sat on the other wingback. Basil propped his hip on the sofa arm beside Lilly.

Danny pulled a kitchen chair beside Poppy and turned the back toward his family. He straddled the seat, the same position he chose whenever the need to lecture his children arose.

Lilly eyed her dad. "We're dying to find out the reason for the last-minute supper invitation."

"Danny won the lottery." Pansy's matter-of-fact comment spilled out without a hint of emotion.

Lilly's eyes widened. "You're kidding, right?"

"Not exactly." Danny propped his arms across the top of his chair. "I suspect you've all questioned why I never allowed any mention of my father in this house. It's time you understood the reason." He peered at Poppy, his brow furrowed as if he was mentally debating how much to say. "Fact is, I had a younger brother. His name was Bobby. I loved that kid. We spent hours together every day after I came home from school or after our latest nanny finished tutoring him. Our parents ignored my brother. Worse, our old man was too arrogant to admit he had a special son like Bobby."

Danny paused amid wide-eyed stares. "The day he turned fourteen our parents hosted a party for their rich friends. When Bobby crashed their event—believing he was the honored guest—the man he called Daddy rejected him publicly." Danny's voice cracked.

Poppy swallowed the pain attacking the back of her throat and placed her hand on his shoulder.

"Later that night...my brother took his own life."

Daisy and Lilly gasped.

Basil and Andy mumbled under their breath.

Pansy stared at Danny, her head tilted as if she was trying to figure out what he was talking about.

"Our parents worshiped wealth and status. Nothing else mattered." Danny lifted off the chair and dropped to one knee beside his sister-in-law. "You are the most special member of our family, Pansy, and we'd never do anything to hurt you. When I was growing up, I learned that too much money destroys families."

"Hold on." Lilly scooted to the edge of the sofa. "You're trying to tell us you don't want to claim your winnings, aren't you?"

"There's a lot more you need to understand." Danny repeated every detail Poppy had shared about his sisters.

Andy shook his head. "Talk about one screwed-up family."

"Curtis Butler's family is a mess, not ours." Lilly's brows pinched. "How much money are you planning to turn down, Dad?"

"The amount doesn't matter."

Lilly huffed. "Of course it matters."

Basil reached across Daisy and gripped Lilly's arm. "The ticket was a gift to Dad. The decision belongs to him, not to you or anyone else in this family."

Andy clasped his wife's hand. "Your brother's right, sugar pie. We need to respect your dad's decision."

Lilly sank back, her shoulders slumped forward. "If you ask me, turning down however much money you're talking about doesn't make a lick of sense."

Silence engulfed the moment until Danny lifted off his knees. "It makes sense because accepting more money than we all need to live a comfortable life is a curse I won't inflict on the people I love."

Pansy tugged her ball-cap visor to the side and peered up at her brother-in-law. "Money's not bad if it's used to do good things and help people."

Danny stared at her, seemingly speechless.

Lilly elbowed Andy. "Aunt Pansy understands."

Basil scratched his head.

Daisy steepled her fingers and pressed them to her lips as if suppressing a grin.

Poppy grabbed the wine and lifted off her chair. "I suggest we all go to the kitchen and enjoy supper as one happy family." She handed the bottles to Basil. "You pour while Pansy, Lilly, and I set food on the table. Daisy, go invite David to join us."

Grateful for her mom's take-charge move, Daisy dashed out to the front porch and across the lawn. She found David leaning back against his camper cradling the greenhouse cat. "Except for Pansy and Mom, our four-legged mousetrap rarely lets anyone touch him, much less pick him up. Maybe you should add *cat whisperer* to your resume."

The feline sprang from his arms and slipped under Danny's delivery truck.

"Seems my new avocation is short-lived. How'd your dad's revelation go?"

"There were two. The first was tough to hear." She shared his story about Bobby. "I can't imagine the guilt he's carried on his shoulders."

"No kidding. How'd the rest of your family react to his lottery-ticket rejection?"

"Everyone except Lilly seemed to come to grips with his decision." Daisy plucked cat hair off his shirt. "Until Aunt Pansy, the one person we didn't believe would understand, claimed that money wasn't bad if it was used for good."

"She's right."

"Her comment could tear our family apart."

"Maybe your dad will change his mind."

Daisy shook her head. "Not one chance in a million."

"Same thing you supposed about his ticket coming up a winner."

"That was random. Dad's decision is deliberate." She looped her arm around David's bicep as they headed toward the house. "At least we can count on Mom keeping everything under control tonight. Tomorrow is another story."

Chapter 38

Saturday morning, a bark outside Daisy's window jolted her from a dream bordering on a nightmare. A young boy dressed in a superman costume sitting on the floor in a dark attic watching cartoons on a tiny out-of-focus television. A noose dangled from the rafters over his head.

Daisy threw off her blanket and climbed out of bed. Did her dream and dark clouds threatening a storm foreshadow today's events? She donned her robe, tiptoed to the kitchen, and found her mom and aunt alone. "Am I the last one awake again?"

Her mom closed the refrigerator. "Unless David's sleeping in."

"I'm gonna write a new story." Pansy tapped her fingers on a detailed drawing of a storefront with Pansy's Bakery and Flower Shop artfully scribed across the window. "This one's about my new store and all the people who come in to buy cakes and flowers." She sprang to her feet, popped on a pink ball cap, and snatched a matching sweat jacket off the back of her chair. "It's time to go help Danny in the greenhouse." She scooted out back with Boots bounding behind her.

"Seems Dad's announcement didn't stifle Aunt Pansy's dream." Daisy's grumbling stomach sent her to a cabinet for a jar of peanut butter. "Maybe you could convince Dad to set up a little shop for her in the greenhouse."

Her mom set a fresh cup of coffee on the table. "You know he doesn't like strangers coming around."

Daisy dropped a slice of bread in the toaster. "He's turning down the money, so in a way he owes her."

"Maybe I can come up with enough money to rent one of those vacant stores in town for her."

"Even if you could, there's a lot more to opening a business than renting space."

Her mom collapsed onto her chair. "What a big mess one tiny little ticket has created."

"Tell me about it." Daisy spread peanut butter on her popped-up toast and took a bite.

Basil traipsed in from the back porch. "Glad you're finally awake, Daisy. When you finish breakfast, I want to run something by you."

"Must be important. You didn't call me noodle-noggin."

"The day's still young."

"Can you contain yourself until I shower and dress?"

"Yeah, meet me in my room." He spun and strode out.

A half hour later, Daisy entered her brother's private space and sat on the leather sling chair he'd bought at a garage sale years earlier. "What's up, knucklehead?"

"It's Lilly." Basil closed the door. "She tried to call you—"

"My phone's on silent."

"She wants us to meet at her house to talk about last night."

Daisy eyed her brother's high-school athletic trophies displayed in a bookcase. "I knew she wasn't about to accept Dad's decision. The question is where do you stand?"

"I was onboard until Aunt Pansy made that comment about doing good. Now, I don't know what to think."

Daisy trilled her lips. "In fewer than twenty-four hours, we've let money divide our family."

"I didn't say I wouldn't support Dad, but I'm not convinced he's making the right decision."

"If you as much as hint one little doubt to Lilly, she'll never come around."

"She might not anyway, especially if Andy backs her up."

"You know he will." Daisy's attention drifted to the family photo displayed on the bookshelf between a football and a baseball trophy. "We shouldn't tell Mom where we're going until after we talk to Lilly."

"She'll know something's up when she sees us driving off together."

"Maybe she won't notice." Basil pulled a jacket from his closet. "No need to keep stalling."

"I'll meet you at your Jeep." Daisy returned to the kitchen, relieved to find her mom gone. She rushed to her room and pulled on a jacket, then dashed out to the Jeep. "I hope I'm ready for this."

"You and me both." When Basil reached the end of the driveway and turned onto the road, drizzle deposited droplets on the windshield. By the time he parked in Lilly and Andy's driveway, they were in the midst of a downpour. "Do you want to wait a few minutes?"

"Is there an umbrella somewhere in here?"

"Nope."

"Guess Marines don't mind getting soaked." Daisy reached for the door handle. "Neither do attorneys." She dashed to the carport and brushed water droplets off her shoulders.

Basil raced close behind. "Remember the strategy we discussed?"

"Yeah. Listen before presenting the facts." She thumped his arm. "You'll make a great police officer."

Lilly stepped out from the back door. "Sorry about the weather."

"A little rain can't stop a soon-to-be cop and a lawyer." Daisy wiped her feet on the doormat, embraced her sister, and stepped into the eat-in kitchen. Basil followed.

"Thanks for coming." Andy gave them each a quick hug.

"Coffee's still hot." Lilly poured two cups, adding sugar and creamer to one. She handed them over. "This will take the chill off."

Daisy followed her sister into the living room and settled on the gray sectional sofa adorned with red and white throw pillows. She pointed to a seascape highlighted by a pale blue sky peeking between billowing clouds. "I like your painting."

Lilly chose to sit on the short end of the sofa. "My latest garage-sale find."

"Your sister has a good eye for bargains." Andy sat beside his wife.

Daisy smiled. "Mom taught us well."

Basil set his cup on the glass coffee table and dropped beside Daisy. "So, what's up?"

Lilly exchanged glances with Andy. "We stayed up late last night talking about Dad's decision...and, well...we believe not claiming the money is a huge mistake." She crossed her arms as if to ward off an anticipated squabble.

Daisy set her cup beside Basil's then leaned back. "We're listening."

"First off, the ticket was a gift. Which means turning it down dishonors Aunt Pansy. Then there's Mom. After everything she's lived through, she deserves to have an easy life. Maybe a bigger house, or at least new furniture and an updated kitchen."

Daisy pressed her lips tight to keep comments from spilling out.

"Andy and I want our children to have everything we didn't. Fancy vacations and a house with a pool." Lilly paused. "So, we came up with a plan Dad can live with. Starting with him giving each of us five million and keeping five for him and Mom. As Aunt Pansy said, 'money isn't bad if it's used for good.'" She lifted a sheet of paper off the end table. "We made a list of good things Dad can do with the rest of the money." She scooted forward and passed it to Daisy. "The thing is, we need you two to help us set Dad straight."

Daisy scanned the list then handed it to Basil. She swallowed the condescending comment begging to roll off her tongue. "You've obviously given this a lot of thought, and your suggestions make sense. The problem is, you haven't considered Dad's perspective."

"What perspective? That he's letting his messed-up family keep us from enjoying the good life?"

"Looks to me like you and Andy have a great marriage and everything you need to have a happy, fulfilling life."

Lilly glared at her. "Easy for you to say. You have two degrees and a huge salary, and you don't live in a rented house."

"You're absolutely right." Daisy tempered her harsh tone. "I live in a rented apartment not much bigger than this room."

"Then you should want the money."

"I hear what you're saying, Lilly, but this isn't about what any of us want."

"Daisy's right." Basil set the list down. "The question is whether we honor Dad and accept his decision."

Daisy nodded toward her brother-in-law. "You haven't told us your opinion, Andy."

He breathed deeply and slowly released the air. "I believe I know where everyone's coming from. As for me, I grew up with four brothers and two sisters in a house with three bedrooms and one bathroom. Mom stayed home while Dad did the best he could to put food on the table and clothes on our backs." Andy reached for Lilly's hand. "We want a big family, three or four kids. Lilly plans to quit her job and be a full-time mom, which means we'll need more income than my salary."

His tone challenged Daisy's resolve. She broke eye contact as her mind drifted to her dad's pained expression when he shared the details about Bobby. Maybe wealth had contributed to his brother's death. "You wanting the best for your family is understandable and honorable, Andy. But, we owe it to Dad and the memory of his brother to honor his wishes."

Lilly pointed to Basil. "Whose side are you on?"

"Out of respect for Dad, I'm not taking sides."

"Then I guess it's up to me and Andy to change his mind, or—"

Basil's eyes narrowed. "Or what?"

"Nothing." She pulled her hand from Andy's and bolted off the sofa. "Come with me, Daisy, I want your opinion on a color for the nursery."

Daisy's suspicion escalated as she followed her sister down the hall to a bedroom. While listening to Lilly carry on about a row of paint swatches taped to the wall, she came to one undeniable conclusion. The sudden distraction was meant to cover her sister's unintended utterance of the word *or*. She also knew her well enough not to engage in a useless probe. By the time they narrowed the color choices to three, Daisy understood what she had to do.

Chapter 39

Poppy's jaw tensed as she stuffed her phone in her pocket. The call could only mean one thing. The prospect of instant wealth had infected at least one of her children. She rushed from the greenhouse and sidestepped a puddle. Grass squished beneath her feet as she strode past Basil's Jeep and trekked to the back the porch. After slipping off her wet sneakers, she walked into the kitchen.

Daisy set her glass of lemonade on the table. "Some rainstorm."

Poppy gripped the back of her chair and eyed her daughter, then her son sitting beside his sister chomping on a bite of sandwich. How long would it take them to admit where they had gone? "Lilly called. She and Andy are bringing pizza for supper in two hours. Any idea why?"

Basil swallowed. "Lilly told you, didn't she?"

"That you and Daisy drove to their house this morning?" Poppy grabbed a bottle of water from the fridge before dropping onto her chair. "What did she want?"

Daisy exchanged glances with her brother. "They tried to convince us that Dad should take the money."

"And?"

Basil cleared his throat. "Daisy and I believe they're misguided."

At least two of her children still respected their father. "What should your dad and I expect when they show up tonight?"

"Something akin to a closing argument from a defense attorney." Daisy explained Lilly's reasoning and her do-good list.

"Danny's right." Poppy twisted the cap off her water bottle. "Money tears families apart."

Basil pushed his plate aside. "What are you going to do, Mom?"

"One thing's certain." She locked eyes with him. "I won't let them ambush your father."

"Do you want me to call and tell them not to come?"

Poppy shook her head. "We need to deal with this before it gets out of hand. I don't want them to confuse or upset Pansy. I know it's a lot to ask, Basil, but will you take her somewhere and treat her to supper?"

"Aunt-sitting again?" He chuckled. "What a way for a good-looking, eligible bachelor to spend Saturday night."

"You're a good son." She eyed Daisy. "You and I will deal with your sister and brother-in-law."

"How do you suppose Dad will react?"

"I know what he won't do. When you three were growing up, no matter how much you misbehaved, he never once raised his voice."

"He didn't need to." Basil scoffed. "His you're-in-a-heap-of-trouble glare was enough to set us straight."

"Because you and your sisters never did anything to break his heart." Poppy took a long sip of water. "When I tell him what Lilly is up to, chances are he won't set foot in the house until she and Andy leave."

"Who can blame him?" Basil popped up. "I'll find Aunt Pansy, take her on a long drive, and stop at a Cracker Barrel. She'll spend hours shopping for a treasure to add to her collection." He waved over his shoulder while meandering out the back door.

Daisy caught her mom's eye. "I'm sorry Basil and I didn't tell you about Lilly's call before we left."

"You meant well. Invite David to join us for pizza. His presence might keep Lilly in check." Poppy took a long sip, then capped her water bottle. "It's time to break the news to your dad." She trudged to the porch, dropped onto a bench, and pulled on a pair of rubber boots. Two weeks ago life was predictable. Her fingers massaged her temples as the weight of potential consequences to her family pressed down on her like a hundred-pound rock. The urge to retreat to her room, crawl into bed, and pull the covers over her head loomed large. Somehow she forced her legs to lift her off the bench and carry her to the steps. Outside, a patch of blue sky peeked through the gray clouds. Maybe it was a sign.

Ten feet from the greenhouse, her son opened the door. Pansy rushed past him, her face flush with excitement. "Basil's taking me to Cracker Barrel. Want me to bring you something?"

"You go and have a good time, sweetie."

"I gotta go get my money." Pansy dashed through the puddle sending a spray of muddy water splattering Poppy's boot-clad feet. Boots followed his mistress straight through the water.

"Sorry about the splash." Basil walked around the puddle. "Dad's all the way in the back. He doesn't know what we're up to."

"Thank you, honey. I'll pay you back if you need to subsidize Pansy's treasure hunt."

"No need. I'm living rent free 'til after New Year's." He leaned down and kissed her cheek. "Call me when it's safe to head back home."

"I will." She entered the greenhouse, headed up the center aisle, and found Danny loading laurels onto a cart. "Monday delivery?"

"Eight a.m. New subdivision."

She pinched a yellow leaf off a bush. "I need to tell you something."

He hoisted a plant onto the last vacant spot, removed his cap, and swiped his hand across his forehead. "Go ahead."

"About Lilly and Andy."

"Did something happen to them?" His tone hinted of alarm.

"Not exactly. I mean no." She struggled to find the right words.

His brows pinched.

As Poppy let the morning's events pour out, Danny's expression morphed from concern to anger. When she finished, he spun away and headed toward the exit. She followed, keeping her distance. Her heart sank as she watched him storm out, climb into the family truck, and drive away. She knew in the depth of her soul that his middle child's underhanded action had broken his heart.

Ten minutes before five o'clock, footsteps on the back porch announced her sister and brother-in-law's arrival. Daisy's eyes shifted from David to her mom sitting across the table. "Are you ready?"

"I don't have a choice."

"We're here." Lilly strolled in from the back porch. "I hope everyone's hungry." Andy followed carrying a large pizza box. "Thanks for turning the oven on, Mom. This will warm up in a flash."

Daisy sniffed the pepperoni and cheese aromas wafting across the kitchen and stared at her sister. Had she failed to notice that Basil's Jeep and the family truck were missing?

Andy slid the box into the oven then leaned back against the counter. Lilly hung her purse on the back of a chair and sat beside her mom. "When are Dad and Basil coming in?" She pointed to David. "Is he staying?"

"They're not coming and, yes, David's staying."

Lilly waggled her finger at Daisy. "You and Basil squealed, didn't you?"

"We told Mom."

"And I told your father, which is why he isn't here."

Lilly shrugged then faced her mom. "Maybe that's for the best. That is, if you're willing to hear what I have to say."

"I'm listening."

Lilly ticked off the reasons she and Andy wanted her dad to claim the winning ticket. When finished, she removed a sheet of paper from her purse, unfolded it, and placed it on the table. "This is a list of ways Dad can use the money he doesn't keep."

Her mom stared at the paper. "Have you even tried to understand your dad's decision?"

"You mean his crazy notion about money destroying families?"

She stared at Lilly. "Please don't take this the wrong way, honey. But this list and you and Andy showing up to convince me to take your side is proof you dad is right."

Lilly huffed and turned toward David. "You're an outsider. What's your opinion?"

"I did a little research." He leaned forward. "Are you aware that a large percentage of lottery winners burn through their money and go broke in fewer than five years?"

"Because they're fools." Lilly placed her hand on her mom's arm. "You have to convince Dad to take the money. For your grandchildren's sake?"

"Playing the grandparent card won't work." She pulled her arm away. "Your father doesn't want the money for good reasons. Which means *everyone* in our family needs to respect his decision."

"If you refuse to talk to him, I will."

"Don't you see what's happening?" Her mom's tone hinted of disappointment. "Money we don't have is already pitting you against your own family."

"Andy and I want what's best for you and us."

"It's time you both accept reality. Unless your father changes his mind—on his own—this subject is closed." She stood and walked out of the kitchen.

"This is your fault, Daisy. If you hadn't blabbed, she might have listened to reason." Lilly bolted from her chair and headed straight to the hutch. "Where is it?" She opened every drawer and slammed each shut before spinning toward the table. Her eyes shot daggers at Daisy. "You moved the tin with all the lottery tickets, didn't you?"

"When you muttered the word *or* this morning, I hoped you didn't mean you'd go behind our backs. Now I know my hunch was right. I love you. Lilly, and I always will. But I won't let you destroy our family. The tin is where you'll never find it."

"You had no right."

"The ticket doesn't belong to you."

Lilly's nostrils flared. "It doesn't belong to you either." She yanked her purse off the chair and stormed out the back door.

"Try to understand." Andy pushed away from the counter. "The idea of being rich has your sister all messed up."

Daisy released a heavy sigh. "This lottery debacle is messing with all of us."

"Given enough time, she'll figure out what's important."

"I hope we all will before it's too late," Daisy murmured as her brother-in-law walked out.

"Smart move hiding that tin, Counselor." David nudged Daisy. "You prevented Lilly from committing a crime."

"A tactic I wish wasn't necessary." Her eyebrows gathered in as her shoulder's pulled low. "Chances are I'll face more unpleasant tasks before this all blows over."

Chapter 40

S andwiched between David and Basil on the last church pew, Daisy folded her hands in her lap. Her mind wandered from the pastor's message to her dad's pained expression when he heard how Lilly had stormed out of the kitchen. The way he refused to speak and headed straight to the bedroom hinted that his middle child had broken his heart. Daisy peered around her brother at her mom's pinched expression. A clear indication her mind was focused on her husband skipping his Sunday-morning newspaper-reading routine to seek refuge in the greenhouse. Maybe she should talk to her dad. Except she had no idea what to say.

A toddler two rows up propped her chin and fingers on the back of the pew. Daisy crinkled her nose and winked. The child spread her hands across her face and peeked through her fingers. Daisy played along until the girl's onset of giggles compelled her mother to lift her onto her lap.

Basil nudged his sister and leaned close. "Does playing peek-a-boo reflect your opinion about the message?"

The toddler peered over her mother's shoulder. Daisy made a silly face, triggering another nose-scrunching giggle.

David held his hand in front of his mouth. "Your sister's practicing her new role as Aunt Daisy."

"You're both wrong," Daisy whispered. "I'm misbehaving to prove corporate attorneys are full of mischief."

A woman sitting at the end of the toddler's row peered over her shoulder. She pressed a finger to her lips and released an audible shush. Daisy pressed her lips together to suppress a laugh and attempted to focus on the message.

Ten more minutes passed before the pastor stepped away from the podium, signaling the final song and the Butler family's exit cue. On the front sidewalk, Daisy and David lagged behind. He gripped her elbow. "Does your family always escape before the service ends, or only when one of you misbehaves?"

"Old habit from way back." She kept her voice low. "Which is also why Mom is taking us miles out of the way for ice cream and lunch."

"To keep Pansy from going to Willy's and leaking news about the winning ticket?"

"You catch on fast."

"Maybe your family needs to keep a guy like me around full-time."

"Would you like me to draw up adoption papers for Mom and Dad, or do you have something else in mind?"

Basil spun around and motioned them to get a move on.

David chuckled. "Seems Marines aren't fond of anyone bringing up the rear."

Daisy rolled her eyes. "No kidding." She and David stepped up their pace and slid onto the truck's back seat beside Basil. During the drive her brother shared hilarious and obviously embellished-to-the-hilt stories about his military shenanigans. He kept Pansy in stitches and the topic of lottery tickets and money off the table. His stories continued during lunch.

After devouring burgers, fries, and shakes, David provided the entertainment during their ride home with his own humorous tales.

The moment Daisy's mom parked in their driveway, she, Pansy, and Basil headed to the back porch. David climbed out and held the passenger door open for Daisy. "I've written the first chapter about your grandmother's case. Do you have time to read it?"

"Absolutely."

He escorted her to his camper. "Will your parents mind if you come inside?"

"They're both too preoccupied to notice. My brother's another story."

"I'm up for a good ribbing." He opened the door.

Daisy climbed into the small space which hinted of lemon and turned in a slow circle. "Compact living quarters. Uncluttered and clean."

"Are you surprised?"

"I remember Basil's room before he enlisted. It gave new meaning to 'mess hall.'" She ran her fingers along the smooth dinette table. "Am I the first female you've invited into your private sanctum?"

"The one and only." He pointed to his laptop lying on the table beside a printer. "You're also the first person other than an editor I've asked to read a work in progress."

"Do you want my opinion or validation?"

"Candid feedback."

"From an attorney?"

David placed his hand on her arm. "From a woman I trust."

Daisy's skin tingled beneath his touch. "I'll do my best." She slid onto the bench.

He sat across from her, booted his laptop, and turned the screen toward her.

She read the first paragraph. With each new sentence her heartbeat accelerated. At the end of the chapter, Daisy pressed her hand to her chest. Her eyes met David's. "Your words are far beyond anything I could ever have expected. The way you portray Mom and Aunt Pansy—" She spoke past the lump in her throat. "You reached into their souls and discovered the depth of their devotion and beauty."

"My story is about far more than a mysterious disappearance. I want to touch readers' hearts and encourage them to see beyond the surface to who people are at the core."

"I had no idea you're such a brilliant writer."

A smile lit his face. "Amazing people bring out the best."

Should she ask him again if he had something else in mind?

David nodded toward the window. "Looks like we have company."

Basil knocked on the open door. "Sorry for interrupting."

Daisy's brows rose. "My brother has a habit of showing up at the most inconvenient moments."

"Not my fault, noodle-noggin. You can blame the other guy."

"What other guy?" Daisy slid off the bench.

"The one on the front porch looking for you."

"Did one of my high-school boyfriends find out I'm home?"

"Never seen him before. He looks like some FBI or CIA dude." Basil grinned. "Are you sure your lawyer gig isn't a cover for your double-agent status?"

David laughed. "If she was a double agent, she'd put all those James Bond chicks to shame."

"At least I have two big guys to protect me from the mysterious man." Flanked by a Marine and an investigative journalist, Daisy headed down the driveway toward a white SUV. "My guess is this mystery man is a salesman looking to meet his Sunday quota."

David nodded. "Or a kid claiming to sell magazines to put himself through college."

"Better yet." Basil nudged Daisy. "He's some religious nut who's come to save the heathen New York lawyer."

"Very funny." Daisy's curiosity piqued as they reached the end of the house and cut across the lawn.

The tall man standing on the porch with Pansy spun toward them.

Daisy gasped. Her heart jumped to her throat.

The man climbed down the steps and stopped three feet in front of her.

She sensed the blood draining from her face. "What are you doing here?"

"I left a dozen messages—"

"My phone's turned off for the weekend."

Basil elbowed her. "You obviously know this guy."

Daisy breathed deeply to slow her pounding pulse. "Basil, David Lambert, meet Michael Warner."

Pansy skipped down the steps and tugged on Michael's sleeve. "Are you Daisy's special friend, too?"

He stared at Pansy as if she'd grown a third eye and he'd forgotten how to talk.

"What's going on out here?" Her dad's voice boomed from behind.

Daisy spun in his direction. "Michael is one of the law firm partners, Dad."

His eyes narrowed as he planted his feet between Daisy and the newcomer. "You came all the way from New York to do what?"

Michael faced her dad eye to eye. "Discuss a case with your daughter."

"On Sunday?"

Daisy tapped his shoulder. "It's okay, Dad. He tried reaching me. I didn't respond."

"Excuse us a moment, young man." Her dad grasped Daisy's elbow and led her out of earshot. "Do you know why he showed up?"

She swallowed the bitter taste of regret assaulting her throat. "I think I do."

"Regardless of the consequences, you need to do what's right and level with him."

"You're right, Dad."

"Okay then, I'll leave you to it." He headed back toward the greenhouse.

Daisy gathered her courage, returned to the gathering in the front yard, and flashed her best I'm-the-lawyer-in-charge expression. "If y'all don't mind, Michael and I need a few minutes alone."

Basil touched her arm. "We're here if you need us."

"Thanks, but I'm fine." She slid her hand around Michael's bicep and led him toward the tree line while struggling to force the colliding emotions cluttering her brain into submission. "I'm sorry you had to come all this way."

"I thought something might have happened to you."

Was he worried about losing Curtis Butler's business, or did he show up because he cared about her? "I simply wanted to spend the weekend enjoying my family."

He placed his hand over hers. "I drove by twice before turning onto the driveway. Your family's home is not what I expected."

Daisy pulled her hand away. "Because it doesn't have an insane number of bathrooms?" She cringed at her glib, verbal slap. "I'm sorry, Michael. I don't mean to come across as disrespectful. It's just, you're the last person I imagined would show up on our front lawn, and I had no idea the firm expected a senior associate to remain on call twenty-four seven."

"Fair enough." He remained silent for a long moment. "When you interviewed for a position with our firm, the partners were split between hiring a Yale and a Stanford grad—both men had higher honors and more credentials than you brought. I convinced them you were the better choice."

"Because Curtis Butler is my grandfather?"

"Every attorney we hire is selected for what they bring to the firm. Sometimes it boils down to connections."

Was that all she meant to him? "What about the invitations to your mother's fundraising event and her New Year's Eve party? Were they motivated by my connections?"

"The fundraiser was my idea. Mother extended the New Year's invitation on her own."

Daisy stopped beside the oak tree she and David had stood under and eyed her family's humble home. Everyone except David and her dad remained on the front porch. At least she and Michael were too far away for anyone to hear their conversation. Especially since she owed him the truth.

How could she explain without placing her career and reputation in jeopardy? No need to worry about that now. Her deception had driven her way beyond any safety zone. "You need to know that my dad hasn't spoken to his father for more than three decades."

Michael stared at her. "Is that the reason you've failed to connect with Curtis?"

Heat inched from Daisy's neck to her ears. "Truth is...I've never met him, and chances are he didn't know I existed until I showed up at his ranch. He still might not know."

Michael's eyes narrowed. "Are you telling me you lied during your interview?"

"I let assumptions stand."

"Typical attorney tactic."

"For courtrooms, not job interviews." Surprised the admission lifted a weight off her shoulders, Daisy faced him. "I have a question. Was your cappuccino bungle an accident or a slick-lawyer maneuver to invite me to dinner?"

"A lucky break." He locked eyes with her. "I have feelings for you, Daisy."

Her mind spun back to breakfast in his parents' morning room. "I doubt your mother would approve of her son dating a fraud whose family lives in a little house in the middle of nowhere."

"She would if you delivered a big win for the firm."

Success obviously meant everything to the Warner family. "What happens if I fail, Michael?"

"You won't. Besides other than my pilot, no one knows I flew down. So I'll cover for you until you come through."

"That's more than I deserve."

He touched her arm. "Believe me, you're worth saving."

"Thank you for the vote of confidence." She owed him big time. "When is your return flight?"

"Whenever I show up at the airport. The firm's jet is on standby."

Lifestyle of the rich. "Why don't you stay for supper and see how the other ninety percent lives?"

"Are grits on the menu?"

Daisy managed a smile. "At our house that delicacy is strictly breakfast fare."

"Well then, I'd best stay and discover what southerners consider an appropriate dinner."

"Down here we call it supper."

"Sorry. I neglected to bone up on southern terms. What's an appropriate supper menu?"

"You'll love Aunt Pansy's sweet-potato pie. Oh, and humor her if she calls you my boyfriend. She's special."

"Understood."

"Good. Now it's time for you to officially meet my family."

"Lead the way."

They returned to the front porch. "We need to set another place at the table, Mom. Michael's joining us for supper."

"Welcome to our home, Michael."

"Thank you, Mrs. Butler."

"Please call me Poppy."

Pansy tugged on Michael's sleeve. "Do you live in New York?"

"Smack dab in the middle of the city."

"Danny won the big lottery, but it's a secret."

Daisy cringed. She hadn't intended to reveal that bit of news.

Michael winked at Pansy. "I promise I won't tell a soul."

"Do you wanna see the fancy New York hat Daisy bought me?"

"I'd love to."

Michael peered over his shoulder as Pansy pulled him to the front door. "Seems this pretty lady has a captive audience."

The moment they disappeared from view and their mom stepped inside, Basil gripped Daisy's arm. "Is everything okay?"

"I told him the truth."

"Are you still a big-time New York lawyer."

"At least for the time being. Where's David?"

"Back at his camper. He claimed he had work to do and would talk to you tomorrow morning." Basil knuckle thumped Daisy's arm. "My guess is he's jealous of the new guy."

"The new guy happens to be my boss—in a sense anyway."

"What does that mean?"

"He's keeping the truth about my nonexistent relationship with Curtis under his belt until I land the account."

"In that case, he's one of the good guys."

Much to Daisy's surprise, Michael fit in with her family far better than she had imagined. During supper he engaged in lively conversation with Basil and her dad and charmed her mom and Pansy with compliments about the meal. Following two hours of laughter and hardy appetites, he patted his belly. "I must say, Poppy, that was one fine supper. And Pansy, your sweet-potato pie is the best I've ever tasted."

Daisy suppressed a giggle. Probably the only one he'd ever tasted.

Pansy's face beamed. "I'm gonna open a bakery in town. Do you wanna stay here tonight and sleep on the sofa? Sometimes Danny sleeps there."

"Thank you for the invitation, but I need to head back to New York tonight." Michael pushed up and faced Danny. "Do you mind if I steal your daughter for a few more minutes?"

Her dad stood. "You stayed for supper, so we trust you."

Michael extended his hand to the man of the house. "It was a pleasure to meet you and your family, sir."

After Michael bid everyone goodbye, Daisy escorted him through the house and out to the front yard. "I'm glad you joined us."

"Most fun I've had during a family dinner—I mean, supper, in a long time."

"I'm guessing you've changed my family's perception of northerners and big-city lawyers."

He laughed. "They definitely changed my perspective of southerners."

When they reached his car, Michael faced Daisy. "I'm counting on you to keep me updated on the Curtis issue."

"I won't let you or the firm down."

"Plus, I'm still planning to escort you to Mother's New Year's Eve extravaganza." Michael kissed her cheek then slid into the SUV. "Remember to turn your phone back on in the morning."

"I promise." Daisy waited for Michael to pull onto the main road before heading back to the porch. Grateful no one had come outside, she dropped onto a rocker. Confusion over her feelings for Michael and David played havoc with her emotions. Somehow she had to push her relationship dilemma aside and do whatever it took to deliver Curtis's business empire to the Warner firm.

Chapter 41

Following hours of pacing and mental brainstorming, Daisy faced Monday afternoon riddled with apprehension. Cynthia Evans continued to refuse her phone calls. Showing up at the ranch without an invitation a third time could doom any chance to fulfill her obligation to Michael and the firm. Daisy heaved a heavy sigh. Her pricey law degree hadn't helped her devise a single alternative approach.

She trudged to the front-room window hoping a change of scenery would trigger something. Anything. A squirrel perched on the porch railing, clutching an acorn in its front paws. Maybe she should mail Cynthia a certified letter summarizing the law firm's proposal. Fat chance of that working, even if the woman bothered to open it.

A van eased up the gravel driveway. The second unexpected visitor in twenty-four hours. Daisy rushed outside. As she closed the distance, the side door displaying a courier-service logo slid open. A uniformed man rounded the vehicle. "Mrs. Poppy Butler?"

"I'm her daughter."

He reached into the van and removed an elaborate floral arrangement. "Will you accept this for your mother?"

"Yes, of course."

He placed the heavy cut-glass vase in her hands before returning to the driver's side and backing down the driveway.

Daisy carried the arrangement into the kitchen. The vase didn't feel like cheap floral-shop glass. She lifted the flowers overhead. A Waterford logo was etched on the bottom. Definitely not a throwaway.

Her mom strolled in and tossed her straw hat on the table. "Who sent you the gorgeous flowers?"

"They're not for me." Daisy read the name on the gift-card envelope then handed it over. "It seems you have a secret admirer."

"They couldn't be from your dad. He'd never splurge on such an elaborate arrangement." Her mom opened the envelope and removed the card. "Oh my. It's from Michael thanking me for my hospitality and a delicious home-cooked meal." She sniffed a pink rose. "This must have cost him a fortune, and the vase looks expensive."

Should she tell her mom how expensive? "It cost a lot more than the flowers."

"Your Michael is a generous young man."

My Michael? Had he replaced David on her mom's 'who's the best man for Daisy' list?

Her mom's phone pinged. She grabbed it off the counter. "A text from Ginny."

"Aletha's daughter?"

"Says she has information about the key and wants the three of us to meet at her house. Oh my gosh, maybe we're close to a breakthrough in Mama's case."

"Tell her we're on our way. I'll find David and meet you at my car." Daisy dashed out back and slowed her pace as she closed the distance to his camper. How would he react to seeing her for the first time since Michael showed up?

He met her at his door. "Hey, what's up?"

"Ginny wants to meet with us." Daisy relayed the message.

"She could have a missing clue." He grabbed his satchel and escorted Daisy to her car. "Who sent the flowers?"

"Michael—."

"The guy moves fast."

Why that comment? "He sent them to Mom, thanking her for supper."

"Nice touch." David slid onto the truck's back seat.

Daisy climbed behind the steering wheel.

Her mom peered over her shoulder. "We missed you last night."

"Sorry I had to beg off. When the mood strikes, authors have to take action. I began chapter two."

Daisy backed out of her parking space and caught David's expression in the rearview mirror. Maybe Basil had been right about him being jealous.

Twenty minutes after turning onto the road fronting her family's property, Daisy parked in the driveway beside Ginny's white cottage. She met them on her front stoop. "Welcome back." She held the front door open and pointed to the living room. "Make yourselves comfortable. I'll join you in a jiffy."

Daisy followed her mom into the compact living room and settled beside her on a floral sofa. "This seems more like a social call than a business meeting."

"It's both, honey." She patted Daisy's hand.

"Your mom's right." David opted for a side chair and pulled his notepad from his satchel before setting it on the floor.

Vanilla and cinnamon aromas floated around Ginny as she strolled in and set a tray on the coffee table. She handed the plate of sugar cookies to Daisy's mom. "Do you recognize those?"

"The same cookies Aletha brought to our house back in the day?"

"You remember. How she loved to bake. Cookies, cakes, pies. If my dad hadn't walked a couple miles every day, he would've gained a ton of weight."

"Smart man." Daisy's mom passed the plate. "Pansy still talks about those cookies."

Daisy pressed her lips tight to suppress her attorney instincts and resist firing questions at Ginny. She lifted a cookie and handed the plate to David.

He bit into a cookie. "Delicious."

"Mother's special recipe."

"Even better than my mother's, and that's saying a lot." David set the plate on the coffee table.

Ginny handed him a cup. "You must try my hot cinnamon tea."

David sipped. "Also delicious."

"It was my sweet husband's favorite afternoon pick-me-up. God rest his soul." Ginny pressed her palms together. "Don't you just love this time of year? Cooler weather. Pretty fall colors."

Daisy fidgeted. How long would the chitchat drag on before David transitioned into investigative journalist mode? Maybe he expected her to make the first move?

"I could have shared my news over the phone, but these days I have so few visitors." Ginny laced her fingers in her lap. "I visited Mother yesterday."

Finally, we get to the point. Daisy scooted to the edge of the sofa. "How was she?"

"Better than most days. When I told her about the key you'd found, she slipped into one of her lucid moments. She remembered taking Rose to open a bank account and rent a safe-deposit box."

"That's great news." David opened his notepad. "Did she say which bank or what Rose put in the box?"

"Her mind drifted away before I had a chance to ask."

"At least she confirmed our suspicions about the key." He clicked his pen. "Where did your mom bank?"

"Same one where I bank. But there's no use checking. I already called. They never had an account under Rose Fowler's name."

Daisy reached for a teacup. "Maybe Aletha used Mom or Aunt Pansy's name."

"Same thing I figured, so I asked. No accounts or safe-deposit boxes in their names either."

"Contacting the bank was a smart move." David anchored his pen behind his ear. "You have the instincts for excellent investigative work, Ginny."

"Do you really think I do?"

"Absolutely."

Her face beamed. "Well then, the next time I visit Mother, I'll ask more questions about Rose. Maybe a few more memories will break through."

They remained for another hour eating cookies, sipping tea and sharing memories about Aletha and Rose. After their hostess escorted them to the car and invited them to come back any time, Daisy backed down the driveway. "It won't be easy finding out where my grandmother had an account. Banks don't give out private information."

"True." David leaned forward. "I have a question for you, Poppy."

Daisy's mom twisted toward the back seat. "What do you want to know?"

"Do you have power of attorney for your mom?"

"Hmm. I believe I do. Something else Aletha made happen way back."

David snapped his fingers. "That's our ticket to discovering which bank."

Daisy glanced in the rearview mirror and caught David's eye. "Even if we do manage to find out, we have one big problem." Daisy's eyes returned to the road. "At some point dormant accounts are considered unclaimed property and are turned over to the state. Which could be a huge stumbling block."

The three fell silent until Daisy pulled into Willy's for gas. A crowd gathered on the sidewalk in front of the thrift store.

"Oh dear, I hope nothing happened to Maddie or Betty." Her mom dashed across the street while David filled the tank. Daisy stood beside the car observing the crowd's animated gestures. "Something big is going on."

Moments after David capped the tank, her mom rushed back. "Everyone's debating whether old Agnes floated up or dropped down."

"What are you talking about, Mom?"

"You know, heaven or the other place. Yesterday she passed over to wherever she'll spend eternity. Her sons arrived this morning to break the news and put her house on the market. I doubt anyone around here will miss her."

"I suppose we'll never discover what turned her into such an unlikable human being." Daisy's eyes drifted to the vacant storefronts. "Maybe her passing will open the door for some much-needed change around here."

Chapter 42

Tuesday afternoon, Poppy ended another fruitless phone call. "If you ask me, we've spent hours chasing a wild goose." She scooted her chair away from the kitchen table and rolled her head from side to side. Today's failure piling on to her family's conflict over a lottery ticket had triggered a massive tension headache.

David tapped the list he'd printed. "We've only contacted a third of the banks within a fifty mile range, which means that goose is still on the loose."

"If it even exists." Poppy stood and removed an aspirin bottle from the cabinet. "It's possible Aletha's lucid moment was nothing more than her imagination gone wild."

"Except for this." Daisy lifted the mystery key off the table. "Tangible evidence a safe-deposit box actually exists or at least existed."

"One thing's certain. Investigative work takes a whole lot of patience." Poppy plucked her water off the table and swallowed two aspirin.

David leaned back and laced his fingers behind his neck. "We could stop and pick back up in the morning."

"Five more calls." Poppy set down her glass. "Then we'll call it quits."

The back door swung open. Lilly slogged in.

Her middle child's pinched expression sent needles of anxiety racing up Poppy's spine. "I'm surprised to see you back here so soon."

"You mean after I stormed out like a bratty teenager?" Lilly set a gift bag on the table and dropped onto Pansy's chair.

"In case you're wondering." Daisy tapped her fingers on the table. "The tin is still tucked away."

"That's not why I'm here." Lilly's shoulders curled forward, her eyes cast downward. "Yesterday Andy and I had a terrible argument over the lottery ticket. I couldn't believe it when he took Dad's side. He made me so mad I stormed out and drove for hours. Somehow I ended up on Tybee Island. I remembered the time Daisy, Basil, and I tied truck inner tubes together and floated in the surf. We made up stories about being lost at sea and landing on an abandoned island."

Poppy scooted her chair closer to Lilly and stroked her arm.

Lilly splayed her left hand and stroked her engagement ring. "That beach was where Andy and I spent our third date. The night I came home way after midnight and Dad met me on the front porch."

Poppy managed a smile. "Your dad was more worried than angry."

"Not too worried to ground me for two weeks. Anyway, that night Andy kissed me for the first time. I was only seventeen, yet somehow I knew we'd be together forever. Two years later we were married. Those memories reminded me how much we love each other." Lilly's eyes reddened. "That's when I realized that family is more important than money, and dishonoring Dad was wrong."

Daisy popped up and hugged her sister's neck. "I knew you'd come around."

"If we'd made a bet, I would've wagered against me."

"We'll blame that on your middle-child stubborn streak." Daisy pulled her arms away. "You need to talk to dad."

"I know."

"Do you want me to go with you?"

"So you can hold my hand like you did when I had to apologize for giving that big bully a black eye?"

Daisy laughed. "A playground punch from a seven-year-old girl five inches shorter and a year younger shocked the dickens out of that kid."

"And set him straight."

"At least your apology to Dad is for a metaphorical punch."

"Yeah, but way more painful for me." Lilly pushed off Pansy's chair and grabbed the bag. "Will you go with me, Mom, for moral support?"

"Of course, I will, honey."

Poppy linked arms with her daughter as they walked across the back porch and down the steps. Halfway to the greenhouse, she stopped and faced Lilly. "I want you to know how proud you've made me, and what an amazing mother I know you'll be."

Lilly sniffled. "You and dad taught me what family loyalty is all about. I just took a little detour in the wrong direction."

"At some point we all make wrong turns, honey. It's the course corrections that matter." Poppy brushed a lock of hair away from Lilly's face. "Are you ready?"

"As I'll ever be."

Inside, Basil and Pansy were playing with Boots at the far end of the building while Danny tended plants off to the side. Poppy held her daughter's hand as they meandered between rows of winter annuals.

Danny turned in their direction.

Lilly moved close. "Do you have a minute, Dad?" Her voice faltered.

His eyes shifted from Poppy to his daughter. He set his shovel aside.

Tears spilled down Lilly's cheek. "I'm so sorry I disrespected you, Dad. Will you forgive me?"

The man of few words who seldom displayed his feelings opened his arms wide.

His daughter rushed to him.

He folded his arms around her. "You're forgiven, sweetheart."

"Thank you." Lilly sniffled. "I brought you a present."

"Your apology was more than enough." He released her.

"Don't worry, it didn't cost too much." She handed him the bag.

Danny opened it and removed a trowel.

"Read the inscription on the handle."

"*My Dad. My hero who nurtures our family with love.*" Danny swallowed. "I'll cherish this forever."

Poppy pressed her palms together and touched her fingertips to her lips. Happy tears pooled and cascaded down her cheeks. Her daughter and her husband had made their family whole again.

Daisy slumped back in her chair. "Lilly's turnaround is a welcome relief."

David pushed his bank list aside. "It's also a testimony to how well your mom and dad raised you and your siblings."

"They're amazing parents, especially considering all the challenges they faced." She gazed at his profile, the way his hair brushed his collar. His muscular shoulders and arms. "Do you mind if I ask you something?"

"Depends." He propped his elbow on the table, leaned his head on his knuckles, and faced her. "Is it a loaded question?"

"Nope."

"In that case, shoot."

Relieved by his half grin, she tilted her head. "What's the real reason you didn't join us for supper Sunday night?"

"Are you questioning my next-chapter explanation, Counselor?"

"Attorneys worth their salt always question motives."

"Do you have your own theory about my reason?"

Daisy inched closer to David. "My brother claimed you weren't wild about spending time around the new guy."

"Is that your way of telling me Basil thought I was jealous?"

"His words, not mine."

"Typical guy."

"You're not going to answer, are you?"

"Hey, I'm still a new guy, so, nope."

"Smart move."

David winked. "Yep."

Chapter 43

A dull ache attacked the base of Daisy's skull as David drew a line through another name on their list. Two o'clock Wednesday afternoon and they had eliminated all the major banks plus half the smaller ones. Worse, she hadn't devised a single viable plan to connect with Curtis. Her mom's sagging shoulders and deflated tone during the last few calls made it clear she was close to calling it quits.

Pansy wandered into the kitchen and set a basket of potatoes from their garden on the counter. Boots sprawled on the floor beside her chair. "Did you find the bank box?"

David leaned back and laced his fingers behind his neck. "We're still working on it."

"When can we go back to the thrift store?" Pansy sniffed a rose in Michael's floral arrangement. "I wanna buy some pretty vases for my bakery and flower shop."

Daisy eyed her mom. How would she respond considering Pansy remained under the illusion that her brother-in-law planned to claim his winning birthday gift?

"Know what I'm thinking, sweetie?"

"You like your pretty flowers?"

"Besides that." Poppy straightened her back. "Lots of items go on sale after Christmas, so why don't we wait until January?"

Pansy shrugged. "Okay."

Delay the inevitable—an appropriate decision, at least for the moment. Daisy stared at her phone lying facedown on the table. She'd promised to keep Michael informed. Tomorrow she'd have to come up with something to report.

Pansy grabbed a bottle of water from the fridge. "Come on, Boots, we gotta go help Danny." Her loyal companion followed her to the back porch.

David tapped his list and nodded toward Daisy's mom. "Are you up to a couple more calls, or do you want to call it a day?"

"What I want is for this to end with some good news, which will never happen if we quit. What's next on the list?"

"You're a trooper. Here's the next victim."

Poppy pressed the number David called out. A woman answered and transferred the call to the manager who introduced herself as Ms. Campbell. Poppy launched into her well-rehearsed spiel lacking any semblance of enthusiasm. "We hope you can help us."

"Perhaps I can." The woman placed the call on hold.

Poppy tapped her fingers to the beat of the recorded music. "At least she didn't brush me off."

Minutes passed. The music stopped. "Good news, Mrs. Butler. Ms. Fowler has a savings account with us."

Poppy's mouth fell open. "Are you serious? I mean how is that possible?"

"A twenty-dollar cash deposit was made every January, although the last deposit was more than a year ago. Good thing you called. The account was a few months away from being declared as unclaimed funds."

Poppy's brows pinched. "Does she also have a safe-deposit box?"

"She does. All she needs to gain access is to come in and bring her key."

"We might have a little problem."

Daisy pulled the phone close. "Ms. Campbell, I'm Daisy Butler, Mrs. Butler's daughter as well as her attorney. Here's the situation." She explained Rose's disappearance, the key, and the reason a death certificate didn't exist. "We believe the safe-deposit box holds evidence that could lead to solving this case."

"I see." The woman paused for a long moment. "Come in, and I'll see what I can do."

"We're on our way." Daisy ended the call, shouldered her purse, and grabbed her mom's power-of-attorney document. Forty minutes later she parked in the bank's lot and peered over her shoulder at David. "Do you want to go in with us?"

"No point raising suspicion. I'll wait out here."

Daisy tossed him her keys. "In case you need them."

Inside the bank, Ms. Campbell invited them into her office. She pointed to a pair of chairs facing her desk. "Please, have a seat."

"Thank you for agreeing to see us." Daisy handed over the POA and a business card.

The woman eyed the card then studied the document. "I can't imagine what you've gone through, Mrs. Butler. Not knowing what happened to your mother all these years." She gave the POA back to Daisy. "Legally only the person whose signature is on file is allowed access to their safe-deposit box. However, I understand your situation, and unlike some of the larger institutions, we go above and beyond to provide superior customer service. Plus, you brought your attorney." She opened her top drawer and withdrew a key. "Come with me."

They followed her to a private room lined with floor-to-ceiling cabinets.

Mrs. Campbell inserted both keys into slots, pulled out the safe-deposit box, and set it on a table. "I hope you find what you're looking for." She walked out leaving them alone.

Daisy touched her mom's hand. "Are you ready for whatever we discover?"

"Finding anything is better than nothing." She opened the box. Three birth certificates lay on top—Rose's, and her daughters'. "Good thing we haven't needed these. The name of the father on mine and Pansy's is blank."

"Not a surprise." Daisy lifted a small black box holding two gold wedding bands. She held them up to the light. "Based on the initials, these belonged to Rose's mother and father."

"There's one more item." Her mom clutched the manila envelope addressed to Rose Fowler. She removed a single sheet of paper. Seconds passed. She gasped. Her face paled. The document fluttered to the floor. Her trembling fingers gripped the edge of the table.

A chill penetrated to Daisy's bones. She retrieved the paper and read the words. Her challenge with Curtis paled in comparison to what she'd read.

"Maybe you and I should pretend this doesn't exist."

Daisy shook her head. "Our family has suffered from too many secrets and lies. No more."

"It will tear Danny apart." Her mom's voice wavered.

"Dad's strong. He'll survive."

"I don't know what he'll do…" Her voice trailed off.

Daisy slid the document back in the envelope and pushed the box back into its slot. She wrapped her arm around her mom's waist and guided her back to the car.

David stood beside the passenger door. "Any luck?"

She handed him the envelope. "It's possible we're on the verge of cracking Rose Fowler's case wide open."

Poppy fidgeted while her family consumed the take-out supper they'd picked up on the way home from the bank. Pansy and Basil debated about store-bought versus home-cooked chicken. When the chatter lapsed, David filled the void preventing an uncomfortable silence. As usual Danny added an occasional comment. The notion of breaking the news to him released a wave of nausea. Poppy grabbed her glass and swallowed mouthfuls of water.

"You're right, Aunt Pansy, the colonel's chicken isn't as good as yours and Mom's." Basil patted his stomach. "But plenty filling."

"Now that we've devoured the store-bought chicken—" David reached across the corner of the table and touched Pansy's hand. "Daisy and Basil will clean up the kitchen while I tell you about one of the funniest cases I solved."

"Oh goodie."

"Well now." Basil scooted his chair away from the table. "Looks like noodle-noggin and I have been relegated to kitchen duty."

Daisy popped up. "So it seems."

Poppy leaned close to Danny. "You need to come with me, sweetheart." Her heart pounded in her ears as she led him to their bedroom and closed the door.

"Why all the drama?"

"You need to sit down."

Danny's brows gathered in. "Why?"

"Please." Her tone pleaded.

He lowered to the bed.

Poppy lifted the document off the dresser and clutched it to her chest. She drew in a deep breath and slowly released the air. "We found this in Mama's safe-deposit box." She released it into his hand.

He zeroed in on their discovery. His nostrils flared. His left hand curled into a fist. When he finished reading, his lips pressed into a thin line.

"Do you want to talk about it?"

"No." He bolted to his feet and stalked out.

Tears erupted as Poppy dropped to her knees and prayed for Danny to find a way to deal with his anger before it destroyed him.

Chapter 44

Daisy read the text to Michael explaining her next step. What if her plan failed? Too late to back out now. She pressed send, donned her suit jacket, clutched her purse under her arm, and joined her dad in the front room. "Are you positive you want to go through with this?"

"I don't have a choice."

She followed him to the family truck and climbed onto the passenger seat. Basil watched from inside the greenhouse. Her dad had declined Basil's offer to accompany them, claiming he needed him to stay home and comfort his mother.

During the ride, a tangle of emotions collided and sent pain shooting up the back of Daisy's head. The closer they came to their destination, the faster her pulse raced. By the time they parked in front of Curtis's ranch house, her palms had turned clammy and her throat dry. She dug a mint from her purse and popped it in her mouth to ward off a cough.

Her dad gripped the steering wheel. "I never expected to set foot on this property again." He released his grip and climbed out. "Let's get on with it."

Daisy squared her shoulders as they ascended the patio steps and faced Curtis Butler's bodyguard.

The man's eyes shifted from her father to Daisy. "Mr. Curtis isn't accepting any visitors."

Her dad stood toe-to-toe with the man. "I don't care what you have to do, I'm not leaving until he agrees to see me."

The bodyguard hesitated, then motioned them to follow him inside. "Wait here."

Anticipating the next move, Daisy faced the living room.

Within minutes, Cynthia Evans approached. "You don't give up, do you?" She eyed Daisy's dad. "If you're under the delusion that bringing another attorney will grant you access, you're mistaken."

"You're the one who's mistaken, ma'am. My name is Danny Butler, and I'm not leaving until my old man agrees to meet with us."

The woman stared wide-eyed. "You're Curtis's son?"

"Yes."

Her eyes remained glued on his. "I can't promise anything."

"Tell him if he doesn't see me, I'll contact every Savannah television and newspaper reporter and tell them what happened to Bobby."

Cynthia's brow pinched. "Who?"

His eyes narrowed. "Just...tell him."

She hesitated, then nodded toward the living room. "Wait in there."

They strode into the massive space. Daisy sat on the sofa while her dad trudged to the window facing the swimming pool. How many painful memories were racing through his head?

Five minutes passed. Daisy pressed her damp palms against her skirt. Ten more minutes. Would they have to camp out over night? Did her grandfather have an idea why his son showed up out of the blue? Had he called the sheriff?

Footsteps sounded from the hall.

Her dad spun around.

Cynthia faced him. "When did you last see your father?"

"Has he agreed to see us?"

"You need to understand he's not well."

"His health isn't why we're here."

"I'm simply trying to prepare you, Mr. Butler. Come with me."

They followed her down the hall to double doors opening to an office smelling of room freshener. Cynthia pointed to a pair of club chairs facing a massive desk.

Daisy stared at the thin, old man sitting in a high-back executive chair. He seemed but a shell of the man she had viewed in her mom's scrapbook.

"You can leave us, Cynthia." Her grandfather's deep voice belied his physical appearance.

"Yes, sir." She backed out, closing the doors behind her.

Curtis succumbed to a rattling cough. "In case you're wondering, lung cancer." He waggled a bony finger and glared at his son. "Did your daughter bring Daddy to coerce me to grant her an audience?"

Her dad's jaw clenched. "Illness doesn't excuse what you've done."

Curtis drew in a shallow breath. "No matter what you believe, I never meant for Bobby to kill himself."

"Your rejection is the reason he's dead. That's not why we're here." He removed the discovered document from his jacket pocket. "This is." He pushed it across the desk.

Curtis grasped the document and held it close. "Where did you find this?"

He glared at his father. "You knew about it, didn't you?"

"You have to understand, Rose was the only woman I ever loved." He slammed the document on the desk. "You have no idea what it was like growing up with a father who refused to accept any accomplishment short of absolute perfection. An A was never good enough unless it came with a plus sign. From the time I was old enough to talk, he preached the importance of position and authority. The day I told him I had no intention of following in his footsteps, he beat me with his belt. He claimed a son was born to carry on his father's legacy, and if I refused he'd cut me out of his will and destroy any chance I'd ever have to succeed."

Daisy winced at the wrath in Curtis's tone.

"I'm not interested in your sob story." Her dad's eyes narrowed. "Did Rose show you the proof?"

"Is that why you're here? To accuse me of killing her—" Curtis tapped his finger on the letter. "Over this?"

Daisy gasped. "*Did* you kill her?"

He flinched as if realizing he'd made a fatal error. "All you need to know is she fell and struck her head on the dresser."

Something didn't smell right. Daisy crossed her leg over her knee. "That doesn't sound logical."

Curtis glared at her. "It was an accident."

She pumped her foot. "Why didn't you call the sheriff? And what did you do with her body?"

He looked away. "A scandal would have destroyed everything I'd accomplished."

"You didn't answer the second part of my question."

"I don't make reckless comments."

Her dad thrust his finger toward Curtis. "And I don't need a response to know you're guilty. You can count on me doing whatever it takes to make sure you spend the rest of your miserable life behind bars to pay for the pain you've caused my wife and her sister."

"Without evidence, no one will ever prove anyone committed a crime." Curtis slid the document back across the desk. "In case you don't know, the district attorney is a personal friend."

The vein in her dad's neck pulsed. "You're a coward and a criminal."

"What I am is a powerful man who can give your daughter what she wants." He caught Daisy's eye. "I'll have the necessary documents couriered to you this afternoon."

She glared at him. "Hiring my law firm won't excuse what you've done."

"My decision is based on your firm's reputation and your tenacity. I trust you won't do anything to jeopardize your position." Curtis grimaced as if his body had succumbed to a debilitating stab of pain. "This meeting is finished."

"If you think this is over, you're dead wrong." Her dad pushed off his chair and stalked out.

Daisy followed. At the door she peered over her shoulder to catch one more glimpse of a frail old man whose wealth and position still granted him power and influence.

Cynthia led them away from the office door. "Your father is a proud man, Mr. Butler. He doesn't want anyone to know about his condition, so I'm relying on your discretion."

"You can count on us to do what's right, Ms. Evans." Daisy clung to her dad's arm as they returned to the foyer and walked outside. She remained silent until he slid behind the wheel and started the engine. "What do you plan to do?"

"Break the news to the family." He shifted the truck into gear and pulled forward. "After that, I'll give that old man what he deserves."

Chapter 45

D aisy stood at the front porch railing and eyed her watch. Ten minutes to five and no indication her grandfather intended to follow through on his promise to courier a contract. What did she expect from a man who had covered up a crime for more than thirty years? If Curtis Butler reneged on his promise, the prospect of losing her job paled in comparison to the shocking revelations her mom and dad had to endure.

She spun toward the house and stared at the master-bedroom window. Two hours after her parents had entered their private space and closed the door, her dad emerged alone and announced a seven p.m. family meeting. Time enough for Lilly and Andy to show up. How would they react? What about Basil? Would his Marine instincts kick in?

Daisy stole one more glimpse of the vacant driveway and headed to the kitchen to make sandwiches for supper. Halfway through spreading mayo on slices of bread, the doorbell chimed. Her pulse accelerated. Maybe she had underestimated her grandfather. She dropped the knife on the counter, raced to the front door, and faced a man holding a thick manila envelope and a clipboard.

"Daisy Butler?"

"Yes."

"I need your signature, ma'am." He handed her a clipboard and a pen.

She signed. Noting the return address and logo, she lifted the flap and removed a contract hiring her law firm to represent the Butler Empire. Finally some positive news to share. She slipped into her room, grabbed her phone, and pressed Michael's private number.

He answered after the second ring. "I assume a personal call means you succeeded."

"We are now the official law firm for the Butler Enterprise."

"Well done, Daisy. Your family connection paid off."

He had no idea the cost.

"Friday morning, we'll meet with our corporate-law division and select a team for the account, with you as the lead."

In two days? She couldn't leave that soon. "The thing is...my family is dealing with some unexpected bad news. They need me to stay a while longer."

"How much longer?"

"A week, maybe two."

Silence.

A knot tightened Daisy's stomach. Maybe she should have tried a different approach.

"Landing a big account doesn't guarantee a partnership."

Michael's change of tone confirmed what underling attorneys understood. The law firm came first, family and personal life a distant second. What would a smart lawyer who wasn't willing to compromise do in this situation? Use her brain to turn a problem into an opportunity. "You do understand that my extended stay will work to our advantage. I'll participate in Friday's meeting remotely, then meet with Curtis to present our plans and reinforce our commitment."

"Slick move, Daisy."

More like brilliant. "By the way, Mom loved the flowers. She mailed you a handwritten thank you note."

"They were meant for you as much as for her. By the way, I'm still counting on taking you to Mother's New Year's Eve celebration as my date."

"We'll talk about that later."

Michael chuckled. "Back to business. The sign of a dedicated attorney."

After listening to details about Friday's meeting, Daisy ended the call and mentally patted herself on the back. Forget overpriced, ivy-league educations. Good old southern grit made the difference. She shifted from corporate lawyer to daughter and returned to the kitchen where her family was finishing what she had abandoned. "Thanks for helping."

David peered up from slicing a tomato. "We saw the courier and figured you were tied up with work."

"Good figuring."

Pansy twisted the lid off a jar of pickles. "Hey, Danny, how come Poppy's not here?"

"She's resting until Lilly and Andy arrive."

A stab of guilt struck Daisy at the sight of Basil's what-am-I-missing expression. Why hadn't she pushed back when her dad insisted they wait to inform him until after confronting Curtis? "A lot has happened in the past twenty-four hours."

"I'd make a lousy cop if I hadn't figured out that much."

"Sometimes police work requires patience, knucklehead."

"For stakeouts and paperwork, not chasing bad guys."

Pansy set the pickle jar on the table. "Can I ride with you when you chase bad guys with your siren and blue lights?"

Daisy marveled at her aunt's perfectly timed disruption. Her lighthearted banter continued through supper and helped ease anxiety over what was to come.

The sound of a car crunching the driveway gravel sent Poppy to the front-room window. A dizzy sensation forced her to grip the sill while she waited for Lilly and Andy to join the rest of her family in the front room. A hush ensued as she linked arms with Danny.

He clasped his hand over hers. Their eyes met.

She nodded.

He faced their family. "When David showed up a couple weeks ago, up I didn't believe he had one chance in a thousand to discover what happened to Poppy and Pansy's mother. This morning Daisy and I confronted the man whose name I never wanted spoken in my home." He paused for a long moment. "We've discovered that Curtis Butler was one of Rose's clients."

Lilly and Andy stared wide-eyed.

Basil's jaw dropped.

Daisy inched closer to David.

Pansy tilted her head. "Mama's in heaven dancing with the angels, isn't she?"

Poppy nodded. "Yes, sweetie. All these years Mama's been watching over us." She hesitated as doubt about their decision to tell Pansy resurfaced. No matter the outcome, her sister deserved to know the truth. She swallowed past the lump in her throat, strode to the sofa, and knelt beside her sister. "There's something else. Do you remember a little while back when you asked if we'd ever find out who our daddie's were?"

"Uh-huh. You said we'd have to take some kind of test."

"Yesterday Daisy and I unlocked Mama's safe-deposit box." She cradled Pansy's hand in hers. "We found a test that told us you and Danny have the same daddy."

Andy choked.

Lilly gasped.

Basil's eyes narrowed to a slit. "Curtis killed Rose to keep the truth from leaking, didn't he?"

Daisy peered around David. "He claimed an accidental fall took her life."

"The man's a bold-faced liar." Basil's nostrils flared. "You have to make him pay, Dad."

"I intend to."

"You both need to understand something." Daisy scooted to the edge of her seat. "Dad will need concrete evidence proving Curtis committed a crime—"

"You're an attorney and David's an investigator. You need to turn over every rock until you find it." Basil bolted to his feet and stormed out.

Poppy trembled at the thought of what her son might do. She pulled away from Danny.

He grabbed her arm. "Leave him be, sweetheart. He needs time to come to grips with the truth."

Pansy's brow pinched as she chewed on her fingernail. "Curtis is my papa?"

Poppy patted her knee. "Yes, he is."

"When can I go see him?"

"We'll talk about that later, sweetie. For now why don't we all let the news settle while we enjoy sandwiches and slices of your carrot cake."

Chapter 46

Saturday night Poppy meandered to the arbor swing. Alone. Following the family gathering, Danny had gone into seclusion, wandering the property late in the afternoon. At night he carried his supper to the greenhouse and ate by himself. Her heart ached over the turmoil that churned his gut. The magnitude of the decision he'd been forced to make. After struggling with her own anger and despair, a wave of peace washed over her. Even though she'd long suspected her mother was dead, knowing she had most likely died the instant her head struck the dresser brought a sense of calm. She pressed her palms together and prayed for Danny to find his own peace.

A gust of wind sent a chill racing through her limbs. She pulled her down-filled jacket tight across her chest. As her eyes shifted to the stars twinkling between the scattered clouds, she imagined her mother blowing a kiss like those she'd blown every time she sent her and Pansy traipsing across the backyard to hide out in their little house. Somehow she had to focus on all the happy memories.

"Did you think I'd skip date night?" Danny's voice broke the silence.

Poppy's heart jumped. "I'm glad you're here."

He settled beside her and poured them each a glass of bourbon before setting the bottle on the side table.

She wrapped her fingers around her drink and sipped. The smooth liquid sliding down her throat released a warm sensation. Was Danny in the mood to talk? Clouds parted to reveal more stars. Maybe it was a sign he had come to some kind of decision.

Minutes passed.

Danny sipped his drink.

A leaf released from overhead and floated onto her lap. "The fall colors are extra pretty this year." Poppy brushed the leaf off.

Danny set the swing in motion. "Lilly and Andy are meeting you at church in the morning. After you return home, we're all going to the ranch to confront Curtis."

Poppy stared at Danny's profile as he laid out his plan. Not once during the past forty-eight hours had she imagined he would make such a bold move.

At half past noon on Sunday, Daisy sat on the leather sofa in Curtis's living room with David on one side and Mom on the other. She squeezed her mom's hand. "Are you okay?"

"I'll never forget the look of disgust in Curtis's eyes the only other time Danny brought me here."

"He's old and frail now, a shell of the man pictured in your scrapbook photos."

"He still holds a lot of power."

Pansy plucked an equestrian magazine off the coffee table. "Does Papa Curtis have horses?"

"Probably." Daisy's dad stood in front of the fireplace with his arms crossed.

"Can we go see them?"

Basil edged beside his dad. "Not today, Aunt Pansy." He planted his feet a shoulder length apart and hooked his thumbs on his belt. The appropriate power stance for a former Marine and future police officer.

Lilly lifted the lid off a wood-and-ivory inlaid box, releasing a faintly sweet, yet earthy aroma. She removed a cigar and handed it to Andy. He held it close, inhaled, then placed it back in the box.

Footsteps struck the floor behind the sofa. Cynthia appeared and placed a straight-backed chair to the right of the sofa." Mr. Butler will give you fifteen minutes. No more."

Curtis followed her, walking with a cane. A suit jacket hung loosely on his bony frame. He dismissed Cynthia with a hand flick, then lowered to the chair. "I see you brought my company's new lawyer." He scoffed. "Are the rest of these people my judge and jury?"

Daisy's dad tapped his biceps. "When Daisy and I left here Thursday, I vowed to turn you over to the authorities and force you to spend your last days on earth behind bars. Peeing in a metal toilet. Wearing prison garb smelling of other men's sweat."

Curtis scowled. "You know without evidence, the DA won't have a case."

"Which is why I spent hours walking my land." Daisy's dad dropped his arms to his side. "That's when my hatred turned to pity, and I realized what a miserable life you've led. Not because your father demanded you to follow in his footsteps—"

"He didn't give me a choice."

"You could have walked away, like I did after Bobby died." He thrust his finger toward Curtis. "You chose to stay because the money and power meant too much. What did that do for you? The only woman you claimed to have ever loved is dead. Your wife despises you. Your daughters are a mess, and you live alone with your horses and mountains of regret."

Curtis's eyes narrowed. "What's your point?"

"I came here today because I want you to see a legacy that matters." He paused, as if contemplating his next words.

Daisy's shoulder's tensed. What legacy was he about to reveal?

"The family you never knew or cared existed, beginning with my wife, Poppy." He knelt in front of her mom. "This beautiful woman brought your only grandchildren into this world. She's the love of my life who warms my bed with her body and my soul with her gentle spirit and loving heart."

Daisy pressed her hand to her chest. When had Danny Butler turned poetic?

He pushed off his knees. "Our son Basil is an incredible man who's willing to lay his life on the line to protect our nation and our citizens. Our two beautiful daughters, Daisy and Lilly, are each successful in their own right. One is pregnant with your great grandson. Her husband Andy is like our second son. There's another special member of our family." He held his hand out to his sister and led her to the straight-backed chair. "Curtis Butler, it's time for you to meet your daughter. Pansy is a kind and gentle woman who loves everyone unconditionally."

Pansy knelt beside Curtis. "I'm sorry you're sick, Papa. I hope you feel all better soon so you can come visit me."

Daisy's emotions teetered between anger and pity at the sight of Curtis's barely perceptible nod. Did he have any idea how much he had missed? Did he even care?

"This beautiful woman you and Rose created has brought more joy to our home than you could possibly imagine." He gripped Pansy's elbow and escorted her back to the sofa. "The one person I haven't mentioned is this fine young man sitting beside our oldest child. Pansy is responsible for bringing David into our lives. He's an investigative journalist who has my approval to write a book revealing the truth about Rose's disappearance."

Curtis squared his shoulders. "What do you want from me?"

"You don't get it, do you?" Daisy's dad faced his father. "All Bobby and I ever wanted was your love and some semblance of acceptance. My wife—the woman you shunned the day I brought her to this ranch—kept me from falling victim to my hatred for you."

"You have no right to judge me." Curtis glared at his son. "After Rose's accident I paid off her mortgage and sent money to her daughters."

Poppy's mouth fell open. "You're the one?"

"I'm sorry for the pain her death caused you and your sister."

Pansy rushed back to Curtis and squeezed his hand. "It's okay, Papa. Mama's happy in heaven and God loves you."

Curtis stared at her a long moment. "Things aren't always what they seem." A gut-wrenching cough forced him to cover his mouth. When it subsided, he stood and leaned on his cane. "Your fifteen minutes are up. My bodyguard will show you to the door." He limped away.

After her family walked out to the front patio and down the steps, David pulled Daisy aside. "When you and Danny met with Curtis, how much did he say about Rose's death?"

"Nothing other than she fell and hit her head. Why are you asking?"

"I know how to read body language and listen to spoken and unspoken words."

Her brows knitted. "What are you trying to tell me, David?"

"I'm not convinced Curtis killed your grandmother."

She stared at him. "Whether intentional or unintentional, he's the reason she's dead. Which makes him guilty of a crime. The question is, which one?"

"What if you're wrong?"

"What if I'm not?"

Chapter 47

With only five days left before Christmas, Daisy strolled out of her New York apartment building and turned up Broadway. Snow flurries fluttered, melted on the sidewalk, and left wet spots on her rubber boots. There was something magical about the city during the holidays. Thousands of tiny lights strung around tree trunks. Decorated display windows.

She passed by the upscale store where she'd spent way too much money on the red sweater dress she'd worn to Michael's apartment. Maybe she'd wear it again New Year's Eve. A kid sporting a blue stocking cap whizzed by on a skateboard, missing her by inches. Daisy rolled her eyes and pressed her purse to her side. At the roundabout she turned onto Central Park South. A young girl stood on the curb petting a gray horse and chatting with the carriage driver. He tipped his hat as Daisy walked by. She smiled. Everyone seemed a bit friendlier.

When she reached 6th Avenue, she crossed the street and headed to 57th. How many times during the past two years had she followed this same path—dashing to work, then trudging home exhausted from long, arduous hours. Today she merely strolled and enjoyed the view. By the time she arrived at her office building, her coat was damp and her spirits high. She rode the elevator to her floor and spoke to admins as she passed by their desks.

Her assistant held her hand over the office phone. "Welcome back, Ms. Butler."

"Hey, Shannon. Love the new hairdo."

"Thanks, Boss."

Daisy meandered into her office. "How's it going, Walter?"

"You'll need your boots again tomorrow. Snow's predicted to pick up overnight."

"Thanks for the heads-up." Even her too-serious office mate was chattier than normal. Daisy tossed her coat over her chair and exchanged her boots for high heels. She removed an envelope from her purse and slid it into her slacks pocket. "I'll be back shortly."

Five minutes later Daisy exited the elevator bank and spoke to the fiftieth-floor receptionist before heading down a long hall—this time without the receptionist's escort. She meandered past administrative assistants and peered over their heads at engraved plaques beside elaborate doors—names of high-powered attorneys. Partners who had reached the pinnacles of their profession. How long had she dreamed of her name placed above a private office door?

At the last desk, a young male assistant stood. "Mr. Warner is waiting for you, Ms. Butler." He opened the door and stepped aside. She eased into the paneled corner office illuminated by sunlight and table lamps. Michael stood facing the window. He spun around, tapped his earbud, and pointed to a pair of leather chairs facing a massive desk.

Daisy sank onto the chair closest to him. She eyed the abstract painting above the credenza and stifled a giggle. How much had the firm paid for that piece of art that in her mind any first grader could have created?

Michael ended his call and approached her. "Glad to have you back, Daisy. You look amazing." He kissed her cheek before settling on his executive chair. "Did your family solve whatever problem kept you away so long?"

"They're making progress."

"Speaking of progress, we're moving you to one of the private offices reserved for partner candidates."

"I'm curious." She tilted her head. "Am I the first gal or guy who says 'y'all' who's permitted to occupy one of those spaces?"

Michael grinned. "Let's just say you've changed a few minds about southern-educated attorneys."

"I'll consider that an accomplishment equal to landing Curtis Butler's account."

"A noteworthy achievement." He pulled an envelope from his top drawer and pushed it across the desk. "Your compensation for coming through."

Daisy's eyes widened as she removed and peered at the check. "That's a boat load of money."

"Hiring you was a smart move on our part."

"I appreciate the grace you extended after I fessed up about my nonexistent relationship with my grandfather."

"You delivered. Nothing else matters."

"Except I proved that G. R. I. T. S. has a whole new meaning. Specifically that 'Girls Raised in the South' are forces to be reckoned with."

"Like your mother and aunt. Which reminds me, I noticed your reaction when Pansy mentioned your father winning the lottery. Why keep it a secret?"

Daisy hesitated. "Because it's a lot of money."

"How much is a lot?"

"Ten digits. Nine *if* he claims the winnings and opts for a lump sum."

Michael released a long whistle. "That's a ship load of cash." His brows pinched. "What do you mean by *if*?"

How could she make him understand without speaking ill of Curtis? "Dad struck out on his own before he finished high school. I suppose you could say he divorced his parents and everything they considered important. He values family and an honest day's work. In his mind wealth threatens both."

"What about earned wealth? Your bonus is a pittance compared to what you'll make as a partner?"

Daisy eyed the crystal clock on Michael's credenza, a stark contrast to the abstract painting. "When I was studying law, Mom talked about one day visiting me in a big fancy office. She was over the moon when I accepted the position here. It's funny how a few weeks can flip one's perspective."

Michael locked eyes with Daisy. "You're not talking hypothetically are you?"

She peered around the luxuriously decorated space representing an untold number of billed hours. "Astute perception."

"One reason clients pay me top dollar."

"You deserve every penny you earn, and I deeply appreciate everything you've done for me, Michael." Daisy removed the envelope from her pocket and laid it on the desk.

He stared at her for a long moment. "That's a resignation letter, isn't it?"

"My two-week notice."

"What led to your decision? Living in New York? The long hours?"

"At some point we all have to consider what's most important." She paused. "The fact is, if Dad claims the winnings, my family will need serious legal counsel."

"What if he doesn't?"

Daisy shrugged. "There are plenty of good firms in Georgia, and adding Warner Law Firm to my resume is a big plus."

"Would it help if I used my persuasive skills to convince you to stay?"

"Top-billing attorneys know when a case is hopeless."

"Touché."

"To make it official." Daisy slid the envelope across the desk.

Michael pushed the unopened envelope into his desk drawer. "I still want you to spend New Year's Eve with me and my family."

"I suspect your mother will withdraw her invitation the moment she learns that an ungrateful southern chick abandoned a highly-sought-after position in her husband's law firm. Who could blame her?"

"You're an amazing woman, Daisy. I'll miss you personally and professionally. How about letting me treat you to dinner on my veranda. Just the two of us."

"Thanks, but my flight leaves in a few hours and I need to tell a few other people goodbye. Oh, and don't worry about my current projects. I'll finish my last two weeks working from Georgia."

"Fair enough. For now, the least I can do is walk you out."

Michael held her elbow while escorting her to the lobby. He stopped beside the exit and swept his arm in a wide arc. "Will you miss all this?"

"The chance to sit at the table in your fancy conference room at least once? Yeah. The insane work hours and office politics? Not for a nanosecond." Daisy stretched and kissed his cheek. "Thank you for everything."

He took her hand and gazed into her eyes. "The night we dined on my terrace...the way your face glowed in the candlelight. There's still a chance for us—"

"We live in two different worlds, Michael. We'd both have a difficult time adjusting to each other's lifestyles." She touched his arm. "However, you have an open invitation to supper at my parents' home."

"Good to know." He lifted his vibrating phone off his belt and eyed the screen.

"Important client?"

"DA's office. We'll stay in touch, Daisy." He tapped his earbud and headed back toward his office.

"Goodbye, Michael," she whispered while stealing one more glance around the reception area. Her eyes landed on a twelve-foot, professionally-decorated Christmas tree. A fitting symbol for the prestigious Warner Law Firm. Strange how much had changed since she'd last entered this space—hoping for a promotion and fearing she'd been fired. Despite her decision to face another unknown future, a sense of peace washed over her.

Daisy meandered into the elevator bank the moment the first ride on the left yawned open. A partner rushed past her without making eye contact or acknowledging her presence. If she had elected to stay in New York, would she have become like him? Preoccupied? Dismissive? Daisy stepped in and pressed the button for the senior associates floor. As the elevator descended, her mind drifted to her family and one handsome investigative journalist waiting for her back home. No matter what challenges lay ahead, she knew deep in her soul that David would have a profound impact on her future and Danny Butler's family legacy.

Thank you for reading Big Secrets, Little lies. What happens next in the Butler family? Following is a sneak preview of book two in the Butler Family Legacy series.

Truth and Forgiveness

Chapter 1

Six weeks after walking out of the Manhattan office building one last time, Daisy Butler remained suspended in a time warp—unable to move forward until her dad made a decision. She plucked a dried leaf off the concrete walkway running through her family's commercial greenhouse and peered up at the glass ceiling. Dark clouds cast a gray pall across the massive space. Another dreary January afternoon in Georgia soured her mood. She crushed the leaf, let the pieces slip between her fingers, and wandered to the exit.

Outside, she sidestepped a puddle from last night's torrential rain and paused beside the miniature house on wheels parked beside her dad's delivery truck. She imagined David Lambert sitting at the camper's dinette with his laptop open. Had her attraction to the investigative journalist who showed up on her parents' front porch the week before Thanksgiving unduly influenced her decision to abandon a promising career and move back home? After he gathered enough evidence to solve the case and finish writing a book about her grandmother Rose's disappearance thirty-five years earlier, would he leave to chase down another cold case?

A wind gust nipped Daisy's cheeks and tousled her shoulder-length hair. She pulled her jacket tight across her chest and dashed across the backyard to her mom's private retreat. Inside the tiny clapboard building the warped floorboards creaked with each footstep. Sheer white curtains fluttered in the breeze from the open window. A budvase adorned the sill, the white rose symbolic of the ongoing struggle to accept the truth about Rose Fowler.

Daisy's muscles tensed as she dropped onto the hand-hewn wooden bench beside her Mom. She scrunched her nose at the scent of damp wood and eyed the open newspaper on her lap. "At least that article didn't appear on the front page."

Poppy Butler tapped the headline. "*Georgia Mega Lottery Winner Remains Anonymous. Winning Ticket Sold at Willie's Convenience Store.*"

She pressed her palm against the dark wine-colored birthmark staining her left cheek. "One slip of the tongue, and the whole world will find out that your dad claimed the winning number."

Daisy released a long sigh. "There's a huge difference between him accepting the check and actually cashing it."

Her mom lowered her hand from her cheek and touched Daisy's arm. "Are you having second thoughts about resigning?"

"I underestimated the challenge of transitioning from twelve-plus-hour work days to zero."

"Like a race car stuck at an endless red light."

"If I'd had the slightest inclination Dad would take this long to decide whether or not to cash that check...what's done is done. Now I need to find some kind of project to keep me busy."

"You could start your own law practice."

Images of Curtis Butler skated through Daisy's mind. The grandfather she had never met before the Warner law firm assigned her to recruit his business empire. If David hadn't arrived on the scene, her family would never have discovered that Curtis fathered her Aunt Pansy and had a hand in her grandmother's disappearance.

"What do you think, honey?"

"About what?"

"Opening your own office."

"I'm a corporate attorney, Mom. I doubt anyone within a fifty-mile range would need my services."

"Seems these days everyone is specialized." A smattering of raindrops pinged the metal roof. Her mom tilted her face upward. "Years ago when Mama entertained men during rainstorms, Pansy and I pretended this little hideaway was a boat adrift at sea. My sweet sister would peer out the window and describe the whales and dolphins she imagined floating by. One time she wrote a story about landing on an island populated by cats."

Images of dozens of sketchpads featuring her middle-aged, childlike aunt's detailed drawings skated across Daisy's mind. "Her imagination and artistic ability are off the charts."

"Lucky for us one of her imaginary stories about Mama's disappearance brought David into our lives."

"Yes, we are." Daisy leaned her head back against the wall. "Does Aunt Pansy understand why we need to keep the winning lottery ticket a secret, even if Dad never cashes it?"

"The challenge isn't whether or not she understands; it's her unpredictable comments."

"One more reason to continue stalling her goal to open a bakery."

"We can't deny her dream indefinitely." Daisy's mom set the newspaper on the bench. She scooted to the edge, removed a new scrapbook from an ancient trunk, and opened to the first page.

Daisy ran her finger over the title bearing her dad's name. "*Danny Butler's Family Legacy*. The sequel to your first scrapbook?"

"At least I won't have to keep this one secret or fill it with newspaper clippings of relatives who don't know us or care if we exist." She turned the page to reveal the family's Christmas photo and tapped her finger on her middle child's image. "Next year's picture will include Lilly's baby—your first nephew and my first grandbaby."

Daisy smiled at the image of her sister standing between her husband Andy and their brother Basil. A lump rose in her throat as her focus shifted to her mom posing beside her dad. The way she turned sideways to hide the birthmark on her left cheek—the blemish she believed obscured her beauty and brought her shame. Other than the birthmark, there was no mistaking she and her mom were mother and daughter. Daisy swallowed as her focus drifted to her own image—her hair tucked behind her ear revealing her faux-emerald earring a shade darker than her eyes. David stood beside her, their shoulders touching. The only non-family member ever invited to pose for the annual Christmas photo. "What goes on the rest of the pages?"

"Pictures? Mementos? One in particular." She flipped to the next page. "Pansy's last birthday card to your dad."

Daisy touched the card, one of dozens created over the years by her aunt who brought so much joy to their family. "The card that held the winning ticket. Do you suppose her cards will continue to include lottery tickets, all with the same number?"

"I suspect they will. We'll find out when your birthday rolls around."

The rain intensified, drumming the roof with a rhythm akin to brush sticks striking dozens of snare drums. Daisy pointed to the ceiling patch over the window. "Good thing Dad fixed that leak." She paused. "Do you have any idea when or what he'll decide about the check?"

Her mom shook her head. "All I know is he's struggling with his conscience."

"About taking the money or what to do with it?"

"Both."

"What do you want him to do, Mom?"

She remained silent for a long moment, as if considering how to answer. "Whatever he believes is best for our family." Daisy's mom closed the scrapbook and placed it back in the trunk. She moved to the window and pushed the sheer curtains aside.

Daisy closed her eyes, pinched the bridge of her nose, and scoured her memory for clues her dad might have revealed. An offhand comment or question during breakfast or supper. Nothing surfaced. Not surprising, considering Danny Butler was a man of few words. She lowered her hand and opened her eyes.

Her mom stared at her, her lower lip clenched between her teeth. "You gave up a lot when you walked away from a promising career. Especially after all those years you spent studying and working hard."

Daisy eased beside her mom. A spider posed in a web stretching between the upper window frame and a rafter. "Family and personal life come in a distant second for Warner law-firm partners. I wasn't willing to make that choice."

"Love of family is a powerful emotion." Her mom swiped her hand across the window. "So is the appeal of huge sums of money."

A sensation akin to a dozen fluttering butterflies accosted Daisy's chest as she stared at the arc her mom created in the condensation. There was no denying one all-consuming fact. Her dad's indecision continued to strain her family's patience and test their loyalty to one another.

Chapter 2

Grateful for the blue sky and a fifteen-degree jump in temperature, Poppy sauntered from the greenhouse and climbed onto the back porch of the only home she had ever known. Her private world insulated from strangers' cruel stares. She hung her wide-brimmed straw hat on a hook, walked into the kitchen, and breathed in the rich scent of freshly baked chocolate chip cookies—a testimony to Pansy's extraordinary baking skills.

She poured a glass of lemonade and settled on one of six vintage ladder-back chairs—her mama's prized possessions. Gifts from a satisfied client. She traced her finger over the hand-hewn table marred by nicks and spills from years of family meals and school projects. So many memories lived in the room that had served as Pansy's and her classroom after that incident when she was eleven. She pressed her hand to her cheek and squeezed her eyes shut as the painful memory escaped. The older boy pulling up her skirt during recess. His smirk when he said if she planned to be a prostitute like her mom, she'd need to fix her ugly face. That was the first time she had any inkling about how her mama earned a living.

Desperate to shove the painful memory back into its hiding place, Poppy opened her eyes and focused on her sister and children's drawings adorning the wall separating the kitchen from the front room. Danny had always found comfort in their simple life, unencumbered by possessions. She understood that his hatred for his father had compelled him to accept the winning lottery check. At the same time, his disdain for wealth kept him from cashing it. Not knowing what lay ahead sent a cold chill creeping up her spine. One little ticket had hurled a gigantic monkey wrench into her predictable, comfortable life.

Poppy pushed off her chair and pulled a cookie from an apple-shaped jar, Pansy's latest thrift-store find. The chewy rich taste of chocolate and brown sugar delighted her tongue and helped ease her anxiety.

Footsteps struck the floor behind her. "I need to buy lots more cookie jars for my bakery." Pansy set her sketchpad and a box of colored pencils on the table.

"Nice hat. How many in your collection now?"

"Thirty-seven." Pansy's brown eyes twinkled above pink cheeks as she fingered her Atlanta Braves World Series logo. "Basil gave me this one. He promised to give me a police hat soon as he graduates and gets his badge."

The stark reminder of her son's career choice released a bitter taste and forced Poppy to set the half-eaten cookie on the counter. She brushed crumbs into the sink. Obviously the family's potential wealth hadn't altered Basil's plans.

"Maybe tomorrow Danny will give me some money to open my store." Pansy plopped her plump body onto her chair at her end of the table and opened her sketchpad. "It'll look like this."

Poppy pulled a chair beside her sister. Boots, Pansy's black sixty-pound rescue dog with white front paws, padded in and laid his head on her lap. She stroked his ears while studying the drawing of mismatched cookie jars lined up on a counter. Behind the display an elaborate flower arrangement sat on a cabinet beneath a sign reading *Pansy's Bakery and Flower Shop*. Somehow she had to stall her sister without crushing her dream. "This looks real fancy."

"I'm gonna paint the walls yellow like sunshine and the ceiling blue like the sky."

Boots lifted his head off Poppy's lap, yawned, and sprawled on the floor under the table.

"You know we'll need to do a lot of planning before we're ready to open a store, sweetie."

"We have to buy baking ovens and get some kind of license, like if I was gonna drive a car. Daisy's a lawyer, she'll help me. We need to go to town tomorrow so I can put this picture in the window of my new store, the one across from Willie's house."

So much for stalling. Poppy reached for her sister's hand. "Do you remember what we told you about keeping Danny's lottery ticket a secret?"

Pansy nodded. "That if people find out he'd won, they'd want us to give them lots of money." She set her ball cap on the table beside her sketchpad and brushed bangs away from her eyes. "But isn't it okay to give people money if they don't have any?"

Poppy swallowed against the tightness in her throat. How many times had she explained reality to the woman who had the mind of a child and the heart of an angel—the family member whose wisdom sometimes belied her mental capacity? "You know Danny hasn't decided what to do with the check."

"He can put it in the bank." Pansy stood, then poured a glass of milk and pulled a cookie from the jar. "Boots wants a cookie, but chocolate makes dogs sick." Her canine's tail thumped in anticipation as she plucked a dog biscuit from a box and tossed it under the table. "I can bake good-tasting doggie treats and sell 'em in my store." She settled back in her chair and bit into a cookie. "If Papa Curtis loved Mama Rose, how come he didn't marry her like Danny married you?"

Poppy stared at her sister. Where did that question come from? She hadn't mentioned Curtis Butler since her family confronted him and introduced Pansy as his biological daughter. How should she answer? With the truth, that's how. "Because he already had a wife."

"Danny's mama?"

"Yes."

Pansy washed down her cookie with a sip of milk and took another bite. "Is Papa still real sick?"

The image surfaced of Curtis Butler sitting in the straight-backed chair, gripping his cane—the way his suit jacket hung loose on his thin frame. "He is."

"When he dies, will he go to heaven so he can be with Mama?"

Poppy wrapped her fingers around her lemonade glass. Was her question prompted by Sunday's message or simple curiosity? "That depends on who's in his heart, honey."

"Oh." Pansy removed a colored pencil from her box, flipped to a blank page, and began sketching a picture of man sitting in a chair.

"Who are you drawing?"

"Papa Curtis." She drew a face surrounded by a heart shape on the figure's chest. "I'm giving him the right kind of heart."

Poppy's eyes moistened. If the man who managed a gigantic business empire had one smidgen of Pansy's compassion, he would never have denied her existence or had a hand in their mother's death.

"Is Daisy still David's special friend?"

Poppy suppressed the anxiety-riddled giggle threatening to escape. Her sister's random thoughts unconstrained by a mental filter made family conversations unpredictable as well as entertaining. "You'd best ask David."

"Okay." Pansy pushed away from the table. "Come on, Boots, we've gotta go talk to him."

Poppy grabbed her sister's arm. "Not now, sweetie."

"'Cause he's busy writing his book about Mama?"

"Exactly."

Pansy pulled her chair back to the table and continued drawing. "How come God didn't make me smart like you?"

Poppy brushed a lock of hair away from her sister's cheek. "There are lots of different kinds of smart."

"What's my kind?"

"The way you know how to write good stories and draw and make people happy."

"Tomorrow when I hang my picture in the window, I'll make lots of people happy." Pansy closed her sketchpad. "It's time to go help Danny in the greenhouse." She finished her milk and scooted out the back door with Boots scrambling behind her.

Poppy slumped in her chair. Maybe she should come up with a good reason why tomorrow wasn't a good day to go to town.

Chapter 3

Daisy stood beside the porch railing as David closed the distance to the steps. Warmth infused her body the moment he climbed the steps. She breathed in the fresh scent of soap and shampoo while resisting the desire to run her fingers through his thick, light-brown hair. "I assume the laptop tucked under your arm means you're ready for me to read your masterpiece."

"From the beginning for continuity."

"Perfect." She settled on the first of two rocking chairs outside the front room.

David sat beside her. "I've rewritten the first page three times since you first read it."

"Because it's the most important, or because you can't make up your mind?"

"Little bit of both." He opened his laptop and placed it on Daisy's lap.

She eyed the screen and read aloud. "*Chapter One. She was thirty-two-years-old the day she disappeared without a trace. A prostitute authorities deemed unworthy of investigation. A woman who in the opinion of many existed in life's dark underbelly, undeserving of compassion. And yet the measure of a life isn't defined by a profession, but by the character of those left behind. Such is the case of Rose Fowler.*"

Daisy pressed her hand to her chest. "Even if she wasn't my grandmother, I'd already care about her."

"The rewrites paid off." David pushed up. "I'll wait in my camper and let you read the rest without me hovering over you."

Her eyes followed David as he climbed off the porch and disappeared around the side of the house. How had she fallen in love with the man who first kissed her New Year's Eve but not since? A man perhaps destined to spend his life on the road? Maybe her feelings were more akin to infatuation, inspired by the way he treated her mom and aunt with dignity and respect. She couldn't think about that now.

Daisy set her chair to a gentle rocking motion and resumed reading. The world around her faded as the story drew her in. David's words tugged on her emotions and held her captive through each chapter. Her grandmother's tragic childhood. How as a fifteen-year old she was left alone to fend for herself. The desperation that drew her into prostitution. Poppy's and Pansy's survival before and after their mama's disappearance. Their love for each other and their family. Three times tears blurred her vision, forcing her to blink and sniffle.

At the end of the chapter revealing the mysterious safe-deposit key that unlocked the truth about Curtis being Pansy's biological father, her heart pounded. She scrolled to the next page, eager to read David's depiction of Curtis Butler's confession and crime. The page was blank. She pressed the page-down key. Nothing happened. Was the rest of the story in another document? She checked his desktop. Nothing there.

Daisy closed the laptop, dashed to the camper's open door, and stepped inside.

"What's your opinion?"

"It's brilliant." She slid onto the dinette bench across from him and set down his laptop. "But where's the rest of the story?"

"The final chapters haven't been written."

She studied his expression. Was he stalling because he wanted to stay around longer or because doubts about her grandfather's guilt had resurfaced? "I thought you'd come to grips with the truth about Curtis."

"What is the truth, Daisy?"

Was that a trick question? "He admitted killing Rose."

"He claimed she fell but didn't say anything about pushing her."

"Do criminals ever admit their crimes?"

"When cornered or facing death, sometimes they do."

"Not if they're cowards or evil to the core."

"Men like your grandfather who control business empires aren't cowardly. Granted he's cold, but evil?" David propped his forearms on the table. "You're an attorney, so you know subtleties matter. Body language. Facial expressions. What is left unsaid."

"I also understand the meaning of beyond a reasonable doubt."

"Then wouldn't you want me to explore every possibility?"

Daisy thrust her thumb toward her parents' home. "He admitted being in Rose's bedroom, David. The only way she could have fallen and hit her head with enough force to sustain a life-ending injury is if someone shoved or slugged her."

"I'm not saying he wasn't in the room."

"Then what *are* you saying?"

"It's possible he's covering for someone."

"Are you serious? The man whose rejection led to his youngest son's suicide? The same man who denied Aunt Pansy's existence because she also failed to meet his standards of acceptability? How could that man have enough heart to protect anyone other than himself?"

"Self-preservation? Guilty conscience? Any number of reasons."

Daisy stared at him for a long moment. "You're not going to let this go, are you?"

"I can't. Journalistic integrity."

Daisy squeezed her eyes shut and mentally replayed the day she and her dad confronted the man she'd first met two months earlier. She pictured her grandfather's demeanor and expression. The words he'd spoken. The sense that something seemed off.

"I suspect somewhere deep down you also have doubts."

Daisy opened her eyes. Had David read her body language? "I admit there was a moment." She turned toward the window and caught sight of the tabby cat charged with keeping the greenhouse rodent free stretched out on the driveway. "What's your next move?"

"Reopen the investigation."

Daisy cringed.

"I could use a partner."

"What are you suggesting?"

He reached across the table and touched her arm. "Help me to uncover the truth and find justice for your family."

Daisy's skin tingled beneath his touch. Should she agree because he needed her, or because she longed to spend more time with him? Did the reason matter? Especially since she was desperate for a project to keep her busy. "Similar to Sherlock Holmes and Dr. Watson?"

"More like Sherlock and Mary Russell."

Daisy's eyes widened. "Holmes had a female partner?"

"Different author, a century later. So, are we a team?"

"How could I resist—David Lambert and Daisy Butler, modern-day supersleuths."

He grinned. "Our first decision, should we tell your parents what we're up to?"

"You mean poke a hornet's nest before we find out if it's packed or empty? Although I had hoped the days of keeping secrets from my family had passed." She glanced around the small space. The tiny kitchenette. His bed, neatly made. "We'll tell Mom and let her decide whether or not to tell Dad."

"Now that we're on the same page about the investigation, how about an honest critique on what you read. Don't hold back. I can take plenty of criticism."

"Do you want to hear that you captured my imagination from the first paragraph and held it fast until the last word? Or that the way you portrayed Rose, Mom, and Aunt Pansy reached in and touched my soul?"

"Any constructive feedback?"

"Your writing is brilliant, David."

A smile lit up his face. "Now that we're partners, you'll be a key character in the rest of the story."

Would she also become a key part of his life beyond the investigation? Would he kiss her again?

"Question." David tapped the table. "What do lawyers and authors have in common?"

"Hmm. They provide ample joke material?" Daisy tilted her head. "On a more serious note, they both understand the power of words."

"Indeed, they do."

Movement outside the greenhouse caught Poppy's eye. Why was Daisy carrying David's laptop to his camper? Had he finished writing his book and asked her to read it? If she'd known about the winning lottery ticket, would she have agreed to let him write her mama's story? She spun away from the window and spotted Danny at the far end of the building loading plants onto a flatbed cart. Another late delivery meant he would skip supper with the family. Again. She set her garden shears beside a row of boxwoods and walked out of the greenhouse.

Poppy paused beside David's camper. Resisting the urge to knock on his door, she strolled around the side of the house and into the front room. She dropped onto the sofa, lifted her mama's photo off the end table, and stroked her beautiful, flawless face. The day she showed the picture to David he claimed she favored her mother. Had he spoken out of pity, or had he recognized something she didn't? Or couldn't? The last time she looked in a mirror, she'd cringed at the sight of her birthmark. Did she dare take another peek and see if by some miracle the dark color had faded? Why bother? Even if it had lightened, the blemish would still draw stares from strangers.

She set the photo on the coffee table beside the scrapbook displaying her childhood poems—another of her mother's treasures. If Rose had chosen a different way to earn a living, maybe she'd still be alive. On the other hand, if Mama hadn't disappeared, David would never have come into their lives.

Poppy's fingers found a worn spot on the sofa's velvety upholstery. Not surprising given every piece of furniture in the room dated back to her mama's childhood. How many strange men had sat on one of the mismatched wingback chairs before Rose led them to her bedroom? If Danny cashed the check, she could buy a new sofa and maybe a pretty rug and a fancy coffee table.

Caught off guard by the mental musing, Poppy curled her fingers and pressed her nails into her flesh. Was this how money changed people? One small purchase? Then another and another after that until accumulating possessions became an all-consuming quest?

Startled by her vibrating phone, she pulled it from her pocket. Lilly. Her middle child. The one member of her family most susceptible to self-indulgence. "Hey, honey."

"Hi, Mom. How's your day going?"

"Same as always. And yours?"

"Andy and I need to buy a bigger car. You know, with the baby coming and all. The problem is, we don't know how much we can afford."

Could she be any more obvious? "If you're asking for my advice, I suggest you decide based on what you can afford today."

"But...what if...I mean, Dad's going to cash the lottery check, isn't he?"

"My answer hasn't changed since yesterday or all the days before."

A sigh resonated through the phone. "I thought by now he would've made some kind of decision."

"Believe me, honey, I'll call you the moment he decides."

"I hope it's soon." After chatting for a few more minutes, Lilly ended the call.

Poppy leaned her head back and closed her eyes. She and Danny had raised their children to respect the value of family, honest work, and humility. Lilly's unrelenting questioning confirmed his fear and the reason he struggled with a decision. Wealth held the power to undermine everything they'd worked to achieve and destroy their family. Much as it had destroyed Curtis Butler's family and led to the death of one son and planted seeds of hatred in the other. One fact remained clear. Danny's choice would have a lasting effect on the people she loved.

Will Danny cash the check or rip it to shreds?
Will Pansy keep the winning lottery ticket secret?
Will Daisy and David's relationship evolve to romance?
Did Curtis kill Rose?
Find out in book two, *Truth and Forgiveness.*

Afterword

A Note From the Author

One of the most rewarding aspects of my writing journey is interacting with readers and book club members. I would love to connect with you and send you a free copy of *The Vet and Valentine's Day*, an award-winning short story:

Go to:
https://www.subscribepage.com/pat-nichols-newsletter

I'd be honored if you'd follow me on BookBub and it's free. https://www.bookbub.com/authors/pat-nichols?follow=true

Want to learn more about my books: https://patnicholsauthor.blog

You can also find me on Goodreads, Face Book, Twitter, Instagram

Acknowledgments

The road to publication is never traveled alone. A heartfelt thanks to my friends who have joined me on this journey.

Sherri Stewart, my editor and mentor, for her expertise and commitment to excellence.

My beta readers Pat Davis, Beverly Feldkamp, Kitty Metzger, Kathy Warner, and Carlene Dunn for their critique and suggestions during the writing process.

My launch team members for their reviews and to all those readers who aren't on the team but take the time to write reviews.

My author friends at American Christian Fiction Writers North Georgia Chapter for creating a warm and welcoming environment and for providing valuable education. My Word Weavers International, Greater Atlanta Chapter partners, for their critiques and positive reinforcement.

A special thanks to my amazing family for believing in my journey and encouraging me to continue pursuing my dream.

Above all, as a Christ follower I thank God for His grace and the gift of eternal life.

www.ingramcontent.com/pod-product-compliance
Lightning Source LLC
Chambersburg PA
CBHW061231310726
48971CB00007B/2013